THE
DESTROYER

GRAHAM P. CLARKE

UK Book Publishing.com

Design, typesetting and publishing by UK Book Publishing

www.ukbookpublishing.com

ISBN: 978-1-917329-30-9

THE
DESTROYER

INTRODUCTION

E ighteen years and nine months ago, an alien-like being is on
Earth. It was dark apart from a street lamp outside the village
pub, where he saw a couple of drunks just leaving, holding
each other up and merrily singing and laughing.

"They look like nice people," he said to himself. "I'll make
myself look like them."

He then used an alien power which enabled him to camouflage
himself to blend in naturally with any situation or surroundings he
may find himself in. Looking very similar to the drunks, he went into
the pub and asked the barmaid not for a drink, but a one night stand.

The barmaid was fascinated by his dark eyes and velvety
voice. Where was the harm?

"Sure," she said. "Why not?"

The alien smiled, revealing perfect teeth, so white that they
dazzled her.

"I'm Sarah, by the way. What's your name?"

He paused and at that moment overheard someone with a
cockney accent watching a televised football match saying, "Man,
he's brilliant..."

"Manny," the alien said. "My name's Manny."

"Well, hello Manny," Sarah replied with a seductive wink,
"nice to meet you. I'm off duty now, shall we, er...?" She tossed
her head towards the door marked 'Private' and the alien followed
her upstairs to her room.

Next morning, before daylight broke, the alien is happy on Earth.

Sarah subsequently discovered that she was pregnant, but of course her baby was no ordinary child. Her son was to grow up to be the person expected by the other God to find certain friends who, along with himself, would become the saviours of Earth.

However, if he did not fulfil the expectation of God then he would probably end up as a mental patient.

* * * * * * * * * * * * * * * * * * * *

The son of the alien-like being, Greg Carter and his friend, Steven Jamieson were just coming out of college.

"Hello mate," said Steven.

"Oh, hi. So did you finish your exam?"

"Yes. Did you take yours or did you forget about it?"

Greg laughed. "Oh yes, Steven; I remembered to do mine because I don't want to end up as one of your psychology patients."

"Fair comment," Steven laughed.

"So, do you want to have a kick about?" asked Greg.

"Sure... and I'm going to beat you this time."

Greg grinned, but then suddenly became serious. "That's odd," he said.

"What is?"

"I've just sensed someone in danger."

"Really? Are you sure you're not cracking up, mate?"

Greg laughed. "Yes, I'm sure; I definitely sensed someone in danger."

"Right then, we should go and help that person out," suggested Steven.

"Yes, we're going to play heroes." He pointed ahead. "Come on, we need to go in that direction."

Steven followed Greg across the college grounds and, turning a corner, they did indeed discover someone in danger – from a student. Greg approached the student.

"Hey! Idiot! Stick your ass out, because I'm going to give it a beating."

The offending student stopped and faced Greg. "Oh yeah? Okay then, bring it on."

Greg threw a right hook in the face of the idiot, who threw a punch back but Greg skipped neatly out of the way and then pushed the idiot, face down, to the ground.

"Kiss the ground," ordered Greg.

"No..."

"Kiss it, I said!"

The idiot kissed the ground and Greg was triumphant, but only for a moment as his opponent seized a dustbin lid and hit him over the head with it.

"Nice move, but not as good as the one I've got for you," Greg said coolly and landed him a martial arts kick.

"Oh, you like Bruce Lee, do you?"

Before the idiot could retaliate, Greg kicked him again...where the sun doesn't shine.

"No, I prefer football." Greg then reached into his backpack, pulled out an orange and rammed it hard into the idiot's mouth.

Choking and spluttering violently, the idiot finally managed to eject the orange and ran off. Greg stood and watched him, feeling pleased with himself and looking proud.

Amy, the person who was in danger from the idiot, went to Greg to thank him.

"That guy was a jerk," she said.

"You can say that again," Greg replied.

"That guy was a jerk," said Steven, grinning at Greg and Amy.

The three laughed.

"So do you want to come with us for a drink to celebrate end of college, Amy? Greg asked.

Amy said she would love to and in that defining moment, the three of them knew that they were about to embark on something special.

Meanwhile, in an academy in Romania, a scientist was receiving an award for accomplishing a scientific project.

"I would like to dedicate this award to my family and my girlfriend," declared Adrian, the scientist, to the audience which included his family and girlfriend.

After everyone else had gone home Adrian, his girlfriend and family left the academy building and paused for a few moments outside, chatting happily about the occasion. Suddenly a car screeched to a halt and the driver gunned them down.

"NO!" Adrian glared angrily at the gunman, instantly recognising him.

"That's for turning us in, Adrian," the gunman said, his voice raised against the sound of the idling engine.

"That robbery is in the past and I did the right thing turning you in to the police. You should have shot *me* because they didn't deserve this," Adrian protested, looking down helplessly at his lifeless loved ones.

"Maybe. That wasn't what we wanted though; we wanted you to experience the loss of something, just like we lost the chance to get away with the robbery. So you would know how it feels."

The man engaged first gear and sped off noisily with his three passengers as Adrian watched, distressed and angry. As he noticed the car's registration plate, he let out an agonised scream.

Back in England Greg, Amy and Steven were in the club finishing their drinks.

"D'you want to dance, Greg?" Amy asked.

"Yeah, go on, then," Greg replied, getting up.

"I should find someone to dance with," said Steven, looking round for someone to partner him. "Oh yes, there's a hot blonde at three o'clock... Hi, dance with me?"

Adrian, in Romania, was still enraged and went to see a policeman friend of his, to see if he could help him find the killer of his family and girlfriend by searching for the registration number.

"Hi, I was wondering if you could look up police records and trace a registration plate?"

"Yeah, course I will, mate. What's the code?"

"It's R, two, nine, zero, C, Z, U."

The policeman and Adrian made their search and found that the code belonged to a stolen vehicle.

"Bingo! I knew that car was stolen. They always make mistakes and that's the last mistake they're going to get away with." Adrian shook his friend's hand. "Thanks, mate... I owe you one."

At the local police station Adrian told the officer on duty he had some information.

"I've got some information regarding a stolen car. I saw some people stealing it. The registration code is R, two, nine, zero, C, Z, U."

The duty officer took a few more details. "Right, sir. Thank you for that. I'll get someone on to it."

From the police station, Adrian went back to his laboratory and began making a bomb, together with a remote control device. He took the finished bomb outside and attached it to the underside of his car.

"Now I've got to collect those idiots and blow them up," he said. Next, he searched the Internet for a disused warehouse. Having found one, he then visited a website explaining how to resurrect people. It told him that in order to get what he wanted he had to find four souls and incant a spell to regenerate the Ku

Klux Klan. He must then throw a potion in the direction of the souls. It stated that if the spell were successful, the person who regenerated the KKK must order them to cause mass destruction to the ends of the earth to attract the attention of '*the chosen ones.*'

It also said if *the chosen ones* kill **KKK**, the person who regenerated them would receive their powers and their victims' souls so that he could regenerate more evil doers until he had enough powers to bring people back to life. However, if the KKK killed *the chosen ones* they would receive their powers and have the ability to destroy the earth. If this situation arose, the person that regenerated them had to kill them to prevent them from succeeding.

He read the recipe for making the potion and then concocted it. For some mad reason, he then broke into song:

#You took all that I had and now I'll destroy you.
I want you to know I'll make you suffer for what you have done.
From now on you're my demons and I'll make
you pay for what you took from me.

(Chorus) I want payback; payback is what I want,

payback is what I ask for and payback is what I'll get.
I want to see your faces when you know I'm going to destroy you.
Then you might be able to understand what I'm feeling.
You will perish for what you did.

(Chorus)

When you are gone I'll have justice on my side, but I won't stop there.
I'll have the world suffer so I can have my loved ones back.

(Chorus)

(Repeat chorus)

Adrian's anger was etched on his face. On the television screen, the people who destroyed his family were being arrested. He heard the location of the police station mentioned. "It's showtime," he said. And went to collect them.

Back in England Greg, Amy and Steven were leaving the club.

"That was fun," said Greg.

"Yeah," Amy and Steven agreed.

As they began to walk home, Steven had a premonition of mass destruction around the world.

Greg and Amy noticed a change in him.

"What's up?" asked Greg.

Steven blinked at his friends. "I've just had a vision of mass destruction around the world."

Amy gasped. "Really?"

"Yeah, it's really strange. I know why I had it, though." He paused, becoming completely inanimate for a few moments.

"I've just had another vision, Greg. According to my vision, you're half alien with great powers... and Amy, I've also got some information about you. You are a good witch."

Amy scoffed at Steven. "That's ridiculous," she said, flapping her hand at him dismissively.

But Amy's hand movement had inadvertently moved Steven against the wall. She then she realised that she was, indeed, a good witch. As the three looked at each other in confusion, they were suddenly enveloped by an amazing bright light. They had been merged into 'the chosen ones.'

In Romania, Adrian had arrived at the police station where his family's and girlfriends's killers were being held. Getting out of the car, he stopped a passer-by and explained his situation to him.

7

The stranger was baffled by Adrian's behaviour, and even more so when he offered him one thousand pounds to pay for their bail.

"But why don't you do it yourself?" the stranger demanded.

"Well, because I was the one who informed on them to the police,"Adrian replied. "So will you do it? Please?"

"Okay, I will, but only if you give me another one thousand pounds."

Adrian didn't argue. "Yes, anything to pay them back," he agreed, giving the man a further one thousand pounds.

The passer-by disappeared into the police station to pay the bail. Adrian waited for him to come out.

"Any problems?" he asked.

"No problems. Thanks for the money," the man said, patting his pocket and smiling broadly at his good fortune.

Adrian nodded and went back to his car to wait for the killers. Minutes later they appeared.

"Hey!" he shouted through the open window. "Come over here."

"What are you doing here?" said one of them, approaching the car.

"I'm the one who paid your bail and I'm here to pick you up and take you back to my place to discuss our next job." Adrian replied.

"Aren't you mad at us for killing your family and girlfriend?" another one asked.

"No, I forgive you for that. I just want to get back to how we were."

"Okay, welcome back, Buddy," said the first one, getting into the car and signalling to the others to do the same.

Adrian drove off to the warehouse, where he stopped the car and got out to open the sliding doors.

"So you really are back?" one of the killers said.

"Yeah, of course," Adrian replied. "We'll discuss our plans inside, okay?"

He closed the car door, but made no attempt to open the warehouse.

One of the killers tried to open the car door. It was locked.

"Adrian, what's going on? I thought you said you weren't mad and that you forgave us?"

Adrian smirked. "Oh yeah, I lied. If you try to get out you won't be able to, because along with the security locks I've put on all the doors, the windows are all bullet proofed as well."

"You tricked us!" shouted one of the killers to Adrian.

"Yes, I did, so I've got something to be proud of, but you haven't." He turned on his heel and walked away, hearing their shouts of protest behind him. From a safe distance, he turned round to see them all wrestling with the door handles. He then took a pocket sized detonator from his jacket and pressed the button. As the car exploded, Adrian took out a special, magically prepared test tube into which their souls were sucked instantly. He then placed a bung in the top of the tube to prevent them from escaping.

"It's a pleasure doing business with you, lads," he murmured, slipping the test tube into his pocket.

When he reached his laboratory, he incanted the spell to regenerate the Ku Klux Klan. Then, taking a potion he had made earlier, he flung it into the air and at the same time removed the bung from the test tube, casting the souls of the killers amongst the potion. An explosion occurred and four members of the Ku Klux Klan appeared in demonic form.

"How did I get here?" one of them asked.

"I cast a spell to regenerate you so that you can do what you did all those years ago," replied Adrian.

"Okay, that's good, but the police will know I've gone and come to get me."

"Well, in that situation a person who looks like you will automatically be installed in your place. He will look, think, sound and act just like you."

"So we're here to stay?" asked another one.

"Absolutely," Adrian confirmed. He then gave them instructions what to do and where to do it.

"Go," he commanded them, with a dismissive wave.

"Right, let's go and destroy everyone from white niggers to Paki-lovinfuckwit bastards."

And with that demonic utterance, the KKK members were gone.

In England, Greg, Steven and Amy were in Greg and Steven's rented apartment. Still amazed about what had happened to them, Steven tried to break the ice.

"Does anyone want to watch television?"

"Yes," Amy and Greg replied in unison.

Steven clicked the remote and the news came on.

"We have just received distressing images of mass destruction in Germany, South Africa, Japan, Australia, Tunisia, United States, Mexico, Brazil and India. We go first to our live reporter, John Ikeman, in Germany," said the newsreader.

"Thanks Gabby. Well, I'm here in Germany where, as you can see, there is real devastation on a grand scale. The people here can't understand why anybody would want to cause such mass destruction. We understand that the people who did this are four members of the original Ku Klux Klan. From what we gather, someone has regenerated them and they have come back as demons with twice the mission they had the first time they were on this planet... to overcome the four corners of the earth and ultimately destroy it. This is John Ikeman for BBC News in Bonn."

"Oh, my goodness!" Steven exclaimed.

"What?" asked Greg and Amy.

"I saw this in my premonition. We could have prevented this. So I am a psychic."

Greg switched the television off. "Okay then, lets go and stop the Ku Klux Klan and the person who brought them back and stop them doing any more damage," he suggested.

"I agree," Steven said.

"Me too," said Amy, nodding at Greg.

"Alright then, we're in. Now, we need suitable costumes." As the words left Greg's mouth, his clothes turned into an orange super hero costume with a capital D in the middle of the chest. He looked down at his super hero suit and smiled at his friends.

Amy's eyes had widened. "How did you do that, Greg?"

Greg looked down again, admiring his suit. "I don't know but I like. I like very much. Instant muscles. Impressive. Saves me a trip to the gym." He grinned at Amy who smiled back. "Okay, it's your turn now, Steven," he said.

"Right, so I'm guessing I just think of a suit and it will appear on me?"

"Yep, you got it."

"Okay, here we go." Steven immediately found himself in a blue suit with a capital P on the chest. "That's just awesome," he said, looking down at it.

"Okay, Amy, now you," Greg said.

Amy thought of a suit and got a green one with a capital W on the chest.

"How do I look?" she asked Greg.

Greg whistled. "Oh yeah! You look much better than Steven and me, Amy."

"Um, how are we going to get there? I mean we can't exactly get on a plane because I might accidentally throw someone out of their seat," Amy asked him.

"That's a good point, Amy. I imagine I just have to think about where I want to be transported to; you'll obviously both have to hold my hands and we should be transported to our destination. Shall we try it?"

Amy and Steven each held one of Greg's hands.

"Beam us up Scotty!"

Amy giggled.

"Sorry, couldn't resist saying that," said Greg. "I'm serious now." He then thought of another room and Greg, Amy and Steven were transported to the bathroom.

"Okay, it works," Greg said.

They walked back into the living room.

"Right. Is that all? Oh, I forgot... how we are going to get our weapons? Presumably the same as we got our clothes. He imagined a weapon and looked down as it appeared in his hand. "What sort of a weapon is that?" he said scornfully. "I've seen tennis balls with more menace in them than that."

The spherical weapon hit Greg on the head.

"Ow!" said Greg, amazed that the ball has just hit him.

Even more amazingly, the ball then starts talking to Greg.

"That was for suggesting I wasn't a very good weapon," said the ball.

"That's fantastic!" Steven declared. "A talking ball."

"Yeah, my name's Oddball, right? I work by Greg throwing me into something or someone and then I will destroy the object or the person. I'm going now; if you want to see me again, Greg has to call my name. Byee, everyone." Oddball disappeared from view.

"Well," said Greg, impressed. "I think he will be good, after all. Okay Steven, Amy, your turn."

"Right." Amy imagined a weapon and blades accordingly grew out of her fingernails.

"Okay, lets see what weapon I've got," Steven said, thinking hard. A starfish blade appeared and he tried, without success, to move it.

"I can't move it," he muttered.

"Try moving it with your mind," Greg suggested.

Steven tried that and it narrowly avoided Greg's head. He looked at Greg, stretching his lower lip apologetically. "Oops!"

"Well, if you wanted to kill me you might have warned me first, Steven. Anyway, let's go and beat those pillowcase-wearing freaks."

"Yes, come on. Let's do that," Amy and Steven agreed.

Greg linked hands with Amy and Steven and off they went to find the Ku Klux Klan.

They arrived in Germany, where the Ku Klux Klan were still causing mass destruction.

"Hey, Whitey! Do you want to get it on?" Greg shouted to one of the Ku Klux Klan members.

"Dude, they look like a pretty mean lot. Are you sure we can take them on, Greg?" asked Steven.

"Oh yeah," Greg replied. "They're about as mean as pansies." He turned to the four. "Did you hear that? You don't scare me. You might be able to scare these people because they can't defend themselves, but my friends and I can and we are going to beat you to save these people. Then we're going to save the world by destroying the person who sent you here. That's a promise."

"Yeah, that's right," Steven and Amy shouted in support.

Greg called up Oddball and threw him into one of the Ku Klux Klan.

"Oddball, bounce that scumbag up and down and vanquish it."

Oddball obeyed, bouncing the white clad figure up and down before hurling it into the air and smashing it against the wall exactly like a pro tennis player would smash a tennis ball.

The three remaining Ku Klux Klan members swiftly disappeared.

"Where did they go, Greg?" asked Amy.

"I don't know, Amy, but we sure scared them."

Meanwhile, in Romania, the remaining Ku Klux Klan members approached Adrian Domescu in his laboratory.

"Are you the one who created us?" one of them asked Adrian.

"Yeah, and I'm so *very* pleased to meet you," Adrian replied sarcastically. "What have you come to see me for?"

"Well, there were three people, one of whom possessed a ball-shaped weapon which he used to destroy our friend. So we were wondering if you could tell us how we could kill him?"

"You'll just have to keep a low profile, stop killing people and then when they're least expecting it, attack and kill them," Adrian replied.

"Okay, boss."

They disappeared.

Adrian spoke his thoughts aloud. "Of course, I'm lying. These people are clearly the chosen ones. They'll constantly be on the look out for these morons and they'll kill them. I shall receive their powers just as the spell said. Once they have been vanquished by a chosen one, the person who resurrected them will receive their powers. After all, why would I let such racist scum conquer the earth when I can have my payback?"

The Ku Klux Klan arrived in England where they intended to surprise Greg, Steven and Amy. Luckily, Greg sensed this before they could destroy Amy and Steven.

"Amy, Steven, get down!" he hissed. He then aimed Oddball at one of them.

Oddball flew into the white-sheeted moron and vanquished him. The two remaining Ku Klux Klan members disappeared.

"Okay, you two, we have to concentrate one hundred percent as we look out for them because they could reappear at any moment," warned Greg.

They reappeared at that very moment.

"Over there, Amy," said Greg, pointing.

"I see them." Amy threw them up against a wall.

"Well look who it is... Dumb and Dumber," said Greg, raising Oddball again. "Now say goodbye." He threw Oddball into one of them and Oddball destroyed it. He attempted to finish off the final member but it recovered from being thrown against the wall by Amy and disappeared.

"You know, this is getting really annoying," Greg said.

Steven agreed. "You can say that again. I mean, they're more annoying than the most annoying soap opera in the world."

"Absolutely," added Amy. "They are even worse than an episode of *Neighbours*."

Greg and Steven laughed with Amy and then went to look for the remaining Ku Klux Klan member. They spotted it going into a gay bar.

"Well, what do you know? It's a poof," said Greg. "Okay, let's go and get the pillow head case and put it down."

"Well I can't go in there, Greg, not unless you want me to wear a fake moustache," Amy pointed out.

Greg laughed. "That would be terrific fun, Amy, but Steven and I will go and beat the milky bar kid. You can go."

Amy laughed. "Okay, I'm off home. Bye, you two."

"Come on then, Fred. Let's go and dance," Greg said to Steven.

"Okay, Ginger."

They exchanged a glance, clearly enjoying themselves, and walked towards the club. They changed back into their normal clothes before entering.

"Right, Steven, let's blend in."

"Okay, but you've got stop calling them poofs, right, Greg? Even if it was funny when you called that scumbag one."

"I'll try."

They danced whilst looking out for the final member of the Ku Klux Klan.

"Hey, Greg, how can it disguise itself when it couldn't before?" Steven asked.

"It must be learning to adapt better, so it can camouflage itself. It must be learning how to use its powers, like we are."

"Except we aren't evil."

"Yeah, that's right," Greg agreed.

"Okay. We'd better make sure we learn faster, then," Steven said.

Greg sensed danger and nudged Steven.

Steven followed his gaze. "I see him," he said. "Racially abusing someone."

"Yeah, he's given himself away hasn't he? I'm going to get him," said Greg.

"And I'm coming with you," Steven asserted.

"Hey, pop and fresh," Greg said to the final member of the Ku Klux Klan, taking it out back.

Steven followed Greg and shut the door behind them. Greg punched the KKK member.

"Ah, just as I thought. As soon as I punched you, you turned back into crazy pyjama man. Now that I know you are the final member of the Ku Klux Klan I can say goodbye, Casper." Greg changed into his orange costume, called up Oddball and destroyed the Ku Klux Klan member.

"Well, the fat lady has sung for them, the racist scumbags," said Greg, turning back into his normal clothes.

"Hey, Greg, do you want to have a drink in here?" Steven asked.

"You're kidding, right?"

"I just thought it might seem disrespectful if we don't."

Greg thinks about it. "Okay."

They bought drinks at the bar.

"This is good beer," Greg said, draining his glass.

"Yeah. Now are you glad we decided to stop for a drink?"

"Yeah, I think I'll have another one."

Greg has another beer, and another one, followed by another one. A loose grin spreads across his face. "Hey, karaoke! I'm going to try that."

Steven held his head in his hands. "Oh boy." But he looked up and smiled at Greg to give him support.

Greg smiled back at Steven, pointing at him. He took the microphone and sang Atomic Kitten's *Cradle* very badly. After he finished the song, they left the bar. Greg was feeling dizzy and swaying ominously.

"Come on, mate, let's go home," Steven said.

In the morning when Greg woke up he found Amy had come round to see him and Steven.

"Oh I feel terrible," he groaned.

Steven asked him what he could remember about the day before.

"I think I watched Casper," he replied.

"No, you vanquished the Ku Klux Klan and then you called him Casper, which was funny, but then you got drunk and absolutely murdered Atomic Kitten's *Cradle* ... which was not funny; not in the least. In fact I'm surprised one of the people in the club didn't call Atomic Kitten and have them sue you.

Amazingly though, and I thought rather perversely, someone said to me, 'Hey, your boyfriend's great; your boyfriend's awesome, and if you don't watch it I'm going to steal your boyfriend and love him long-time.' That made me feel sick and I was embarrassed because you put me in that position with your drunken antics. Now, I'm your best friend… yeah, even after all that, and as your best friend I think I should give you some advice. Next time we go out, mate, just have one drink."

"Yeah, okay, I'll try. But did all that really happen in one day?"

"Yeah, man, it's a sick world."

"Yeah," Amy and Greg agreed in harmony.

"Actually," said Steven, "another good thing to come out of last night besides vanquishing the last of the Ku Klux Klan was seeing you get along with the people in the gay club, because for someone who is supposed to be homophobic you're halfway to becoming gay yourself."

Greg smiled. "The term is homosexual and I'm not one."

"See? You're correcting me."

Greg laughed. "Okay. I'm going to get something for my hangover." He swallowed some aspirin and then drank a glass of milk to wash it right down. He then grabbed a banana and for some bizarre reason, lit it and smoked it.

"Great idea for an anti-smoking advert. Eat a banana after smoking it and it's still not as stupid as smoking a horrible white stick," he said.

Amy laughed. "You're mad. But you're also really clever and sweet. That's why I love you."

Greg moved in closer to Amy and they shared a moment.

"I've thought of another good thing about last night, too, when I was murdering Atomic Kitten's *Cradle*," Greg said, noticing Steven's mocking smile. "Alright, I know it was really bad. Anyway, I thought about how much I love you as well, Amy."

Greg and Amy were about to kiss each other but Steven interrupted them.

"Hey, lovebirds."

Amy and Greg looked at him. "What?"

"I think there's something on the television you should see."

Amy and Greg were shocked when they looked at the screen. It showed that four members of the original Vikings had been resurrected and had caused mass destruction.

"Oh boy," said Greg, as the three looked at each other.

"Oh boy, indeed," Steven replied, putting his hand on the television as if to steady himself after the shock. He looked at Greg and Amy. "I've just had another premonition. This time, as well as you throwing Oddball, a song has to be sung and Amy has to throw a potion to vanquish them. I don't think we have to do it all in that order."

"Why do we have to do all that?" Greg and Amy wanted to know.

"Well, I'm guessing it's because he's getting a partner so he will have more power to take on our power of three."

"Who is he getting to be his partner?" asked Greg.

"That guy you beat up."

"Oh, the Idiot is helping him?"

"Yeah. The Idiot," Steven replied.

In Romania, Adrian was finishing an incantation and making a potion to bring Greg's enemy to his laboratory. Within moments, the enemy was transported there and stood before Adrian.

"Hello..." Adrian greeted Greg's enemy. He passed his hand over a crystal ball, magically made to tell the future. 'What is his name?' he asked the crystal ball by transference of thought. "... Christopher," he said after the briefest of pauses.

"What? How do you know my name, Slap Head, and how did I get here?" Christopher the Idiot asked Adrian.

"It's Adrian to you. I know your name because I looked into my crystal ball and you are here because I cast a spell and a potion to get you here."

"You're mad," Christopher the Idiot said in a most derogatory manner.

Adrian threw a fireball in the direction of Christopher the Idiot, narrowly avoiding him. He had picked up this power from the Ku Klux Klan.

"Call me mad again in that negative tone, or try to escape, and next time I won't miss."

"What do you want from me?"

"I want you to join me, Christopher."

"Why?"

"It's because you're a bully and being a bully won't get you anywhere in life, except if I offer it to you on a plate and that is exactly what I'm doing. I can give you the chance to get back at at Greg."

Christopher the Idiot considered for a moment. "Okay. What do you want me to do?"

"I want us to say a spell to kill a thousand people in England through the Vikings."

"Okay."

They incanted the spell together and then watched the news to see the people being slaughtered.

"Well done, Christopher."

"No problem, Adrian. Is there anything else you want me to do?"

"Oh yes, but first we wait."

They smiled at each other.

In England, Greg, Amy and Steven were carrying out last minute checks.

"Okay. We've got to go and get them. Amy, have you got the potion?" asked Greg.

"Yeah, got the potion, Greg. Have you got the lyrics to the song?"

"Absolutely," affirmed Greg, beating his chest.

"Right," said Steven, looking at Amy and Greg, "then let's go and get some Scandinavian for value."

Greg and Amy laughed with him as they left on their mission.

"Well, there's one of them," said Greg when they got there.

"Should we go and introduce ourselves?" Steven asked.

"Yes, I think we should," Greg replied.

Amy nodded agreement.

"Hey, Netto," Greg said to one of the Vikings.

The Viking turned round and looked at Greg.

"Yeah, you with the funny hat."

Before the Viking had a chance to do anything, Greg threw Oddball into him, Amy threw the potion into him and along with Steven they rapped:

So you thought you could destroy us? Well all you've done is angered us.
When you anger us you make us dangerous
and we're here to stop all this chaos.

(Chorus) We're going to make you suffer in
silence and make you come undone,

then we're going to annihilate you so you can no longer hurt anyone.

You think you're tough but you're not,
you've killed too many people and that's a lot.
Now we're going to punish you for what you have done,
so from now on you'll never get to hurt anyone.
You took so much away from so many people,

now you're going to regret becoming a rebel.
My proclamation is that those that rebel against
good people don't win, we win,
so now I'm going to tell you, you're fight is over
because we're going to make sure your life is over.

(Chorus)

You'll be destroyed and reduced to nothing,
meanwhile we'll have everything.
You can't go anywhere that is our call,
as we'll rid you of this world once and for all.
You have too much damage and now we've reduced you to cabbage.
So buckle up and take the ride,
as we're about to show you extreme pride.
(Greg smiles)

(Chorus)

After we've vanquished you, you won't go round dressed like an idiot
as you'll be extinguished so you'll be no more
and you won't be able to run riot anymore.

(Chorus)

"Bye bye," Greg sang as the Viking and three others were vanquished.

"What happened, Greg?" Amy asked.

Greg wore a smug grin. "Their powers must be linked to one another, but ours are obviously getting stronger. So if one of them fails to succeed they all fail. The people who sent them here must be getting weaker. While we are getting stronger."

"What was that about them getting weaker?" Steven was looking at the new test with its four World War II Emperors of the Sun being formed demonically.

Greg turned around. "Oh boy." He glanced at Amy and Steven. "Come on guys, we've already fought off the Ku Klux Klan and the Vikings."

We can take them," Amy said.

Greg and Steven both nodded agreement.

"Come on then, Oddball. What have you got for us?" said Greg.

Oddball turns into three samurai swords for the trio to use.

"Okay, nice move, giving us weapons of the legends of the Japan."

"Oh, so you want to have a sword fight, do you?" asked one of the emperors of the sun as the entire group of emperors formed their own samurai swords by the use of demonic powers.

Greg, Steven and Amy took up their own swords that had been formed by Oddball.

"Okay," Steven said, "let's go and win this battle."

"Right then; Oddball, I hope you make good samurai swords," Greg replied.

The three approached the emperors of the sun and started fighting. Greg soon knocked one of emperors to the floor.

"Why can't you have the courtesy to stay extinct?" he asked as the demon lay there on the ground.

Just as Greg was about to slay it, the emperor of the sun and its friends disappeared. Greg screamed with frustration. "Arrgh! Come on, let's go and find them."

They reached the spot where Greg thought he sensed them, but they were not there.

"Where are they?" Amy asked.

"I don't know. I don't get it; I sensed them here but now I don't. Someone must be messing with my powers," Greg replied.

In Romania, the emperors of the sun approached Adrian.

"Well now, look who it is! Japan's most useless export. What's the matter? Can you not think for yourselves? asked Adrian.

"As a matter of fact, we actually just used our intelligence to trick the Destroyer into thinking he sensed us in a place where we are obviously are not, so that he and his friends wouldn't be able to find us. Anyway, we came here to ask if you could give us a power top-up," replied one of the emperors.

"Oh. Well, in that case you can have a power top-up." Adrian then mixed three potions four times. "Here you are; you must each take these three potions," he told them. They will give all four of you the ability to move your enemies to the underworld of the damned where demons might kill them, so then you will have the Destroyer on his own and you will be able to kill him. You will also have the ability to throw fireballs and last but not least, the ability to deflect your enemies' weapons."

"Thanks, boss."

"This should be interesting," Adrian murmured to Christopher as the emperors of the sun left.

Their lips curled as they smiled at each other in an evil way.

In England, the emperors of the sun took Steven and Amy by surprise.

"Steven, Amy, watch out!" Greg shouted.

They swung round as the emperors of the sun threw two fireballs at Steven and Amy and one at Greg. Amy used her power to deflect the fireballs aimed at her and Steven back in the direction of the emperors of the sun. Greg did likewise, but the emperors deflected them back again. Amy and Greg decided to deflect all three fireballs into a nearby wall, thereby destroying the fireballs and the wall.

At that moment two of the emperors of the sun decided to send Steven and Amy to the underworld of the damned with their new powers.

"Steven? Amy..." Greg was confused.

"Nice power, huh?" One of the emperors of the sun smirked at Greg.

Greg reacted to the provocation. "Okay, now you've made me angry."

"Couldn't you have come up with something better than that?" the emperor persisted.

Greg threw Oddball at the emperor of the sun, but the emperor deflected him back at Greg. Oddball went back into Greg and the emperor of the sun threw a fireball at Greg who deflected it back at the emperor, who in turn sent it back at Greg who then decided enough was enough and deflected it into the wall.

He sighed deeply, wondering how on earth to get rid of the emperors of the sun.

"Well, unless we are planning on doing this till doomsday, I suggest we think of a way to settle this once and for all," said one of them.

"Unfortunately, you're right, because without Steven and Amy I don't have the power to vanquish you on my own so I need to find another way to beat you and make you powerless." He thought for a moment. "Okay, I'll challenge you all you to a rugby match. I hear Japan are only getting beat forty nil these days."

"Fine," an emperor replied. "We will do anything to see you beaten and powerless."

"Whatever, Yoko."

In the underworld of the damned, Steven and Amy were still looking confused, wondering where they were.

"All I can think of is that we are where the emperors were originally, in the underworld of the damned," Steven said.

"Oh boy; creepy," Amy replied with a shiver.

"Yeah, so we should get searching for a way out of here."

In England, the rugby match was about to get under way.

"Okay, so that's our referee and your assistant referee," the emperor of the sun was saying to Greg.

"Not to mention the video referee who is neutral and naturally is more powerful than us," Greg pointed out.

"Huh, well we don't see the point of having them."

"Well, I'm not a fan of them myself, but they are here and since we don't trust each other, we should be glad of that. Neither of us can cheat or deceive each other and the best team will win." declared Greg.

"Look, are we going start this match or are you going to keep talking?" asked one of the emperors of the sun.

"Well, excuse me, but you were talking as well, but go ahead, bring it on," Greg replied, gesticulating with hands and arms.

The referee tossed the coin and asked Greg to call.

"Heads."

The coin came down tails and one of the emperors of the sun kicked the ball downfield and Greg caught it. He ran down field, but an emperor came towards him to try and tackle. So Greg decided to throw Oddball at them, who stretched himself to prevent the tackle. As they were deflecting Oddball away from them, Greg sprinted towards the line and touched down for a try. Oddball then went back into Greg's body and Greg successfully kicked the conversion over the bar.

"YES!" Greg celebrated with an air punch. "Seven nil straight away and I will give you a right good thrashing."

"That's what you think. Come on you lot, let's switch into hyperdrive," urged an emperor of the sun.

"Hyperdrive?" Greg said quizzically.

One of the emperors kicked the ball downfield and Greg caught it. However, this time one of the emperors was ready for him and waded in with a crunching tackle, which sent him down, leaving him winded. The ball went loose and was picked up by one of the emperors who ran with it to the try line and touched down on it. The conversion was kicked successfully as Greg scrambled, gasping, to his feet.

"Hyperdrive!" he said, now understanding.

Greg prepared to kick off. First, he took a look around and saw the four emperors of the sun standing ready to catch the ball.

"Oh boy!" he sighed. "Well, I may as well have a go at trying to beat them."

He kicked the ball downfield, directing it to the corner flag, then ran towards the emperor who caught the ball. He commited himself to the emperor but as he was about to tackle, the emperor quickly threw the ball to his nearest team mate, who in turn threw it to the next player, who kicked it downfield for his team mate to run onto. Before Greg could even start to run after the emperor with the ball, he had already run down the pitch and crossed the try line, touching down for a try.

"What the hell!" Said Greg.

Then he sees another emperor running downfield in a flash and taking the conversion successfully.

"Oh great, they've got all the speed of Superman," Greg muttered sarcastically.

"Come and have a go if you think you can score one, but if you do we will score another one!" one of them shouted.

Greg reacted angrily. "I will find a way to beat you, mark my words,"

The emperor of the sun smiled smugly as if to say 'I don't think so!'

Greg picked up the ball and tried something different from the kick off. He kicked the ball down the middle of the field and ran after it in a determined fashion as if to catch the ball from his own kick, but an emperor was too quick for him and caught it first. The emperor kicked the ball over Greg's head; Greg watched the ball in flight then turned his gaze to one of the emperors who, in a flash, ran down the left flank, caught the ball and crossed the try line, running to score beneath the posts. The subsequent conversion kick was successful.

"Oh boy, I'm getting thrashed," Greg said to himself. "That's for being arrogant."

He picked up the ball and kicked it downfield hopelessly. One of the emperors easily picked it up and ran downfield. Greg tried to tackle him but he sidestepped him and sprinted for the try line, touching the ball down. The conversion was kicked between the posts and the emperor of the sun maintained his one hundred percent record.

Greg again had the ball, ready to kick off.

"Well, you must be getting used to that by now," one of his opponents remarked.

Greg gave it an angry look and kicked off. The ball went downfield and an emperor caught it and ran at Greg. Then he passed it to his team-mate who sprinted away from Greg and, seeing his team mate coming full pelt down the pitch, decided to kick the ball along the ground to the try line, where another emperor dived on the ball to score the try. Their kicker again cleared the crossbar successfully.

Greg retrieved the ball and kicked off yet again. One of the emperors caught the ball and drove it down into the corner of the pitch where another emperor ran after it, picked it up, ran to the try line, then touched it down to score the try.

The kicker lined up its kick and looked across at Greg. "Looks like you're going to lose."

"Just get on with the game and kick the damn ball," Greg retorted.

The emperor of the sun kicked the ball and it rebounded off the post. The emperor had a look of anguish on his face.

One of his team mates came up to the disappointed emperor and said, "Don't worry, he'll not be good enough to come back from our unassailable lead."

"Yeah," was all the emperor said.

The half time whistle was blown and the Samurai Warriors were all celebrating and saying, "We're going to win."

Greg traipsed into the dressing room and paced up and down, wondering how on earth to get back into the match. "Okay, Greg, pull yourself together. You're losing forty points to seven at half time, what do you do?" He thought quietly for a moment.

"Well, I've got to score thirty three points to level the match, so that's five tries and four conversions. I just hope destiny does the rest for me."

"Or you could use me as well," a strangled voice said.

"Oddball? Is that you?"

"Yes. I can give you a power boost so that you match them," Oddball replied.

"Why didn't you tell me that before?"

"Well, because if you don't ask, you see, you don't get."

"Oh. Okay then, Oddball, please can you give me a power boost?" asked Greg.

"Yes Greg, I can." Oddball went deep into Greg and began the process of upgrading Greg's powers. "Okay, you're just as fast as they are now," he said.

"Thanks, Oddball, I just hope I can make you proud of me," Greg said.

"Well, actually Greg, I don't have to be the only one whom you feel you should please."

"Whatever do you mean, Oddball?"

"Listen up: I can make a crowd to encourage you and discourage them, because after all, this is your world, not theirs."

"Oh, I'd like that. I'd like that very much. Now then, let's see, how many people do I want? Yeah... I think I will have the biggest crowd in the world."

"Okay, Greg, but first I'll put an electronic scoreboard by the side of the pitch."

Then Oddball surrounded the pitch with a massive crowd.

"Is that it, now?" Greg asked.

"Yes, so you should get all the support you need to come back and beat those emperors." Oddball told him.

"Okay, I'm going out while they're still being stupid and pathetic in their dressing room," declared Greg who walked down the tunnel leading to the pitch and received a rapturous reception from the fans. He then looked up at the scoreboard and saw that Oddball had put a message on it, 'To The Destroyer, win or I'll leave you.'

"Good one," Greg chuckled, looking down at Oddball who was in his hand. Oddball then disappeared into Greg, who waited for the four emperors to come out.

They came out, slapping high fives with each other. "Hey, look who it is," said one of them sarcastically, "It's the saviour of the world."

"Fine. Be like that, but I'm going punish you for being arrogant," Greg retorted.

"After that first half display? Oh, I doubt it."

"We'll see."

Greg kicked off and just after one of the emperors caught the ball, Greg used his supersonic pace to run towards him and tackle him. The ball went loose; Greg picked it up and used his new found pace to sprint towards the try line and score underneath the posts. He did an impression of a roadrunner, then looked at the emperors.

"I told you," he said, saluting the crowd who were cheering for him.

The scoreboard read: Destroyer 12 points; Samurai Warriors 40 points.

Greg kicked the conversion over the bar successfully and the scoreboard changed to read: Destroyer 14 points; Samurai Warriors 40 points.

One of the emperors kicked off. Greg caught the ball and another of the emperors tried to tackle him but he used one of his new powers to jump over him majestically. All of the emperors turned round and stared at him in shock. He waved at them audaciously and then used his supersonic pace to sprint towards the try line, again scoring underneath the posts. He kicked the conversion successfully.

The scoreboard read: Destroyer 21points; Samurai Warriors 40 points.

The emperors kicked off. Greg again caught the ball and sprinted towards them. He then sidestepped round them, sprinted towards the try line and scored.

His conversion kick was successful. The scoreboard read Destroyer 28 points; Samurai Warriors 40 points.

Again, the emperors kicked off. Once more Greg caught the ball and ran downfield. As the emperors approached him, he supersonically bounced around them, hurtled towards the try line and touched down beneath the posts.

He turned Oddball into a carrot and ate it, therefore putting Oddball back where he came from. "What's up doc?" Greg said, and then successfully kicked the conversion. The scoreboard showed 35 points to the Destroyer and 40 points to the Samurai Warriors, or emperors of the sun.

Again the emperors kicked off. The ball went downfield and again Greg caught it and then literally flew down the left wing and touched down under the posts. He then, with rather disappointing arrogance, put his hands on his hips.

"Is it a bird? Is it a plane? No, it's the Destroyer kicking your big fat sumo butts," he jeered, making a sarcastic salute towards them.

He kicked the conversion and it looked good but then a gust of wind took it wide and it rebounded off the post, went the wrong side of it and dropped to the ground. Greg then looked up to God as if to say, "I know... there's no place for arrogance."

The scoreboard read 40 points all.

The tension was building as the emperors again kicked off. Greg caught the ball and ran at them, trying to take them on with one of his fancy tricks, but this time they had wised up to him. They tackled him.

Steven and Amy were in the underworld of the damned trying to keep away from some demons they had encountered. They were behind a cave wall, which they came upon after narrowly avoiding capture by the demons.

"Amy, I can't hold them off forever. Have you finished with that spell to go with the potion?" Steven said.

"Yeah."

"Great. Say it, then, and I'll hold them off with my blade."

Amy completed her incantation and handed the potion to Steven.

He threw it amongst the demons, vanquishing all of them.

"Ciao," he said with a mock salute. "Come on, Amy; let's try and find a way out of here."

They went off together to look for a way out, spotting what they thought was an exit but as they approached it, a new set of demons came out.

Steven threw his blade at one of them, wounding it, and attempted to wound the others.

However, they disappeared and then surprised Steven and Amy by capturing them from behind and taking them into a waiting area which was behind the door they thought was the exit.

"Detain them here while I go and tell the source that we have captured a couple of people to be sacrificed," one of the demons ordered.

"This is almost laughable," Steven said as the demon left. "The source of all evil has a waiting room, just like a dentist."

Amy smiled. "Yeah and I can't wait to fill these idiots in."

"That's a good one."

"I've been working on a spell to give us extra strength," Amy whispered.

"Well, let's go ahead and do it; come on."

They linked hands. "Give us the strength to beat these demons so that we can beat them off and turn them into lemons," they intoned together.

The spell worked instantly, giving Steven and Amy the strength to beat the demons, enabling them to escape.

They threw the demons up against a wall and in an instant the demons turned into lemons. They picked the lemons up, escaped and hide behind a nearby wall.

"Do you want to know what the demons taste like?" Steven asked.

"Yeah, why not?"

They both tried some lemon, spat it out and threw the fruit to the ground. "Yuk! That's sick," Steven spluttered, wiping his mouth.

"Ooh, chronic, yeah," said Amy, screwing up her face.

Steven grinned. "Beating those demons was brilliant, though."

"Yeah, I know, but it's not the same without Greg."

Steven nodded. "I agree; so we have to try and find away out of here so we can be reunited."

"I know a spell that might get us out of here... if it works," Amy said.

"Try it, please."

"Okay, here goes. Amy took a deep breath. "Send us back to where we came from, so we can help Greg and be as happy as Larry and as cheery as Dom."

The spell didn't work.

"Why hasn't it worked?" Steven asked.

"I don't know... oh, hang on, it's probably because we weren't in contact with each other and both of us didn't say the spell."

"Oh, I see. By the way, what was that about being as cheery as Dom, Amy?"

"Oh, that's referring to my older brother, Dom. He's a comedian and always happy."

"Oh, I get it. Right, the spell makes sense now."

"Yeah? Good. So are you ready to say the spell along with me, Steven?"

"Yeah." Steven closed his eyes and began to hum softly.

Amy giggled. "What are you doing?"

"Just meditating."

"And I thought Greg was the only mad one."

"Well, I am studying to be a psychologist; there'll be a lot more mad people to make me mad. Anyway, let's say the spell."

"Sure you've finished meditating?"

Steven grinned. "Yes."

They held hands and together repeated the words of the spell, but it still didn't work.

"Now what?" asked Steven.

"I don't know."

They both stared blankly at each other, wondering what they had to do to get out of the underworld of the damned.

Back in England, Greg and the emperors had sussed each other out. So they were used to each other's powers and had not managed to score any further tries. They had scored only penalties, four a side. So the score stood at 52 all. With only thirty seconds left on the clock, Greg was in possession of the ball. He decided to try and sidestep round one of the emperors. However, one of them tackled him, knocking him to the ground.

The ball went loose and the emperor picked it up and began to run up the pitch. Greg picked himself up and ran after the emperor. He caught up with him just before he reached the try line and tackled him hard enough to put one of his legs into touch.

The emperor continued, touching down, thinking it had scored a try.

In the midst of much celebrating, Greg went to the referee.

"Surely you can't give that? His foot was over the touchline."

The referee looked to the assistant referee for clarification.

"No try," said the assistant referee.

"The assistant referee agrees with you, but I did not see it. So I'll have to call upon the video referee."

The video referee was summoned.

"The assistant referee and I have different views on the last passage of play. We need your help in making the right decision."

The video referee viewed the video several times to make sure he was not making a mistake. Greg, the emperors and the crowd waited for the verdict and all stared patiently at the scoreboard to see what the video referee's decision was. When the result flashed up on the scoreboard: 'no try,' there was an almighty sigh of relief from Greg and his fans.

Greg restarted with a lineout played straight and good to himself, using his supersonic speed. He then sprinted right up the pitch and, seeing that there was nothing to be had in terms of a try, with a strong defensive line of emperors in his way, he decided to attempt a drop goal. He kicked the ball confidently between the posts, therefore gaining three points and leading 55 to the emperors' 52 points.

The emperors' kicker restarted the game. Greg caught the ball and the emperors advanced towards him.

"Come on... try and beat me now, you good-for-nothing manure heads," Greg shouted to the emperors. He then threw the ball out of play, knowing that the whistle would go as time was up. The whistle blew for full time and the metaphorical crowd exploded with cheers of excitement. Greg fell to the ground with an expression of relief that he had finally beaten the emperors.

After composing himself, Greg rose to his feet and began to rap the song that would help vanquish them:

> #At first I didn't think I had the strength to beat you,
> but when I found the strength I also found
> hope to carry on and destroy you.
> With hope in my heart and destiny on my side,
> I know I can take you and whatever comes my way
> then destroy them after Oddball takes them for a ride.
>
> (Chorus) Finding strength wasn't easy,
>
> but once I found it I was able to beat you
> and in a moment you'll be feeling queasy.
>
> My job is to give as many people as possible the strength to carry on,
> so they can live as peacefully as possible and be united as one.
> When the world is united it will be a much safer place,
> and then everyone in it will be able to laugh at it and its evil face.
>
> (Chorus)
>
> What we should do is try to do as much good as possible,

because doing good makes us feel confident
and that helps us turn our dreams into reality
instead of thinking they're impossible.
If we can all pull together we can help each other through the bad times
and celebrate the good times.

(Chorus)

Then Greg smiled. "Okay, Oddball, do your thing."

Oddball then appeared and Greg slammed him into one of the emperors and, because their powers were connected to each other, Oddball was able to merge them together and turn them into a basketball which he bounced about wildly before throwing it out of the stadium. Oddball then vanquished them. The crowd cheered again, gradually quietening down.

"Six," pronounced Greg.

The crowd laughed and many of them whistled with delight.

Greg turned to the crowd and waved his thanks for their support.

As their laughter died down, the next contender appeared and there was a gasp of surprise. It was their former king.

Yes... you guessed correctly; it was King Henry VIII.

Greg turned round. "Henry the Eighth? This is getting even more ridiculous by the minute."

"You won't be saying that when I beat you at tennis," Henry retorted.

"Oh, you want to play tennis? Well you'll have to lose weight if you want to beat me, chunky monkey," Greg replied.

"I'm not fat; I'm just big boned."

"Oh? Big boned? Well in that case, I'm terrified," said Greg sarcastically.

"You will be, but first of all an umpire has to appointed... and not a good one."

"Well, isn't that a surprise? Henry the eighth, the evil bigamist, wants an evil umpire, but unfortunately for you, I want a *good* umpire. So we can't both have what we want."

"Technically, we can both have what we want."

Greg was suspicious. "What do you mean?"

"Well… come on, we need a neutral umpire." Henry gazed upwards to the sky.

A two-headed alien appeared.

"A two-headed alien; I might have known. All umpires are in two minds about everything," said Greg.

The evil head spoke. "What I propose is that for every game Greg loses, one hundred fans will lose their lives."

"No! I'm not having that," the good head replied.

"I agree," said Greg.

"Well I don't, because I'm the executioner," the evil bigamist declared, looking smug.

Greg laughed. "I can think of a better name to call you, but it's before the watershed so I'll refrain."

The two-headed umpire intervened. "Okay, that's enough. Because we can't agree with each other, we'll toss a coin to decide it. If the coin lands on tails, one hundred fans could lose their lives and if it lands on heads this rule will not be implemented."

The coin was flipped and landed on tails.

"So it has been decided if Greg loses, then one hundred fans will lose their lives," the umpire announced.

"Fine. I'll just have to thrash Mr Blobby in straight sets: six-love, six-love, six-love."

"Now we'll toss a coin to find out who will serve first. So Greg will get heads and the evil bigamist will get tails," said the umpire.

The coin landed on heads.

The umpire gave Greg the ball to serve with, then made an umpire's chair appear from somewhere and climbed up to sit in it.

Greg walked away to prepare to serve, getting the crowd behind him.

"Okay, folks, let's humiliate that murderous Michelin man."

Greg threw the ball up and served a fine ace. "Oh yeah, what a serve," he said.

"Fifteen-love."

The ball, being of alien origin, magically came back to him from the other end of the court.

Greg served another ace.

"Thirty-love."

"Well, what do you know? Another ace,"

Greg gets the ball back and again serves an ace. "This is getting even better for me and more humiliating for you," he said, looking confidently at the evil bigamist.

"Forty love."

"Okay, Oddball, we're just one point away from winning the first game. I think we should serve up another ace."

With Oddball's help, he delivered another ferocious ace.

"Game to the Destroyer. Destroyer leads, one game to love, first set."

"Well! Well! Well! You didn't even win a single point on that serve and now I'm going to humiliate you on your serve," Greg taunted.

"That's what you think, but I think you're the one who's going to be humiliated," the evil bigamist replied, preparing to serve. Clouting the ball in mid-air, he attempted an ace but inadvertently sent the ball too far.

"Fault!"

The second attempt was no better and again the ball missed its target.

"Double fault! Love fifteen," the umpire shouted.

"Wow, you really are humiliating me," Greg commented.

"I will win, trust me!" the evil bigamist replied.

"Trust me and end up like your wives," said Greg jokingly.

The evil bigamist glowered with rage at Greg as he served. He managed to get the ball in this time, but Greg smashed it devastatingly down the line, thus winning the point.

"Love thirty."

Greg clenched his fist. "YES!"

The evil bigamist served again and the ball was good. Greg returned it down the line but his opponent reached it and returned it back somehow. Greg delivered a drop shot over the net, but the evil bigamist somehow reached that as well, so Greg decided to lob the ball over the evil bigamist, winning the point.

"Love forty."

Greg again clenched his fist in triumph.

The evil bigamist prepared to serve and with a grunt, sent an easy one for Greg to return; back it came, down the line with some pace, allowing Greg to play a cross-court winner.

Greg was lapping it up. "Yes, I'm just churning away and you'll be burning today," he rapped.

"Game to the Destroyer; Destroyer leads by two games to love."

Greg bounced the ball a few times, preparing to serve. He slammed another ace down at incredible speed.

"Fifteen love."

He quickly built up his lead, serving another ace followed by another and yet another one.

"Game to the Destroyer; Destroyer leads by three games to love."

Greg grinned broadly. "Oh yeah, this is getting even easier for me all the time."

The evil bigamist came to the baseline and delivered a good serve but Greg smashed another winning shot down the line.

"Love fifteen."

Another good serve followed but Greg again smashed an absolute screamer down the line.

"Love thirty."

Greg clenched his fist. The evil bigamist was now serving well but unfortunately for him and luckily for all the good people, Greg again caught him out with a dasher down the line.

"Love forty."

"Oh yeah, I'm getting even better."

The evil bigamist was becoming increasingly frustrated. He calmed himself down and tried to reach an ace but stood no chance against Greg's confident cross-court winner.

"Game to the Destroyer; Destroyer leads by four games to love."

Greg then waved to the crowd and began to sing to the tune of Rod Stewart's *If you think I'm sexy*.

"If you think I'm super and you want to cheer, can you say 'go Destroyer.'

"GO DESTROYER!" roared the entire crowd.

"Thank you all very much. The evil bigamist will be leaving the building as soon as I've beaten him, trust me," he said.

"Quiet please. The Destroyer to serve," the umpire called.

Greg served another scorching ace, clenching his fist in delight.

"Fifteen love."

Another ace followed.

"Thirty love."

"Well I'm just a couple of points and a game away from taking the first set and I'm not even sweating yet."

He served another ace.

"Forty love."

With another ace, he won the game.

"Game to the Destroyer. Destroyer leads by five games to love, first set."

"Oh yeah, the sweet spell of a wounded, evil scumbag," Greg chanted.

"That's always what people say before they lose," said the evil bigamist, holding his racket against the ball before serving.

His serve was good but Greg's adrenalin was still pumping and he sent another unstoppable winner down the line.

"Love Fifteen."

The evil bigamist served the ball to the line and this time Greg performed a Boris Becker-style dive to whip the ball over the net and sharply across the court to win the point.

"Love thirty."

Greg returned the next service straight at the evil bigamist's body so he had no chance of hitting the ball.

"Love forty."

"Oh yeah, three set points."

The evil bigamist's next serve was delivered with with speed and accuracy, but Greg's confidence was high and he flipped his unreachable return across the court to claim the point.

"Game and first set to the Destroyer."

The crowd began to cheer with delight.

"Yeah I am great, good, pure... and so undoubtedly better than you, you evil jerk." said Greg.

"Just get on with the game, you orange freak," the evil bigamist replied.

"Call me that again and I'll put my hand down your throat and rip your heart out."

The umpire, nervously watching the two from his elevated seat, thought it was time to intervene.

"Just get on with the game," he hissed. "Play!"

"Okay," said Greg, who served, deliberately aiming it at the black heart of the evil bigamist, making sure that he couldn't return it.

"Oh yeah. Sweet. Just as I planned, straight at your little black heart." "Fifteen love."

"Time to serve again. Ready?"

The ball bounced furiously, striking the evil bigamist.

"Oh yes, straight at your little black rock."

"Thirty love."

The crowd cheered, wanting more.

Greg served once more at the body of the evil bigamist, ensuring that he could not return it, and won the point.

"Forty love."

The crowd cheered even louder.

"I am just getting better and better," Greg said, elated by his performance.

He served again at the black heart of the evil bigamist and clinched the game.

"Game to the Destroyer; the Destroyer leads by one game to love and by one set to love."

"Oh yeah and that's the game."

The evil bigamist received the ball and served, putting some effort into it, but Greg's judgement was perfect and he returned the ball swiftly across the court and out of reach of the evil bigamist who was breathing heavily.

"Love fifteen."

"Again I am great."

Greg returned the next serve in emphatic winning fashion.

"Love thirty."

"I've said it before, I am great and to add something to that, I'm absolutely fantastic," Greg sang out.

The evil bigamist served, looking utterly frustrated. His serve was just in and might have been a winner, but not against Greg on his present form. He deftly smacked the speed out of the spinning ball and feathered it over the net so that the evil bigamist had no chance of reaching it.

"Love forty."

"Oh yes, three more points."

The evil bigamist delivered another good serve, only to find the ball hurtling straight back towards his face, forcing him to duck.

"The Destroyer leads by two games to love in the second set and by one set to love."

In the next game, Greg served four brilliant aces in succession.

"Yes, yes. I'm just getting better by the game."

"The Destroyer leads by three games to love in the second set and by one set to love."

"So what are you going to do now that I'm thrashing you?" Greg taunted.

Henry the eighth gave Greg an angry look, but in his rage sent his serve too far.

"Fault!"

Henry the eighth served again, resulting in another long shot.

"Double fault."

Greg laughed and gave the evil bigamist an ironic burst of applause as the crowd started cheering.

"You know, you are making this match too easy for me.

"Love fifteen."

The evil bigamist's next service came back at him like a bullet as Greg smashed it down the line.

"Love thirty."

The crowd cheered, quietening down for the next serve which again was returned forcefully by Greg, defeating the evil bigamist.

"Love forty."

"Well, look what we have here. I am three points up again."

The evil bigamist, red faced and sweating buckets, glared at Greg. In his anger, he thrashed the ball across the net at great speed and the crowd gasped. Was it to be the old king's first point of the match? No chance. Greg reached it easily and again returned it just out of Henry's reach.

"Game to the Destroyer; Destroyer leads by four games to love in the second set and by one set to love."

In the next game, Greg's four perfect aces didn't give the evil bigamist a look in.

"Oh, I am on fire."

The crowd went wild as the excitement grew.

"Quiet please. The Destroyer leads by five games to love in the second set and by one set to love."

"Well, I'm on course to win the match now," said Greg.

"That's what you think," replied the evil bigamist.

"I do, and I also think you're an idiot who's wasting my time, so just get on with the game."

The evil bigamist merely gave Greg an outraged glare and then served. There had been very little wrong with Henry's serves, but Greg's returns had been brilliant. Again, he slammed a cross-court winner home to gain the point.

"Love fifteen."

"If I haven't said it before, I really should have... I am great."

The evil bigamist served again and, just like last time, Greg hit a cross-court winner.

"Love thirty."

The evil bigamist served again. Once more Greg hit a cross-court winner.

"Love forty." Said the umpire.

The evil bigamist served again, straight into the net. Taking the ball again, he bounced it twice on the court before his second service, which also went into the net.

"Game and second set to the Destroyer; Destroyer leads by two sets to love." The crowd cheered madly and then settled again for the start of the next set.

Again, Greg served four aces in succession.

"Game to the Destroyer; Destroyer leads by one game to love and two sets to love."

The evil bigamist prepared to serve, jogging on the spot. After the first foot fault of the match, he served rather cautiously and failed to reach Greg's spinning return.

"Love fifteen."

The evil bigamist served solidly enough but Greg again returned the ball down the line, out of reach.

"Love thirty."

Greg clenched his fist, smelling victory.

The evil bigamist's next serve bounced aloft and Greg leapt up to smash the ball way out of reach of his opponent.

"Forty love."

Then Greg decided to play a rally with the evil bigamist to get his hopes up so that when he won the point he could crush him and hurt his little black heart. Greg won the point with a lob.

"Game to the Destroyer; Destroyer leads by two games to love in the third set and by two sets to love."

Greg turned to the crowd, hands held aloft. "Hail me, full of grace, hallowed be my name!"

The crowd cheered rapturously.

"Say my name."

"Destroyer!" they shouted.

"Can't hear you? Come on, I want you to say it really loud."

"Destroyer!"

"Again?"

"Destroyer!"

"Once more, and this time I want you to up the volume even more. In fact I want you to shout to the heavens."

"DESTROYER!" The crowd responded with a mighty roar.

"Go Tim!" came a voice from somewhere in the crowd and Greg and the rest of the crowd laughed with delight.

The evil bigamist prepared to serve and his delivery was fast and accurate but Greg returned it down the line and won the point.

"Love fifteen."

As the crowd cheered Greg did a little dance for them and they went even wilder.

"Quiet please!"

The evil bigamist's second serve was treated in the same ruthless manner.

"Love thirty."

With the crowd cheering, Greg clenched his fist.

A hush descended again as the evil bigamist served and this time Greg returned a half volley over the net, clinching the point.

"Love forty."

Greg again raised both hands to the crowd. "Am I great? Or am I great?"

"GREAT!" they roared back.

"Quiet, please. Henry VIII to serve."

The evil bigamist served and Greg clouted the ball back at him, winning the point and another game.

The umpire had to shout to be heard above the cheering crowd. "Game to the Destroyer; Destroyer leads by three games to love in the third set and two sets to love."

Greg won the fourth game with four successive aces.

"Game to the Destroyer; Destroyer leads by four games to love in the third set and by two sets to love."

The evil bigamist served but an exhilarated Greg returned the ball past him and well out of reach.

With his fist clenched, Greg saluted the cheering crowd. "YES!" He was just a few shots away from winning the match.

"Love fifteen."

The evil bigamist served and amazingly produced an ace.

Greg looked shocked.

"You didn't think I had that ability, did you?" the evil bigamist asked.

Greg was too stunned to reply; worse still, the evil bigamist served another ace, followed by yet another one.

"Forty-fifteen."

At that moment the crowd began to jeer the evil bigamist to try and put him off.

Greg lectured himself. "Okay Greg, stay cool; you have to get the shock out of your system."

His opponent jeered. "You do know talking to yourself is a sign of madness?"

"No; you winning this match would be madness. So you've just made me angry enough to make myself come back to beat you in straight sets, you chunky not so spunky monkey."

The evil bigamist served but Greg, now enraged, returned a ferocious winner. The crowd cheered and clapped thunderously.

"Yeah, how do you like that?"

"Quiet please! Forty-thirty."

The evil bigamist's next serve was good but Greg slammed it back out of his reach.

The umpire struggled to be heard above the noise of the crowd. "Deuce. Quiet please!"

The evil bigamist served and Greg returned it but misjudged the distance and the umpire called it out.

"Advantage Henry VIII."

Greg thought the ball had bounced on the line. "You cannot be serious! Titanium pigment flew up. You have to amend your decision, you two-headed freak!"

"I am giving you a warning: one more outburst like that and I will disqualify you and award the match to Henry VIII. Do you understand? Destroyer?"

Greg faced the umpire. "Yeah, sorry for my outburst." He walked quietly back to the base line knowing he must control his anger.

The evil bigamist's serve was clean but Greg's swift forehand down the line again defeated him.

"Deuce."

Again the evil bigamist served; the ball bounced high and Greg sprang up to smash it past him in some style.

The crowd was rapturous.

"Advantage Destroyer."

The crowd quietened down to see the evil bigamist serve another ace.

"Deuce."

Greg won the next point with a brilliant cross-court backhand.

"Advantage Destroyer."

Greg clenched his fist, but refrained from commenting.

The evil bigamist promptly served another ace.

"Deuce."

The evil bigamist's next serve was good and Greg returned it down the line, but the evil bigamist reached it and played an artful shot that landed just over the net. Greg reacted quickly and lobbed the ball back over. Evil bigamist couldn't reach it in time so Greg won the point, to the crowd's delight.

"Advantage Destroyer."

Greg clenched his fist as his confidence returned. He would *not* let this monster humiliate him.

The evil bigamist served a good ball, which the Destroyer returned down the line where Henry was weakest.

The umpire waited for the applause to die down. "Game to the Destroyer; Destroyer leads by five games to love in the third set and by two sets to love. Destroyer to serve."

Greg's serve would have been an ace but for a foot fault.

"Fault!"

Undaunted, Greg tossed the ball up for his second serve which was a killer, beating any of the match so far.

"Fifteen love."

On a roll, Greg served another ace, followed by another ace and then the final one of the match.

The crowd was ecstatic.

"Game, set and match to the Destroyer. The final score is six-love, six-love, six-love."

"I killed Henry the eighth I did, I did, I did, I did, I killed Henry the eighth, I did, I did, I did, I did, I did, all forty minutes long," sang Greg.

"That one's for free but this one's for me," he rapped, and then continued:

I am the one, I am great because I am good as well as pure
and once I'm done getting rid of you, you'll be nothing but manure.
I am the one who can't be beaten, but you just have been
and to add to what I've said before;
when I send you down there you'll be tortured by Satan
so therefore you'll be further beaten.
I am the best hero in all of the land and you are like a bad boy band.

(Chorus) I am the one who took you on.

I am the one who beat you hard and you will
go down so deep in the ground,
so no one here will see you around.

I will go on to be even greater than I already am
and if you're lucky the people down there
might give you a leftover tin of Spam.
The best I can be is ten times as good as you ever will be
and when I've fulfilled my potential with you,

down there I'll be sipping Earl Grey tea.
I hope you will be as miserable as sin,
while I'll be as cheery as a drunk drinking gin.
I will sleep even better once you are gone
because once again I am the one.

(Chorus)

Then when all of us good people in the world
get up in the morning I'll be fine
and you'll be in a place unfit to house a swine.
You are a filthy scumbag that never amounted to much
because you never had and never will have a good human touch.
So all I want to say to you to round all this off
is you do not have what these people are made of.
They are good, they are pure and they will always choose me
over you as the one they want to cheer.

(Chorus)

The crowd responded with rousing applause and he applauded with them, showing his appreciation of their support. Then he noticed that Oddball had appeared.

"Take it away, Oddball and kill that evil bigamist, he said," about to throw Oddball into his hated opponent, who interrupted.

"I am not a bigamist; I divorced those who didn't die," he protested.

"Oh, you just had to try and have the last word didn't you? But I've got something to say to you to shut you up. You *are* an evil bigamist, because they didn't die naturally, did they? You had them beheaded, so you are also a murderer. I can call you a murderous, vindictive and oh, so evil bigamist." Greg then turned towards a section of the crowd and put his hand to his ear. "Do I hear a halleluiah?"

"Halleluiah!" replied that section of the crowd.

"Again!" he asked the next section of the crowd.

"Halleluiah!"

"Again?"

"Halleluiah!"

"Thank you all very much," said Greg, throwing Oddball at the evil bigamist.

"Okay Oddball, do your stuff."

First Oddball flew into the face of the evil bigamist, making his cheeks expand. "Chubby cheeks," he said, and then dropped down to where the sun doesn't shine. "Oops... too far," said Oddball.

Greg and the entire crowd laughed at that, but then Oddball went to the black heart of the evil bigamist and stretched it until it blew up, therefore vanquishing Henry VIII.

Everybody in the crowd rose to their feet and cheered; they had just gotten rid of one of the most evil beings in their country's history.

The cheering came to an abrupt end when the evil beings arrived to challenge Greg. There were four of them; all had swastika emblems on their clothing... they were Nazis.

The crowd gasped.

Greg looked at them in disbelief.

"We are too strong for you. You might have been able to beat those useless monkeys that preceded us, but you can't beat us because we will annihilate you, just as we did with all those people over sixty years ago," one of the Nazis declared in his demonic voice.

"You are sick and I'm going to punish you for saying that," Greg replied.

The umpire came down from his high chair. "If you're all quite finished with the rubbish talk, I'd like you to listen to me."

Greg and the Nazis looked surprised. "Yeah? And what have you got to say?"

"Well, what I've got to say is that both teams now get to add something." He looked at the Nazis. "What do you guys want to add?"

"We'd like to add a commentator who can turn the crowd against the Destroyer, " the Nazi captain replied.

"Okay, so we need a Moaning Minnie. The SportsLive commentator would be just perfect for you. His name is Alan Peace; ironic for someone who stirs up trouble."

The umpire created a press box and put the commentator in place in the stadium. He turned to Greg. "Destroyer?"

"Well, I think I'll have floodlights, because it's getting dark," said Greg.

The umpire immediately put floodlights in place around the stadium. "Right," he said, "all that's left for me to do now is change into my football referee strip."

His grey flannels and blazer were instantly replaced by a black shirt and shorts.

"Right. I'm now in my referee's outfit; that makes me official, so let's get this match started."

Greg and the Nazis took up their positions and the crowd started cheering in anticipation of what promised to be a truly great match. The referee took a coin from his back pocket ready to flip it and placed his hand on the good half of his head.

"Oh, I almost forgot; we need a name for this tournament which Greg has been competing in and will now try to win by beating the Nazis. So, just off the top of my head, I'll call it the Destroyer Cup."

Then the evil half of his head responded. "Yeah, I'll go for that because I would love to see the moment when the Nazis beat the Destroyer and become the destroyers."

"In your dreams, you evil and ugly version of something from the Addams family," the good head replied.

"Me ugly? You're the one who looks like the back end of a bus."

"Whoa, you guys; you're behaving like us instead of like a responsible referee. So pull yourself together! No pun intended," said Greg.

"Yes, sorry," the heads replied, looking ashamed of themselves. They then looked at Greg and the Nazis.

"Nazis, which side of the coin do you want?" the referee asked.

"Heads!"

The coin came down heads, so the Nazis won the toss. The Nazi striker kicked off, his captain took control of the ball and then kicked a devastatingly good Steven Gerrard like pass to the to the Nazi striker waiting to receive it at the bottom of the pitch. The striker took the ball on towards the goal and had a shot but Greg made a brilliant save.

The commentator described the action.

"... oh, that was a brilliant save by the Destroyer. He just tipped it round the post. Now the captain of the Nazis will take the corner. Here it comes; it's a brilliant out swinging corner, the defender attacks it with a towering header that goes into the bottom corner of the net. Its one nil to the Nazis and the wheels may be coming off the Destroyer's challenge to win the Destroyer Cup now..."

Greg's fans disagreed. "Hey, shut up! The Destroyer is going to come back and win."

"No, you shut up. The commentator's right; the Destroyer's burnt himself out," the Nazi fans retaliated.

Greg kicked off and some of the fans cheered him, but others were jeering and Greg heard them.

"After all I've done for them, and some of them are jeering at me." Greg looked dejected and immediately gave the ball away. The Nazi captain passed it to the striker, who volleyed it from the edge of the box into the top right hand corner of Greg's net.

"... oh, what a corker, and the Destroyer has gone in sixty seconds. It's two nil to the Nazis and hopefully the world will be coming to an end so I won't have to do this Godforsaken job any more..." the commentator said.

"Yeah," remarked a negative fan of Greg's. "I'll second that thought, because I don't like my job either."

"Oh will you shut up, you moaning Minnie Mouse? I don't like my job either but I don't want the world to end because I'm a fighter and I think about saving up enough money so that one day I can buy my own business. Then I can go to see my former boss to flip him the bird and say how well I've done. That's my plan in life, so if all of you good and positive people would like to abide with me?"

He sang Amazing Destroyer to the tune of Amazing Grace. After he had sung it once, all the positive people in the crowd started to join in.

"Amazing Destroyer, how sweet the name that gave us so much hope," they sang.

Greg looked up at them and smiled in appreciation of the song they had made for him. They cheered him but the no-hopers in the crowd interrupted with jeering.

"Come on, everybody that wants to cheer the Destroyer! Let's drown the boo boys out," urged the fan that made up the song.

All the positive fans did just that, giving Greg a warm feeling.

Greg smiled and kicked off. He had a confident swagger about him as he took the ball up the pitch. He headed towards the goal, beat the Nazi striker and captain with a nutmeg and a step over respectively. He then shot at the left side of the goal, but the Nazi goalkeeper made a brilliant one-handed save to turn the ball round the post.

"... that was an absolutely brilliant save by the Nazi goalkeeper..." the commentator declared.

Greg prepared to take the corner kick and once more, the negative element of the crowd started jeering.

One fan stood up. "Hey! What are we doing?" He looked around at the faces turned towards him. "I mean why are we jeering the Destroyer? After all if the Destroyer loses to these idiots, the world and the people in it will cease to exist and while I admit I was one of the negative fans who didn't mind that happening, I've just come to my senses. I've realised that we shouldn't be negative, wanting the world to end, and that the only reason the Destroyer hasn't done very well in this match so far is because he hasn't had the support of the entire crowd. So I say all we negative people should stop being petty and give the Destroyer our support. Even though I'm not a strictly religious man I do believe in karma and that doing as much good as possible will rewards us with many riches. So that is surely as good a reason as any to get behind the Destroyer and support him? After all, he has just won a corner after showing some sublime skill with only half of the crowd's support. Imagine, then, what he could go on to achieve with the support of us all."

"I agree with you," said somebody in the crowd.

"Yes, I agree, too," another said.

"Yeah, and I agree three," someone wisecracked, making them all laugh.

"Okay, are you ready to cheer the Destroyer on to make up for us booing him?"

Several voices shouted "Yes!"

"Good. Oh, and I almost forgot... my name's Oliver, just in case you decide to join the new support group that I've just decided to form."

All of the people in the stadium smiled.

One fan called out, "Yeah, I might get back to you, Oliver, mate. Anyway, should we chant the Destroyer's name?"

"Yes, indeed. Right, now on the count of three I want you chant, 'Go, Destroyer! One... two...three!"

"Go, Destroyer! Go, Destroyer! Go, Destroyer! Go, Destroyer!" The entire crowd was soon chanting in unison.

"Wow, it worked, being positive and having a go at the Nazis got all of the crowd back on my side," Greg said, taking the corner from the left .

"... Oh!" the commentator exclaimed. "What a corner by the Destroyer, which is fortunately saved for another corner. It takes a player of real skill to be able to curl a ball like that from a corner kick. I have to admit that the Destroyer is back in my favour and that is not a comment I make lightly..."

Greg was cheered as he prepared to take the corner kick from the opposite side of the pitch.

"... Here comes the corner kick from the right... the Destroyer again curls it brilliantly into the direction of the goal but the keeper saves it, expertly hanging onto it..."

The Nazi goalkeeper kicked the ball up the pitch. The Destroyer ran back towards his goal and the ball was collected at the feet of the Nazi captain who tried to catch the Destroyer out by trying to lob the ball over him as he was still off his line. The Destroyer cunningly used Oddball, who stretched himself to give the Destroyer extra reach to brilliantly tip the ball over the bar.

The captain of the Nazis took the corner kick. It was an in-swinging one. The Destroyer took it comfortably and dropped the ball on the ground so he could dribble it. He dribbled it round the Nazi striker then nutmegged the captain of the Nazis and finally, a step over took it round their defender. The Destroyer aimed to the right of the goalmouth. The Nazi goalkeeper deftly saved it and turned the ball right round the post.

Greg then received a huge roar of appreciation from the fans. He took the corner and curled it brilliantly at the top left corner of the goal but the goalkeeper made a brilliant one-handed save, tipping the ball round the post for another corner. He tried to take it quickly, but rather embarrassingly, he slipped on his backside. The Nazi defender gathered the ball with his feet and played it along the ground to his nearest team mate, the Nazi captain, who in turn played a neat and tidy pass to the striker.

At that moment Greg chose to speed towards his goal just in time to save a brilliant curling shot by the Nazi striker. It was a corner to the Nazis and the captain ran up the pitch to take it.

It was pinpointed towards the Nazi defender, who expertly jumped to place a bullet header past the outstretched Greg into the bottom corner of the net. The Nazis began to celebrate as the scoreboard flashed three-nil in their favour.

"... Oh no, it's three nil to the Nazis and I have a horrible feeling in the pit of my stomach. Of course, it could be that mince pie I ate earlier, but I think it's because I know what will happen to these innocent people if the Nazis beat the Destroyer. I just hope for their sakes that Greg can do what Liverpool did against A.C. Milan in the Champions' League final that took place in Istanbul..." the commentator continued.

"Okay, I'm three-nil down so I have to wake up and smell the coffee or all these people who have supported me so well throughout the Destroyer Cup will die," thought Greg.

"Come on, Destroyer! You can beat those useless scumbags. You can do it, we believe in you," one of the fans shouted and then looked around the crowd. "Well, are we with him? Come on..."

His words were drowned out as all the fans began to cheer and chant.

Greg, heartened by the show of support, kicked off and then followed up by dribbling the ball around his four opponents. "Okay Greg, you can score," he told himself. "Just hit the ball so damned hard that you slam that swastika-bearing freak into the back of the net; not only that, you'll claw back a goal. Here goes..."

His shot at the goal from the edge of the box was indeed forceful and fierce, just as he intended. However, his plan didn't work.

The Nazi goalkeeper gathered the ball up effortlessly.

"Bugger!" said Greg.

The Nazi goalkeeper kicked the ball out of the goal but Greg reacted quickly and charged the kick down. The ball went agonizingly wide.

"Oh, how bloody lucky can you get, you son of a bitch!"

The Nazi goalie snorted. "I'm not lucky; you're just rubbish. You're beating yourself, therefore making it easy for us to just brush you aside and win the cup to end the world."

"Oh, really? Well, funny you mentioned rubbish and the end of the world because you smell like rubbish so much so that your stink alone could end the world, and quicker than expected. So I can at least stop you from doing that. Come on, Oddball, I need you to turn into a can of deodorant."

"Why do you want a can of deodorant?"

"Why do you want a can of deodorant?" Greg mimicked in a demonic German accent.

Oddball appeared and turned in to a can of deodorant which Greg pointed directly at the goalkeeper.

"Okay, it's time to get rid of Uncle Stinky."

As Greg proceeded to spray the Nazi goalkeeper with deodorant, the commentator tried to stay calm.

"... well, this is getting silly now. The referee needs to step in before the Destroyer does something stupid and gets himself sent off, or even kills us all. Oh, the Nazi goalkeeper has just laid his hands on the Destroyer. I hope he's punished for that..."

The referee then did step in.

"You two need to calm down. I'm giving you both yellow cards," he told them, brandishing two yellow cards.

"Goal kick!" the referee said, pointing to the Nazi goalkeeper.

The commentator continued. "... the Destroyer returns to his goal... the Nazi goalkeeper boots the ball down the field; the striker latches onto it and shoots... oh, what a brilliant save by the Destroyer to keep himself in the game!"

Nothing came of the corner kick. There was just a lot of boring passing of the ball by the Nazis. Finally, after what seemed an eternity of boredom, Greg intercepted the ball and dribbled it around them. Then he drew the goalkeeper out of his goal and tried to lob the ball over it, but the goalkeeper tipped the ball over the bar. Greg curled the corner in with pace, but the goalkeeper took it coolly.

Greg then decided to swear in German.

"Sheiss! sheiss! sheiss!" he repeated.

The commentator concentrates on the action. "... the keeper has the ball and releases it to his nearest team-mate..."

Greg then tackled his opponent, the Nazi defender, therefore winning the ball. He took the ball into the box.

"... this is a good opportunity for the Destroyer to get back into the match. The Nazi goalkeeper comes out... spreads himself to try and block the shot. The Destroyer shoots at the goal but the goalkeeper blocks it, and the Nazi defender is in the right place at the right time and clears it out of play. Well, I really don't know what more the Destroyer has to do to score. I just hope he thinks of a way to get back into the match..."

Greg took the throw-in to himself at supersonic pace and kicked the half volley into the top right corner of the goal. Unfortunately, the Nazi goalkeeper made a brilliant save, tipping the ball over the bar. Greg then took the corner, which was good. However, the Nazi defender cleared the ball out of play for another corner. Greg curled the corner in brilliantly.

"... what a great corner and it agonizingly hits the bar then goes out of play. How unlucky can the good guy get? I just hope the ball will break kindly for him to get back in the match... I'm sure he can then go on and win the game..."

The Nazi goalkeeper took the goal kick and as it travelled down field, Greg tried hitting it on the half volley from the halfway line, but the keeper made a brilliant save to turn it over the bar. Greg took the corner with an in-swinging ball to himself, promptly took the ball up the pitch, dribbled around the Nazi defender and had a shot at goal. The keeper spilt the ball but pounced on the rebound and then kicked it away up field.

Greg charged down the kick in yet another attempt to score but the ball went agonizingly wide. The goalkeeper took the goal kick and the referee checked his watch and then blew the whistle.

"Drei zu nil! Drei zu nil! Drei zu nil!" The Nazis chanted, exchanging high fives with each other.

In the changing room, Greg brought Oddball out.

"Well, Oddball? Got any bright ideas?"

"No. Unfortunately I used up all my special powers making you more powerful than the emperors."

"So that lot of evil idiots could win the war? Just listen to them chanting, 'drei zu nil.' I bet that's the only German they know."

"Yeah. You're probably right."

"I probably know more German words than they do. Like: Ich heisse Greg Carter. Ich bin achtzehn jahre alt. Ich mochte zu gewinnt, and... check this out for size... Liebe Nazis, du eine nein wunderbar. Then there are other languages that I know of like Japanese: kanichiwa, nomo arogato, and... oh, what I would love to say to those idiots next door, sianara." Greg brought his hands together, looking towards his opponents' dressing room.

"Then there's Italian. Arrivederci and ciao, which is what I am planning to say to them when I beat them."

"Okay, if you're finished going mad are you going out to the pitch because it's nearly the end of half-time?" Oddball said.

"Yeah, okay... and can you bring your non-existent powers," Greg replied with the words non-existent in air quotation marks.

"What's with the air quotation marks?"

"Oh, come on, Oddball; I know you. You always like to hide your talents and then surprise people with them."

"Sure, I was just messing with you. I was hoping you wouldn't work me out so fast so I could have a bit more fun."

Greg laughed. "Well I wouldn't be a superhero if I couldn't work things out with one of my best mates."

Oddball smiled at Greg and went back into him.

"Right, time to face the music," said Greg, leaving the dressing room and entering the tunnel leading to the pitch.

The Nazis followed and took up their positions.

The commentator held the mic to his lips. "Welcome back to this match all you brilliant fans. I'm so flaky that I've decided to switch to supporting the Destroyer. It hasn't gone well for us so far, but if we all get behind the Destroyer he can hopefully come from behind to beat the scumbag Nazis..."

The second half of the match kicked off.

Steven and Amy were still wondering how to get out of the underworld of the damned.

"Well I'm fresh out of ideas. What about you?" asked Amy.

"I don't have any ideas either, unfortunately," Steven replied. Then suddenly he had a premonition about how to get out of there.

"Was that a premonition, Steven?"

"Yes, it was!"

"What did you see?"

"I saw us taking fragments of our clothes as they are from earth and that's where we want to be. I also saw me taking a piece of Satan's flesh using my blade, and I can only assume in the future which is about to become the present, you put a spell on me to make me look like a demon, because Satan or whatever that red freak is called seemed to think I was one of its demons. Then we both said the spell."

"That sounds too dangerous though. Perhaps I could think of another spell to get out of here?" Amy suggested.

"No, Amy. I think what I saw in my premonition is really the only way we can get out of here and back to Greg."

"But are you sure you want to do that?"

"Of course, yeah!"

"You're certainly a brave guy."

"Well, fortune favours the brave and we certainly need fortune in order to get out of this place."

"Okay," Amy agreed. "In that case I'll just think of a spell to disguise you as a demon." She closed her eyes. "Disguise Steven as a demon in this place so that he can do what he needs to do to get us out of this place."

Steven was magically disguised as a demon.

"How do I look?"

"Scarier than hell," Amy replied with a grimace.

Steven smiled. "Perfect. Will you be here behind this cave wall when I get back?"

Amy nodded. "I'll be there."

"Okay, I'm off to scratch that thing that is mentioned in Queen's Bohemian Rhapsody."

Amy laughed. "Good luck."

Steven entered what resembled a dentist's waiting room and waited there until a demon called him in to see Satan Himself.

"You called for me?" Steven asked in a demonic voice.

"Yes, because you are a new demon and I have an obligation to give you an assignment that will make you a full demon," Satan replied in his satanic voice.

"Okay, what do you want me to do?"

"I want you kill the Destroyer." Said Satan.

Steven's first thought was, 'No way, you red idiot with a giant cutlery set,' referring to Satan's giant fork and knife amongst other tools. But he didn't want Satan to realise he was an imposter...

"Okay; that's not a problem. Do you want to shake on it to seal the deal?"

"I like your style," Satan replied.

They shook hands and Steven chose that moment to scratch a piece of flesh from Satan.

"Sorry, I'm such a klutz," he explained, to make it seem accidental.

"That's okay,"

Steven then walked out of Satan's den, holding his head up high. Smiling, he passed through the waiting room and went directly to the cave wall where Amy was hiding.

She looked amused. "So did you literally get a piece of Satan's flesh?"

"Yeah. I made that red nitwit look absolutely bloody stupid." Steven gave the sliver of Satan's flesh to Amy.

She put it on the ground and held her hand out. "Quick, give me a fragment of your clothes."

Using his blade, Steven cut a piece off his shirt off using his blade.

Amy then cut a piece off her shirt, using her finger blades. She started a fire by striking her blades on the ground and then put the fragments of their shirts on the ground.

"Wow, that's clever," Steven remarked.

"Yeah, well, I thought since I didn't have a frying pan it would be a good idea to cook the ingredients the old fashioned way and as there was no way of breaking a piece of rock off this cave wall, I decided to rub my finger blades against the floor that has Satan's flesh on it."

"Super witch."

"I don't know if I'm that good," said Amy, modestly.

"You are; trust me."

"Now we have to say the spell that we said earlier. That, along with the potion, should get us out of here and back home to Greg."

Steven and Amy held hands and repeated the spell they had chanted earlier. They began to disappear, but just before they did a gang of mean-looking rats came out of nowhere. They were rats that sought out good beings to kill.

Steven gasped. "Bloody hell! Where did they come from?"

"I don't know, but hopefully the spell can take us back to Greg before they get to us."

To their immense relief, Steven and Amy were able to disappear before the rats reached them.

Greg, meanwhile, was still losing three nil to the Nazis. He had the ball but lost it to the Nazi captain.

"Oh boy, it doesn't look like it's going to be the Destroyer's day. At least he has had a go at trying to comeback from three nil down, so I suppose that's all we can ask for," said Oliver, who was now officially the most popular fan in the ground even though he used to be the Moaning Minnie.

"Yeah," the crowd agreed with a huge, communal sigh.

"The Destroyer's back on the ball but we can't show our disappointment, so I suggest we cheer him on in the hope that he can somehow come back and beat those idiots into the ground," Oliver said, watching the Destroyer.

The crowd all cheered the Destroyer who had the ball at his feet and skipped majestically past the captain of the Nazis. As he was about to shoot from outside of the penalty box he was deliberately tripped by the defender of the Nazis who was the last outfield man on the pitch.

Greg was in a bad way.

"Oddball, my left leg's bust. Have you a power to heal it?

Oddball appeared. "Your leg is broken. I'll just run myself through it and heal the break."

Oddball swiftly summoned his powers and healed Greg's leg. "Don't get up too quickly, otherwise the leg will break again," he warned.

"Oh... I was going to get up slowly anyway, for dramatic effect."

Oddball sniggered before disappearing back into Greg.

After rising to his feet in slow motion, Greg went to the Nazi defender and glared down at him as if he were scum.

"Oh, and what are you going to do? Stare me to death?" the defender asked.

"I'm merely looking at an evil, good-for-nothing-scumbag who I want sent off by the referee." Greg shifted his gaze to the referee and waved an imaginary card at him. "Send that freak off, now."

"Don't tell me how to do my job. I know I might look like an idiot, but I'm not!" both heads replied in unison. The referee then showed the Nazi defender a red card that vanquished him.

The crowd roared their approval.

Greg gasped with surprise. "How the hell did you do that?"

"Well, contrary to what you think, I am good at my job. And just remember, I can also do the same to you if you get on my bad side and we both know you won't like that."

"Yeah, sure," Greg agreed, preparing to take the free kick. The remaining Nazis had lined up to make a wall. He took the free kick which was good, but so was the wall, which did its job. Greg was disappointed. Then the captain of the Nazis played the ball towards the goal in an attempt to score.

"... the captain of the Nazis has just played the ball towards goal in an attempt to score and it looks like curtains for all of us. Oh... what's this? There appear to be two new superheroes and one of them has just cleared the ball off the line..."

Hearing the commentator's words, Greg, still looking disappointed, turned round and looked with disbelief at Amy and Steven. Then he saw that the ball had been magically placed on the spot where the corner kick was to be taken from.

"Wow, it's amazing what can happen when you're feeling sorry for yourself," Greg thought, going over to greet Amy and Steven.

"Well, it's about time," he said.

"Yeah, we know," Steven said. That's because we accidentally landed in a weight loss clinic."

"Explain?"

"After what we just saw, mate, I never want to eat a cheeseburger ever again."

Greg and Amy laughed.

"So where did the emperors of the sun send you?" asked Greg.

Steven took a deep breath. "The underworld of the damned."

"The underworld of the damned? Is that... down there?"

"Oh yes," Steven and Amy replied in unison.

Greg smiled at Amy and Steven and then looked at the Nazis. "So that's what they call hell..."

"Yeah."

"Okay, guys, are you ready to rock 'em with our high football tide?" asked Greg.

"Readier than ready," Steven replied.

"I bet you're glad to be back on earth, even if those scumbags are currently on it."

"Yeah," Amy agreed.

"And I'm certainly glad to have you back because I was feeling sorry for myself and they almost scored. So I'm guessing one of you saved me from further embarrassment by clearing the ball off the line?"

"That was Steven," said Amy.

"Oh, right." Greg looked at Amy and Steven in turn. "Thanks."

The three of them shared high fives. They heard the commentator posing a question.

"... I wonder if these new superheroes can help the Destroyer beat the scumbag Nazis?"

"Come on, then; let's line up for the corner to stop the Nazis going further in front," Greg said.

Greg took up position between the posts and Steven and Amy went into the six-yard box to help Greg out.

The corner came in from the captain of the Nazis, looking for the head of their striker, but Greg came to take the ball before the striker could head the ball towards the goal. He released it with a long throw to Steven, who takes the ball to the by-line. He looked across to see Amy running up the pitch and crossed the ball for her.

"... and the green girl rises above the six foot four Nazi captain and plants a brilliant header past him into the top left corner of the net to finally claim a goal back. The superheroes now have a platform from which they can build," the commentator said with satisfaction in his voice.

The crowd cheered their new heroes as Greg ran up the pitch to congratulate Amy and Steven.

Greg then returned to his position between the goalposts while Steven and Amy also prepared for play to continue.

The captain of the Nazis kicked off and passed the ball to their striker, who took the ball up the pitch. Steven tackled and took the ball back up the other end, bouncing the ball on his feet. He then played a neat one-two with Amy who had also run all the way up the pitch. Steven then took the ball and kicked it hard and low past the outstretched Nazi goalkeeper into the bottom right corner of the net to make the score two goals to the Destroyer's team; three to the Nazis.

Greg, Steven and Amy celebrated with more high fives.

"... the superheroes are only one goal down now and there is a real chance that we can finally see the back of these horrible beings..." the commentator said, but his words were barely audible, with the crowd cheering wildly for their superheroes Greg, Amy and Steven.

The players took up their positions and the captain of the Nazis kicked off, passing the ball to the striker who tried to run with it but Amy made a brilliant tackle to win the ball. She then laid the ball off to Steven who was standing by the touchline. He went on a mazy dribble with the ball at his feet and when he approached the penalty box he deftly flicked the ball into the box with his heel. The crowd watched his amazing skill in awe.

"... and the green heroine takes the ball down on her chest from what was simply a breathtaking show of skill by the blue superhero. The girl in green tries to take the ball around the Nazi captain... oh! He has brought her down... she's okay, she's up on her feet and the referee has pointed to the spot. A penalty to the superheroes..."

The crowd went wild with excitement as the ball was then magically placed on the penalty spot for Steven to take the penalty. He looked extremely calm as he walked a few paces backward and then ran towards the ball. He hit the ball at the keeper's bottom right corner; unfortunately the keeper saved it from going into the net by pushing it out in front of him. However, Steven had enough energy to get to the ball before any of his Nazi opponents, to score into the roof of the net, leaving the goalkeeper beating the ground in annoyance that he and his team-mates had thrown away a three goal lead. But nobody in the stadium had any sympathy; the fans were cheering even louder than before in the Destroyer Cup.

The scoreboard confirmed they were equal at three goals each.

"... It's three all now, and miracles do happen. That goal caps an amazing achievement by these three brilliant superheroes, who have now scored three goals in just six minutes. A simply miraculous six minutes. Now, the question is, can they go on to win this match and end the suffering of all these fantastic supporters...?"

The crowd was still cheering, knowing that if they kept it up, they would give their superheroes the confidence they needed to defeat the three remaining Nazis.

The captain of the Nazis kicked off and passed the ball to the striker, who took the ball around Amy with a Ronaldinho-style step over. He took the ball up the pitch and into the penalty box and was about to shoot, but Greg came off his line in a heartbeat and took the ball right off the feet of the Nazi striker.

"... good goalkeeping there by the Destroyer. He releases the ball to the blue boy; I'm sure he won't mind my calling him the blue boy..." the commentator said, looking into the crowd.

"Yo! Blue boy," shouted some fans.

The commentator smiled."Great; I'm glad you like the nickname. Anyway, back to the game now. Blue boy is just trying to embarrass the captain of the Nazis and does just that by bamboozling him with his fancy footwork to the extent that he falls on his backside. What a shame, not! Blue boy then crosses the ball into the penalty box for the green girl to brilliantly head the ball with extreme pace at the goalmouth, and it's... oh! That was so close, but the Nazi goalkeeper just got to that one to turn the ball round the post for what will be a corner kick to the superheroes. I have to say, green girl is just as good at playing football as she is at turning me on. She is definitely an asset and I wouldn't mind getting my hands on her assets, if you know what I mean?" The commentator smiled at his own joke and looked at the fans sitting next to him.

They stared at him, unimpressed with his comments.

He looked embarrassed. "Oops, I fear I may have gone too far in mentioning my fantasy. No offence intended there, folks..."

Oliver stood up. "Okay, but from now on I suggest you only talk about her football talents as opposed to her other talents. I like the name 'green girl' though. In fact all the names you have given the superheroes are good, but nowhere near as good as the superheroes themselves." He turned to address the entire crowd. "As a matter of fact, I've thought of a song for our new superheroes. So if everyone in this terrific stadium could repeat each verse after I've sung it, that would great."

"Y-E-E-E-S-S!" roared the crowd.

"You are the hope of our lives... no, that's no good because it'll make us look as if we've got nothing else but sport in our lives. Ah, that's it, I've got the song... okay, here goes:"

> # *You give us so much hope so that we can carry on,*
> *so that we can be like you and bind the good in this world as one...*

The fans responded and repeated the first verse as Oliver had requested.

> *(Chorus) You are our beautiful superheroes*
> *and we support you in your quest to make these good for nothing Nazis*
> *as obsolete and dead as Dodos.*

All the fans repeated the chorus and rapped together, repeating Oliver's verses.

> *the Nazis are suckers for embarrassment;*
> *we thought they'd had enough of that*
> *and forfeited the game, deciding enough is enough.*
> *Blue boy is looking good strutting his stuff,*

> *(Chorus)*

71

Green girl receives the ball at her feet;
after the Destroyer had launched a long kick
so he must have had his shredded wheat.
Green girl then has a shot at goal,
And although the Nazi keeper saves it
Our superheroes are still on a roll.

(Chorus)

Now can the superheroes score one more goal for us,
so we can celebrate it with one more chorus?
You've done so well to get this far,
now can you remove these Nazis from this earth
because they have been to the people on this earth
nothing else but a terrible scar.
If you do as we as we ask you will be ridding the world
of so much hate and that will be something
we can all cheer as well as appreciate.

They ended with a final chorus and Oliver thanked the fans for their fine performance in support of the three superheroes.

The commentator resumed. "Well, follow that, Peace! What a wonderful display of support from such dedicated fans. That was a simply great composition from Oliver that has put us all in the mood to cheer these brilliant superheroes on, hopefully to victory against the most ugly and hated race ever to walk this most beautiful of worlds. The ball is in play and the Destroyer has it, releasing it to blue boy who takes the ball up the pitch. He takes the ball to the by-line, crosses it for green girl... oh, and that was a brilliant bicycle kick at the goal but the keeper unfortunately turns it round the posts for another corner kick to the superheroes.

"And blue boy takes the corner. The ball is pinpointed to Amy who heads the ball towards the goal; the keeper saves it easily and has the ball in his hands, releasing it to the captain of the Nazis, who takes the ball to the penalty box and shoots... no, the green girl tackles him, where on earth did she come from at that speed? And the ball goes out of play for a throw in..."

"Wow, Amy, that was impressive," Greg said.

"Yeah, well I couldn't get back to save your bacon the conventional way, so I decided to cast a spell to magically get me there to help you."

"Doesn't matter; I'm glad you saved my Babe Johnson, because I wouldn't want to lose him," replied Greg, who referred to his pride as Babe Johnson.

They both laughed.

Steven then came down the pitch to help Greg and Amy with the throw in.

"... the Nazi captain takes the throw in, directs it to the striker of the Nazis. Blue boy heads it out. Green girl collects the ball at her feet and takes the ball down the line. Blue boy sprints towards the goal ready to take green girl's cross. Green girl gets to the by-line, crosses the ball for blue boy to brilliantly scissor-kick the ball at goal... oh, I say, the keeper only *just* gets to it to turn it over the bar! It will be a corner kick to the superheroes. Blue boy takes it and wonderfully curls it in. Green girl heads it well towards the goal but the keeper makes a brilliant save, tipping the ball over the bar for another corner to the superheroes. Blue boy takes it. It is a good one and green girl again heads it towards goal. The keeper again saves it with a tip over the bar. Blue boy again takes the corner, this time trying a new move. He chips the ball up to green girl, who scissor-kicks the ball towards goal. Unfortunately, the captain of the Nazis heads the ball off line..." The commentator pauses to take a breath and a quick sip of water.

Steven volleyed the ball back at the goal but the Nazi keeper held on to it easily and then kicked the ball up the pitch. Amy chased it and collected it at her feet.

"Green girl runs with the ball; she dribbles it past the captain of the Nazis. She's at the the edge of the box, flicks the ball with the outside of her left foot to the on-rushing blue boy who shoots on the volley, but the goalkeeper makes a brilliant save as he has done way too often from the point of view of all the good people in this stadium. With ten minutes to go, the Destroyer is coming up for the corner kick. He obviously feels if there are more people attacking the corner kick, there is more chance of getting a goal from it. Blue boy takes it... it's an in-swinger."

"Over here," shouted Greg to Amy.

Amy brilliantly headed the ball back to Greg who had noticed the Nazi goalkeeper was ever so slightly off his line.

"Oh! And the Destroyer audaciously lobs the ball over the Nazi goalkeeper and into the net..."

The commentator's voice was drowned out as the crowd cheered even louder than before.

"Well, that was even better than Philippe Albert's goal against Manchester United because, you know, it takes a very cool person to be able to pull off that sort of skill when there is so much at stake in a match. I think we can now look forward to more peace on earth than there has ever been before. It's four goals to three in favour of the superheroes. I am going to get as drunk as a skunk with these brilliant fans after the match," the commentator, Alan Peace avowed.

"Yeah, you are," said Oliver.

Greg, Steven and Amy were celebrating what they had managed to achieve together. The fans were still cheering and had begun chanting, "Superheroes rule! Superheroes rule! Superheroes rule!" Then they saw that the Nazis were about to kick off and decided to chant obscenities.

"You're sheisse and you know you are!" some of the fans shouted. Within seconds, the entire crowd was chanting, "You're sheisse and you know you are! You're sheisse and you know you are! You're sheisse and you know you are!"

The Nazi captain was angry, so incensed in fact that when he tried to dribble the ball round Amy he fell over onto his backside. A roar went up as the fans gave ironic cheers, enraging the Nazi even more. Then Amy took the ball up the pitch and slammed it at the goal. Unfortunately, the Nazi goalkeeper turned the ball round the post, but then again, the superheroes were winning and that was the most important thing. So there was no need to be greedy.

Steven took the corner kick. He decided to waste time by calling Amy across and passed the ball to her. She passed it back and he kept the ball by the corner flag, managing to keep it there for the remaining ten minutes of the match, plus stoppage time of four minutes due to Greg's injury. However, he didn't just keep the ball by the corner flag like Alan Shearer; Steven now had the opportunity to show off his skills and to give the fans a sideshow event. He kept the ball up in the air using his feet and other parts of his body until the referee blew the the final whistle. Steven then kicked the ball into the stand for someone to catch as a souvenir.

Surprise! Surprise! Oliver, the most popular fan in the in the ground, caught it. The fans were cheering ecstatically.

"At last the match is over, the superheroes have triumphed against the scumbag Nazis and I can go and get sheisse faced with these amazing fans, like I promised earlier. Signing off now, Alan Peace," the commentator said, struggling to be heard above the cheering fans.

The referee walked briskly across the pitch to Greg, Steven and Amy and magically changed his referee strip into a suit. He then magically created a trophy and held it up for all to see.

"Okay," he said to the crowd, "this is the moment all you brilliant fans have been waiting for. The winners of the Make

Peace Through Sport or the Destroyer Cup are... oh, I don't know what to call you."

"Oh, well we don't know what to call ourselves either," said Greg, as the crowd laughed.

Just at that moment, Oddball appeared. "How about the name of Oddballs F.C?" he said.

"Yeah, that's a good name," replied Greg, Amy and Steven in unison.

"Okay, then. The winners of the Make Peace Through Sport cup are Oddballs F.C.," announced the alien in the suit, aka the referee and umpire.

The crowd then went absolutely crazy with joy.

"Wow! What terrific support," Greg said.

"Yeah," Amy and Steven agreed. "Unbelievable."

"The only thing that's missing is Queen singing 'We are the champions' while those loser Nazis stand useless as statues," Greg said.

Oddball had a suggestion. "I could temporarily turn into an mp3 player with speakers as a substitute for headphones so that everyone in this stadium can hear it. It will have 'We are the champions' downloaded onto it."

"Oh, but that would be fantastic," Greg said.

"Yeah," Steven and Amy agreed. "Cool."

The fans stopped cheering and began to sing along with the great Queen recording and Greg, Steven and Amy linked arms and joined in as well. When they reached the words 'no time for losers,' Greg pointed at the Nazis.

When the song was over the fans started cheering again, the mood even better than it was before. Oddball then returned to its usual state.

"Now I would like to reward you three by conjuring a bottle of champagne," declared the alien in the suit and a bottle of classy champagne flew into his hands, apparently out of thin air.

Greg accepted it on behalf of his team and thanked the alien.

"Do you want me to turn into a corkscrew so you don't have to waste any energy popping the cork off?" asked Oddball.

"No, it'll spoil the atmosphere," Greg replied. He then pointed the bottle at the Nazi captain's crotch and flicked the cork off at it.

Steven and Amy started laughing along with the entire crowd.

"Oh yeah; get in there!" Oliver said, delighted.

Amy glanced at Greg. "That was brilliant."

"Nice one," Steven agreed.

Greg drank some champagne straight from the bottle, spluttering as the bubbles fizzed all over his face, going up his nostrils.

"There you go, Amy," he said, passing her the bottle. She also swigged the foaming liquid from the bottle and then handed it to Steven.

Steven drank the remainder of it.

"I hope nobody wanted any more champagne because I've finished it off, he said, wiping his face with the back of his hand."

The other two laughed.

"No problem, mate; we've had enough," said Greg. He rubbed his hands together. "Now then, do you want to sing a little song to get rid of those obnoxious Nazi pricks?"

"Yeah!" they agreed.

"Okay. Oddball, can you turn into a laptop?"

"Anything for you, Greg," Oddball replied, instantly becoming a laptop.

"Thanks." Taking Oddball's home made laptop, Greg wrote the song down using the supersonic speed that Oddball supplied.

"Right, here it is." Greg passed the laptop displaying the song to Amy and Steven, who each took it in turn and memorised the song.

"Got it?" Greg asked them.

Steven and Amy nodded.

As Greg took the laptop from them it turned back into Oddball.

"So, are we ready to rock this stadium?" asked Greg, looking at Amy and Steven.

"You bet," Amy replied.

"All right an' ready," said Steven in an American accent.

Greg and Amy laughed and then Greg addressed the crowd.

"Okay, all you brilliant fans, feel free to join in with the chorus once you've learnt it!" He turned to Amy and Steven. "A one, two, three..."

 # We stand united, as well as good and right.
And what we say to you Nazi scum is good day and goodnight.
We good people in this stadium are so powerful and good.
But you Nazis are as useless as a piece of old deadwood.

(Chorus) We are united as one true good
because we have good blood and you have bad blood.
We good people in this stadium are all good and pure
And where there's evil in the world we'll always find a cure.

All of us good people must stand together
to try and make good stay in the world forever.
We can make this world a better place
by erasing all the bad guys who are just a disgrace
from this earth; go in shame and hide your face.

(Chorus)

We will make sure that you never return to this earth
so you're going to go somewhere very hot,
... but not
to Australia on a sunny beach in Perth.
You good for nothings are so useless you cannot work together
We are good at teamwork, but then we are what's called clever.

We will smile the biggest smile when all of you are gone
and take pleasure in the fact that you will be unknown.
The world will be united as it never has before
And happiness will take your place; peace on earth for evermore.

(Chorus)

The crowd responded by clapping, cheering and waving. Greg, Steven and Amy took their bows, acknowledging the ovation.

"And now, the moment we've all been waiting for," said Greg, who then threw Oddball into the captain of the Nazis.

Oddball also stretched itself into the other two Nazis.

"Bye bye," Greg said, putting two fingers up to the Nazis.

Oddball then blew them up and the crowd cheered again as Greg encouraged them with a wild whooping noise.

As the applause died down, an unknown fan came down the stadium steps. He was wearing a black suit and carried a black briefcase.

"Hi. My name's Jack Clarke," he said to the three friends. "I own a chain of businesses all of which are registered on the stock market. My nickname's Blackjack because all my companies make so many people so much money. Anyway, I've come down to tell you that with the money I've amassed I would like to buy your magnificent stadium and enter your team, Oddballs, into the Combined Counties League. I would also like to sign all of you up as players, and I'll hire a manager to pick the rest of the team and other staff members."

Greg smiled at Jack. "Wow, well that's very flattering but I think I speak for all of us when I say we would be a bit too busy to play football and as for the stadium, you can have that for free." He looked to Steven and Amy for confirmation. "Yeah?"

"Yeah," they agreed.

"That is so generous of you all, but are you sure you don't want any money?"

"Positive, yeah," said Greg.

"Well, that's very kind of you, I must say. How about if I make you all honorary presidents? Then you can come and watch the games for free."

"Thanks. That would be great."

"Okay, well I'll just have to ask you all to sign your names on a document. This is to give you official permission to use your stadium and also the name Oddballs F.C. as the name of the team I am going to enter into the Counties League." Jack reached into his briefcase and took out the document, handing it to Greg.

Greg signed his name 'The Destroyer' and handed the deed to Steven, who signed it 'Blue Boy.' Finally, Amy signed it 'Green Girl.'

"Thanks a lot. I'll get this back to my lawyers who can put an extra clause in the contract that will officially make you honorary presidents of the club," said Jack Clarke, stowing the papers away in his briefcase. Then he said his farewells and walked out of the stadium, joining the mass exodus, still buzzing after all the excitement.

The stadium was finally empty. Greg looked around, replaying in his mind their recent triumph. He felt good.

"Well done, guys," he said, taking Amy's and Steven's hands in his. "Let's go home."

"Boy, that was some long night. How about we go to bed and celebrate tomorrow?" Greg said to the other two.

"Good idea," Amy agreed.

"Night then," Steven said, looking at Greg and Amy.

"Night," they replied together.

"Amy, are you coming to bed to... you know?" Greg asked.

"Oh, so you're not that tired?"

Greg grinned. "Yes... not that tired."

Back in Romania, Adrian Domescu is talking to Christopher.

"Okay, it's time to try something different. If we can't beat the superheroes we will just have to find a way to separate them. Now then, if we put the Destroyer, Greg Carter, under a spell, that will make his arrogant streak a hell of a lot worse and he will use it against Steven and Amy who will then disown him, leaving him pretty much alone. You, Christopher, will then be responsible for making him feel completely alone, which means he will have no choice but to join us and then help us to get my family and girlfriend back. However, that part of the plan can wait for now. So, do you have any questions?"

Christopher the Idiot looked confused. "Yes, I do. How can this work? I mean, I thought the only way for you to get what you want is to kill the Destroyer? That is certainly what I want."

"Well, that was only according to a theory on the Internet but the Internet is full of all sorts of garbage. I should have realised that earlier. Although I would say that theory had some useful information because I do believe there is a connection between the Destroyer and bringing back the dead, even if it was rubbish in terms of giving inaccurate information. I think the connection is combining the Destroyer's powers with our powers and that should be enough to bring back my loved ones. As for you, Christopher, and what you want... well, once we have brought back my loved ones the Destroyer will be a disgrace to everyone who knows him. The reason it is good for you is because he will have lost his good nature and, from what I've gathered about him, that will be a fate worse than death," Adrian replied.

"Yes, I like your way of working our plan even better than the original way we were going to do it," said Christopher, the Idiot, smiling in a demonic way.

Adrian nodded. "I thought you would. Right, it's time to put the spell on Greg, the Destroyer."

"Okay," Christopher replied, still smiling.

Adrian wrote down the spell and gave it to Christopher, the Idiot to read.

"Fine. I'm ready to say it."

Adrian and Christopher held hands and incanted the spell.

"Let the Destroyer fall under our spell so we can use him for what we need to do and then make his life a living hell."

"Now we wait," said Adrian looking at Christopher.

As their eyes met, they both began cackling with manic laughter.

It was quite late next morning when Greg, Steven and Amy came out of their rooms, stretching their arms and yawning.

"Wow, that was one good night," Amy said, smiling knowingly at Greg.

Greg was grinning at Amy like a Cheshire cat. "Yeah, cool."

As the trio finished brunch, Steven asked, "Where do you want to go to celebrate our achievements?"

"How about our favourite Indian restaurant? Greg suggested. "Boy, that makes it sound like you and I are gay."

Steven and Amy laughed.

"Well I would love to go to an Indian restaurant," Amy said.

"Yeah, me too. Just so long as you don't start any funny business, Greg."

Greg gave Steven a look of mock horror. "Okay, so let's go off to the home of the best hot curry in the whole of Newcastle. Then maybe we can go clubbing afterwards to burn off the excess calories."

Later that evening they headed for the Indian restaurant just as they planned.

"A table for three, please?" Greg requested.

The immaculately dressed head waiter showed them to a corner table and handed them each a menu.

"Okay," Greg said. Let's get ourselves warmed up for all the clubbing afterwards, yeah?"

"Yeah," Steven and Amy agreed.

They didn't really need the menu; they knew exactly what they wanted to eat.

"Three red hot curries, please," Greg said, when the waiter came along.

The waiter grinned at them. "You sure you can take Vindaloo? Is very, very hot, you know."

"We know... and yes, we can take it," Steven told him, grinning back.

They each drank a cold beer while they waited, but it wasn't long before the waiter returned with three generous portions of the highly spiced, authentic Indian dish they loved.

"Enjoy your meal," he said.

"Thanks very much." Greg held a forkful in front of him. "Open your mouth, burn your gums. Look out stomach, here something fiery comes," he said. Putting the fork in his mouth, his face turned red and his eyes watered as he chewed.

"Oh, that is so good," he said, reaching for his cold beer.

"Yeah, real good," Steven agreed and Amy just nodded, fanning her mouth furiously with her hand. Their faces had turned red as well.

"More cold beer, please," Steven said, catching the eye of the waiter.

In Romania, Adrian and Christopher were watching Greg, Steven and Amy on Adrian's magically modified wide screen television.

"Why hasn't the spell worked yet? Surely Greg should be blowing his top by now?" Christopher asked, impatiently.

"Patience, Christopher. The spell takes quite a bit of time and as for Greg blowing his top, I think technically he is, the hot curry is doing that for him. I think that's why some people like a hot curry, because it's a good way for them to blow their tops without committing an act of violence. Don't worry though, because once the curry has been digested, the spell will take effect and our plan will work," Adrian told him.

Greg, Steven and Amy finished their meal, paid for it and left the restaurant to look for a club.

"Okay, here we are," said Greg, stopping outside an ordinary looking building, the doors of which were being guarded by a giant of a man. *ALLNITE MUSIC*, declared a flashing sign above the doors and as they were opened by the bouncer to admit the trio, a blast of heavy metal escaped into the street.

Inside the club, they ordered their drinks and found a table. Greg and Amy danced while Steven sat with his cold lager.

A few dances and many beers later, Amy and Greg visited the bathroom separately.

"Ah, that is such good beer," Greg declared, falling rapidly under the spell and becoming mortally drunk; not his usual self at all. As he turned his head he saw a woman eyeing him up. Cool, yeah. He staggered up to her.

"D'you wanna get on board the Greg train?"

"Oh, yeah; don't mind," the woman replied.

Greg and the woman went off together and he bought her a drink, after which he led her to the bathroom for sex in one of the cubicles.

Steven came out of the adjacent cubicle and washed his hands. He could hear voices coming from within the cubicle.

"Oh, yeah," Steven said, "someone's getting it on." Then he heard a moan and a breathy female voice murmuring, "Oh, Greg..."

"Oh boy. Greg, what have you done?" Steven said. He left the bathroom, looking shocked and bumped into Amy, on her way in.

"What's the matter? Did you see a ghost in there?" Amy asked him.

"No, of course not, it's... there's some horrendous graffiti in there."

"So what?"

"So, you don't need to see it."

Amy wasn't impressed. "You're a terrible liar, Steven. So I'm going in, because my intuition tells me there is something I do need to see in there."

Steven quickly positioned himself between her and the bathroom.

"Get out of my way, Steven."

"No!"

"Okay; I'm going to count to three and if you're not out of my way by then I'm going to do horrible things to your private parts." As she opened her mouth to start counting she heard a woman's voice.

"Oh, Greg," the voice was saying, "you're one fast train going through my tunnel..."

"What? That's it, I'm going to kill him!" Amy announced.

"I can't let you do that," Steven said, still standing between her and the bathroom door.

"Steven, let me come past, or else I will..."

Steven skipped out of Amy's way, fearing what she would do to his treasured parts.

"Oh Greg, mate, what have you done?" said Steven, walking away and out of the club.

Amy stood on the toilet seat and looked down into the next cubicle to catch Greg and the woman in the act.

"How could you, Greg?" shouted Amy in disgust.

Greg did not even have the grace to look guilty "Well," he said, looking down at his genitalia, "that's because everything down there works."

"You pathetic excuse for a human being," replied Amy, storming out the bathroom.

Greg and the woman followed her out and he shouted after her..

"Amy, I'm sorry for that remark."

Amy turned round. "Oh, you're sorry, even though you're still with her?"

Greg suddenly rounded on the woman. "For God's sake, haven't you got a home to go to?"

"Oh, how charming," the woman replied.

"I know, because I did literally charm the pants off you earlier."

"Don't flatter yourself..."

"I'm not, I'm flattering you."

"You arrogant pig."

"Yes, I am and you're a thick whore."

With that, the woman spat in Greg's face.

Greg took out his hanky, shook it and wiped the spit off his face, glaring down at her.

"Oh, you like spitting do you, you little bitch..."

"Hey! Don't call my girlfriend that ever again or I'll hit you." The woman's boyfriend was just coming to the bathroom to look for her.

"Your girlfriend? So you're going with this female dog? Well, she can't think that much of you since she's just had it off with me," Greg boasted.

"Right," the boyfriend growled. "That's it, you're dead!"

Greg advanced towards the boyfriend, looking down at him like he was scum.

"Ooh dear, I'm really scared!" whimpered Greg.

"You should be."

"Yeah, in your dreams maybe, but in reality I'm not."

"Don't say I didn't warn you!" The boyfriend then rushed at Greg, attempting to hit him.

Although he had drunk a lot, Greg's reflexes were still sharp and he intercepted the punch, pushing the boyfriend to the ground.

"Now then, that was a big mistake of yours to think you could beat me in a fight because nobody beats me at anything, especially a fight," he said, and then kicked the man in the stomach.

"Nobody messes with me because I am the great and powerful Greg Carter, unlike you, you're nothing. Nothing!"

Greg was yelling at him and was about to kick him again when the hefty bouncer came along and stopped him.

Amy, shocked at Greg's behaviour, stormed out of the club.

The bouncer escorted Greg out of the club, but as he tried to break free, he broke the bouncer's nose.

"Ow, you bastard, I'll get you for that," cried the bouncer, holding his painful and bloodied nose.

"I don't think so. That was just for throwing me out of the club, and now I think I'll kill you," Greg retorted, taking hold of the bouncer by the neck. "And the method I'm going to use will make you wish you had never been born, you earringed, tattooed freak. Greg then squeezed the bouncer's neck until he began to go limp. That was when Steven, waiting outside, had to step in to save the bouncer's life.

"I apologise for Greg's behaviour," he said to the purple faced doorman. "He's not normally like this; he's just clinically insane at the moment."

Greg fell about, laughing manically.

"See? He's laughing like a jackass even though I didn't make a joke; a true sign of madness."

"Yeah," is all the bouncer could say, still holding his nose and looking at Greg with distaste.

Greg continued to laugh.

"Greg, what *is* the matter with you?" Steven asked him.

"Nothing," he replied, still sniggering.

"Well, I beg to differ, because from what I've just seen, your behaviour could not be remotely described as nothing. It's extreme, Greg, and a serious problem to those of us who love you. I've known you for a long time, so I know that you are not yourself. There must be something on your mind. So are you going to share it?"

"No, I'm not, because there is nothing on my mind and as for you saying you know me, well you obviously don't know me as well as you think, because this is absolutely me."

Steven turned to Amy. "Okay, it's your turn to try and knock some sense into him. Just try not to kill him."

Amy smiled. "Greg, do you know how much you have embarrassed Steven and me?"

"You and Steven are only embarrassed because you worry about what people think of you. So you should both be more like me, because then you wouldn't be worried about what people thought of you," he replied, jabbing a finger at her to make his point.

"Oh, I see; so that is why you didn't care about what that woman's boyfriend said and also why you just walked away without caring what he thought of you?"

"Your use of sarcasm shows you have a weak mind. So you're just like me."

"No, I'm not weak like you and the only reason I used sarcasm was because it's the only way to get through to someone who is so arrogantly trying to control people, to get them to do everything his way, he doesn't even see that he isn't taking his own advice."

"Is that so? Well you didn't seem to have any problem with my arrogant streak before today. So how about a kiss to make up for having it off with that tart?" Greg slid his hands around her hips and attempted to kiss her.

Amy wriggled free and slapped his face, the force of it knocking his head backwards.

"If you want to see me again you'd better grow up and start behaving like the man I know you really are?" Amy began to walk away.

Greg replied with a sneer. "Yeah? Well don't hold your breath, darlin' because I am already the man I really am."

Amy stopped walking and turned around. "No you're not; you're a complete idiot," she said and continued to walk, back towards her home.

Greg just laughed at her, proving her point.

Steven also began to walk away.

"So you're leaving me as well, Steven?"

"Yeah, that's about it; you are behaving like an evil, arrogant swine and all I can say to you is that we hate seeing you like this. I just hope you have the sense to revert back to your old self – the good, caring guy that we knew and loved. Goodbye, Greg." Steven gave Greg one last pitying look and walked away from him.

Greg turned away angrily. How dare they leave him? Who the hell did they think they were?

As he walked away a stranger came up to him with an unlit cigarette in his hand.

"Have you got a light, mate?"

Greg was still sore that Steven and Amy had left him.

"What?"

"A light. Are you deaf? I said do you have a light?"

Greg took exception to the man's attitude. He looked him up and down, curling his lip savagely.

"Oh, so you want a light, do you? Well, I'll give you a light alright." Greg then mysteriously set the man alight just by pointing his hand at him. The man screamed in agony.

"Feel the fires of hell burning your insides," Greg said in a most evil voice. He then extinguished the fire in the same way as he had started it, by pointing his hand towards the man. He put his hand down. "Now go, before I do any more damage to you."

The man with the cigarette ran away, scared out of his wits.

Greg, composing himself, looked down at his hand as if he didn't understand what was happening to him and why he just did what did.

"What is the matter with me? I'm doing things that I wouldn't normally do. Maybe it's because there is so much anger inside of me? That could be it, and because all this anger inside of me I have forced my friends to leave me."

Suddenly, he burst into song:

 # All this anger is causing me so much pain;
And that's just driving me insane.
I wish I could find a way to get rid of this angst, get back to my usual self
and help my friends put the bad guys at the back of the shelf.

(Chorus) How is it that I can destroy myself but I can't heal myself?
How can I make the pain go away and make
this nightmare become a good day?

I can feel more anger and pain than I ever imagined
Preventing my success that has been predestined.
I want to stop myself from losing control
To see a clear path to achieve my goal
Of helping Steven and Amy beat the evil on the ground
To flood sinners with goodness in which they will drown.

(Chorus)

I wish I didn't feel this way,
I want to help my friends destroy the decay
And find a way to do what I need,

To rid the world of evil and greed.

(Chorus)

*When will all this hell in the world go away
to leave us with harmony and peace every day?*

(Chorus)

Greg, by now in a remorseful and sombre mood, looked up to see a church in front of him.

"Perhaps my old friend Robbie will help me get back to my old self so that I can help Amy and Steven fight the evil in this world," he said, going into the church.

In Romania, Adrian is giving Christopher the Idiot instructions.

"Okay, Christopher your moment is finally here. Are you ready?"

"Oh yeah, I've been waiting patiently for this very moment."

"Good. Use your new shimmering power that you picked up from the emperors of the sun to get to the church on time. Then when you're there and Greg comes out of the church you must use your new power to blow up that church with Greg's friend, the priest, inside it."

"How do I do that?"

"You just say there's no place like home and think of the location of the church. Did I explain that properly, Dorothy?"

"Yes, crystal clear. Okay, here goes. There's no place like home," said Christopher the Idiot, who then disappeared.

"Oh boy, he's one heck of an idiot," Adrian said.

Christopher the Idiot arrived in England and walked across the road to the church.

Greg was sitting in the confession box.

"Forgive me, Father for I have sinned. I am ashamed to admit that I set a man on fire today," he revealed.

"I'm not the priest," a voice answered.

"What?"

"I'm not the priest, I'm just a fellow sinner wanting to give my confession and you're in the priest's box."

"Oh!" Greg was embarrassed and left the priest's box, keeping his head down to hide his discomfort.

Then Father Robbie came out of the vestry, saw Greg and held out his arms in welcome.

"Greg, what a pleasant surprise; long time no see."

"Yeah, I know. Sorry I didn't come to see you before to congratulate you on becoming a priest, but I've been very busy."

"Oh that's okay; better later than never. So what have come to see me for... and please don't say to catch up on our time in the RAF cadets."

Greg smiled. "I have come here to see my old friend Robbie. Or is it Father Bob now?"

"Father Robbie, actually, and I do know you haven't just come to see me. So why have you come?"

"Okay; I came to make a confession and indeed I did, but inadvertently gave it to the guy already in there. So now I'll have to repeat myself to you."

Father Robbie laughed. "I see. Well, just take a seat for a moment and I'll hear you afterwards."

"After a few minutes, the man left the confession box and Greg heard Father Robbie say, "Take care, now, and I'll see you next Saturday, will I?"

The man mumbled something and walked out of the church.

"Greg? I'm ready to see you now," Father Robbie called from the priest's box.

"And what is it you want to confess?" he asked as Greg closed the door to the confession box.

"Well, I am ashamed to admit that I have set a man alight and I have also cheated on my girlfriend, Amy."

"Alright, I see. And do you know why you did these ungodly deeds?"

"I honestly don't know. What I do know is that I had quite a few drinks before I did these horrible things. I was drunk, actually."

"Well, in that case, your sin was drinking too much alcohol, and not necessarily what you did as a consequence. So what you must do to avoid this situation in future is to practice moderation and cut back on alcohol."

"That's more or less what Steven said."

"Well you would do well to listen to Steven. He is full of words of wisdom."

"He is. You're right, as always."

"Well, no, I'm not *always* right..."

"Now don't be so modest, mate... I mean Father Robbie. You're good at your job."

Father Robbie smiled to himself. "Thank you, Greg."

Greg and Father Robbie came out of their respective boxes.

"Now go in peace, and remember what I told you, Greg," Father Robbie said, looking at Greg kindly.

"Yeah, okay, and just to show my appreciation of your taking time to see me, how about a hug?"

"Of course."

The two men hugged each other; both sincere in their action.

Father Robbie released Greg and stood back. "Now don't leave it so long before you come and see me again, Greg, because I like helping people with their problems and it's what I'm here for."

"Sure. Thanks, then, and bye for now."

"Bye, Greg. God be with you."

Christopher the Idiot had been waiting across the road for some time when he saw Greg leave the church.

"Okay, it's time to test my new power which I picked up from the Nazis," he said. He then made a fireball and threw it at the church, blowing it up and killing Father Robbie instantly.

"No!" screamed Greg who had been flung to the ground by the blast.

Christopher the Idiot curled an evil smile at Greg before vanishing.

The idiot was instantly transported back to Romania.

Adrian praised him. "Well done, Christopher."

"Thanks. So what do you want me to do now?"

"Now we wait a little."

Meanwhile, in England, the emergency services were at the scene of Christopher's devastating crime. Greg, being the only witness, was being questioned by a police officer.

"Did you see who did this?" the police officer asked him.

Greg was distraught. "No, unfortunately I didn't see the scum that did this. All I remember is talking to Rob... Father Robbie, who is one of my closest friends, walking out of the church and then being knocked down by the blast of the explosion. I honestly cannot remember anything else." To his horror, he broke down in tears, and self-consciously turned his face away.

"Okay, we'll leave you alone," said the police officer. "Get in touch if you remember anything, won't you?"

Greg felt his anger returning. "Who would do such a cruel, evil thing to such a good man? I'm going to find the scumbag who did this and make him pay."

This was not good news, because just when it seemed that Greg was coming out of the spell, this latest setback had put him well and truly back under it. He walked away, determined to find the person who had perpetrated this heinous act and, as luck would have it (or, more precisely, as Adrian's plan would have it), Christopher appeared before Greg.

Greg stared at him in anger.

"Amazing grace, how sweet the sound of the explosion that killed the priest, who to me is a disgrace," Christopher the Idiot sang and then laughed in Greg's face.

"Is that the best you can do?" Greg asked.

The idiot has thrust his face right up close to Greg's.

"No. How about this? Your friend the priest is now deceased."

"I am going to beat you to a bloody pulp," Greg replied and in his fury, gave Christopher the Idiot the beating of his life. "This time I'll finish you off once and for all, you son of a bitch," he growled, and raised his arm, preparing to punch the last bit of life out of him.

Then Adrian appeared.

"Leave him alone," he shouted at Greg.

"Give me one good reason why I should?"

"Because I need you to join forces with me and Christopher."

Greg laughed ironically. "You're living in a dream world if you think that is going to happen."

"Have it your way. I'll just count to three. One, two, three..."

Greg held his head as the spell of anger caused an agonising, blinding pain. He struggled with it for a few moments, but eventually had to give in to it.

"Okay, boss, I'm all yours," he said, surrendering to an invisible force.

"Oh, I love that; the feeling of absolute power," Adrian said, grinning with triumph at Greg. "Now then, we need to get back to my lab in Romania to discuss what I want you to do."

Greg changed into his orange superhero costume and he, Adrian and Christopher the Idiot were transported to Adrian's laboratory using their special powers.

"So what do you want me to do? asked Greg.

"I need you to write us a song because a song has to be sung in order to officially make us a team." Adrian told him.

"Okay, no problem. Oddball, turn into a notepad and a pen," commanded Greg, focusing on his hand.

Oddball didn't appear and Greg looked bemused. "That's odd; why hasn't Oddball appeared?"

"Try asking it again."

"Right. Oddball, I know you can hear me, so can you turn into a notepad and pen?"

There was still no sign of Oddball and Greg looked even more puzzled. "That is strange, Oddball has never failed to appear before."

Adrian shrugged. "You'll just have to use my pen and paper."

Equipped with pen and paper, Greg began to compose the lyrics. They sat in silence, allowing him to concentrate and before long, he put down the pen and pushed the paper towards Adrian.

"That's it, I'm finished."

After reading the song, Adrian passed it to Christopher the Idiot who also read it and then gave it back to Adrian. No one spoke.

"Well?" asked Greg.

"Well okay, are you ready to rock?" Adrian replied, looking at Greg and Christopher.

"Sure," Greg said with a relieved smile.

"Yes," from Christopher the Idiot.

"I'll start then," said Adrian.

Payback to God

(Adrian sings the first verse)

I will make God suffer for what he has done

then I will smile as he dies because he will
have lost and we will have won.

(Chorus which only Adrian sings) Payback to God, payback to God.
Payback to God can only be good; we'll pay him back as only we could.

(Greg sings the second verse)

I will have my revenge when God's dead and buried;
if he has a grave I'll plant it with weed.

(Chorus, which only Greg sings.)

(Christopher the Idiot sings the third verse)

When God Is dead I will smile the biggest smile,
A smile that's as big as a crocodile's.
God won't be resurrected like his son
We don't need a god, or anyone.

(Chorus which only Christopher the Idiot sings.)

(Chorus which Adrian, Greg and Christopher the Idiot all sing together.)

"So what do want me to do next?" Greg asked Adrian.

"Next, I want you to make your first kill," Adrian replied. "Are you okay with that?"

"Course."

"Right, then let me find someone to be your first kill." Adrian flicked through the channels on his magically enhanced wide screen television. Eventually he found a channel screening a man smoking a cigarette. He turned to Greg. "There, that is your mark."

"Oh yes, I'm going to enjoy this," Greg said, looking at the television screen. He sauntered up to where the man was. "Hey, Smokey Joe!"

The man swung round. "What? Who said that?"

"Oh, I see you don't go Specsavers," Greg taunted.

"Are you looking for a fight?"

"No, I just want you to participate in my first kill," Greg replied, angry again. He tried to get Oddball to come out of his hand so he could use Oddball to kill the cigarette-smoking man, but Oddball didn't appear. Instead Greg's hand turned into a spike and he suddenly grew into a ten-foot alien.

"Well! Well! Well! That was a nice surprise for me and now I'm going to give you yours."

The man looked up at Greg with fear.

Greg stabbed the man with his spike hand, making him scream.

"Was that painful enough for you?" asked Greg, removing his spike hand and, hearing no answer, left the man for dead and changed back into his orange superhero costume. He then went to Adrian's laboratory.

"Congratulations on making your first kill, Greg," Adrian said.

"Yeah," agreed Christopher the Idiot, "I have to congratulate you too. You know, that was one mean alien you turned into."

Greg smiled at them.

"Now the three of us are united, we can get on with the next part of my plan," Adrian said.

"Fine. What do we do next?"

"Well, you, Christopher and I are going to create animal demons, or demons out of animals, to be more precise."

The other two looked at Adrian and then at each other.

"I will write down a spell that we can all say to summon one hundred stray cats and turn them into a single cat demon," Adrian explained.

Taking the pen and paper, he wrote down the spell and showed it to Greg and Christopher the Idiot.

"Once you've read it, we'll say it," he told them.

Adrian gave them a few minutes to read the words and then took the paper away, putting it on his desk.

"Okay, boys, now let's say the spell."

Together, the three of them incanted, "Send us one hundred cats here today and turn them into a cat demon that can blow people away."

One hundred stray cats magically materialised in Adrian's laboratory and formed a nine-foot cat demon.

"That's some bad kitty," exclaimed Christopher the Idiot with a smile.

Greg and Adrian were also smiling,

"Yes it is," agreed Adrian, admiring the cat demon.

In England, Steven came out of his room and shut the door behind him. He had a premonition as well as a voice in his head. He then went down the street to the bus stop to wait for a bus that would hopefully take him to the people who needed saving. As he waited, he saw Amy, who was walking on the other side of the street.

"Hey, Amy!" Steven shouted.

She waved to him and stopped, waiting for a gap in the traffic so that she could cross the road.

"Hi, Steven. What are you up to?"

"Amy, I've had a premonition of innocent people being blown away by a cat demon and I've also heard a voice in my head that told me Greg only did what he did because he was put under a spell."

"Do you want me to forgive him just because you heard a voice in your head?"

"Well it was a supernatural voice, not a voice that a mental patient would hear," he told her.

She squinted at him. "Do you expect me to believe you?"

"Well, you're a witch and a lot of people wouldn't believe you if you told them, but I know you would want them to believe you. So I'm asking you: will you believe me and help save a lot innocent people? If we do that we can help to return Greg to normal."

"Yeah, okay. Do you want me to write a spell that will magically take us to the innocent people so we don't have to get on a bus?"

"That would be good," Steven agreed, but first we should go into the flat to change into our superhero costumes without anyone seeing us."

They changed into their costumes and were ready.

"You'll have to hold my hand," Amy said.

Steven took hold of Amy's hand and she said her spell: "Take us to where the innocent people are, so we can get to them faster than going by car."

They instantly disappeared to the place where the innocent people were.

In Romania, Adrian was giving the cat demon a pep talk.

"Do you understand what you are supposed to do? Miaow if you understand."

The cat demon miaowed in a chilling way and then disappeared to attempt its first kill.

Steven and Amy in England are waiting for the cat demon to show and it does just that. Then it prepares to throw a demonic fur ball at the innocent bystanders.

"Everyone get down on the floor!" Steven shouted to the innocent bystanders. "Amy, can you say a spell to get us and this mean kitty out of here so there's no danger to any of these innocent people?"

He then had to jump on top of the cat demon to turn its head away from Amy so that it could not hurt her.

"Sure, as long as you can think of a remote place to go to," she replied, giving the cat demon a wary look.

"Yeah, I can, but do you need to make a potion like when we were in the underworld of the damned?"

"No, because my powers have advanced. The reason I know this is because when I went home after having a row with Greg, I tried a spell to take me to a peaceful place without the aid of a potion."

"Okay. In that case I'll think of the lake district."

"And I'll think of the same place." Amy then thought of a spell and touched the cat demon so that it, and she and Steven, could go together to the lake district to fight.

"Take us to a remote place, where we can kill this cat demon and make sure it cannot hurt any of the human race," she said.

They were transported to the Lake District and Amy took her hand off the cat demon.

"Let's see if I can strangle you to death," Steven said to the cat demon. He almost managed it, but did not have quite enough strength.

The cat demon finally produced its demonic fur ball which it pitched into some grass and then threw Steven off its back. Luckily, Steven managed to cling onto the branch of a nearby tree, before jumping down onto the grass.

The cat demon was preparing to hurl another demonic fur ball at Steven and Amy.

"Amy, let's go down that hill, out of its line of fire, and maybe we can think of a way to kill it."

As they began to go down the hill, the cat demon released its fur ball and because Amy and Steven were no longer in its line of fire the fur ball went into a tree, destroying it.

"How many ways to skin a cat do you know?" Steven asked Amy.

"Well, I know they don't like water and there's some water not far from here."

"Okay, you make your way to the water and I'll get the cat demon's attention. Then I'll lead him to you, and the water, where can drown him."

"Well, be careful, Steven."

"Hey, I'm Mr sensible; not like your boyfriend and my best friend."

"Yeah, I know. How could I forget that? Anyway I'll go to the water."

Steven then starts the perilous process of attracting the cat demon towards him.

"Hey, kitty, kitty, bum fluff, come and get me," he called.

The cat demon stalked towards Steven shaking its tail angrily.

"That's it, just as I had anticipated. Now... to run." Steven said, watching the cat demon. He then ran away from it, but the cat demon prepared to throw another fur ball at him. Luckily, the voice in Steven's head warned him and he was able to dodge it. The fur ball hit a tree, reducing it to sawdust. The cat demon growled in annoyance that Steven had avoided its fur ball and then continued chasing after him. When Steven reached Amy by the lake, he let the cat demon think it was going to kill him. The cat demon launched itself at Steven intending to tear him to bits, but at the last moment, Steven jumped out of the way and the cat demon splashed into the deep, dark water and drowned.

Steven and Amy began to celebrate thinking they had vanquished the cat demon, but when they heard a growl they turned round to see that it had magically reappeared.

"Oh no, don't tell me... it's got nine lives," Steven groaned.

"Unfortunately, I have to say it looks likely, so we're going to have to kill it eight more times," Amy said looking at Steven with dismay.

Steven sighed with disappointment. "Yeah, yeah. Oh, look out, it's coughing up another fur ball, let's get out of its line of fire."

"No problem," said Amy, diving behind a rock.

The cat demon faced Steven as it hiccupped, trying eject the fur ball. Just as Steven jumped behind a rock near Amy, the cat demon hurled its fur ball towards him. The fur ball destroyed the rock, but luckily Steven was protected by the rock taking the full impact.

Amy and Steven ran away from the cat demon, losing it in the process.

"Amy, do you know any other ways we might kill the cat demon?"

"Let me think," she said, chewing her bottom lip. "Well there is one. My family has a cat that's scared of bees and wasps because of the fact that they can sting it. Sorry, Steven, I can't think of any more ways to kill the cat demon at the moment."

"Don't worry about it; we just have to take one step at a time." He looked around. "Surely there must be loads of bees and wasps here in the Lake District because of the all the wildlife."

When he looked at a certain tree, the voice in his head told him where there were some bees.

"Amy, the voice in my head tells me there is a colony of bees behind that tree," he said, pointing out which tree it was. "So let's lure Sylvester to another death."

They ran to the tree but the cat demon had seen them. It prepared to hurl another fur ball at Steven. Steven carefully approached the beehive so as not to disturb the bees too early. He carefully lifted the hive and very slowly turned around to face the cat demon, but at that moment, another fur ball came hurtling towards him. Steven froze; he didn't want to drop the bees in case they flew off and away from the cat demon. Luckily Amy used her power to deflect the fur ball into a tree which was instantly destroyed.

Steven breathed a sigh of relief. "Thanks Amy." He looked at the cat demon. It was preparing to discharge another fur ball at him.

"I thought I saw a pussy cat, I did, I did," he taunted, and then launched the beehive at the cat demon with all his strength. The bees flew angrily out of the hive and attacked the cat demon, causing it to swallow its fur ball and therefore inadvertently vanquish itself and one more of its lives.

Steven and Amy looked at each other.

"Yes!" they said, with a celebratory high five.

They had to quickly prepare for the demon to attack again and, just as they expected, it reappeared, more aggressive than ever.

"Don't look at me like that," Amy warned it.

Steven thought that was very funny, but the cat demon was preparing a fur ball to aim at Amy.

She started to run. "Come on, it's time to run like Forrest Gump again!"

"Oh yeah," Steven said, also running. "I'm with you."

They both hid behind some trees that were part of a dense forest, losing the cat demon who threw its fur ball into a tree and destroyed it. It was nowhere near Amy and Steven because they outran the cat demon and lost it.

"So is there a third way to kill Jerry's enemy?" Steven asked.

"I can't think of one just yet. You could try and think of one as well, couldn't you? We might vanquish the cat demon quicker if we *both* try, instead of just me?"

He realised that Amy was serious. "Yeah, sorry, it was unfair of me to expect you to do all that. I need to contribute as well, of course." He looked blankly at her.

"Can you not think of anything at all?"

"I'm all out of ideas, I'm afraid." Steven shrugged hopelessly. "Sorry, but my family have a dog, not a cat."

Amy laughed. "Don't worry, your gift of being patient is much better than my hurried approach, because you can make mistakes by rushing a job."

"I suppose so, but I'm sorry I haven't got any ideas, it's just that I know nothing about cats. Well apart from what names to call them."

Amy laughed again.

"That's okay. Actually, when I was looking at you I thought of an idea to do with your weapon. You could use it to skin the cat demon... you would have to demonstrate your brilliant bravery as well, of course... then, with it being cold the cat demon will surely freeze to death."

Steven stared at Amy in amazement.

"My god," he thought, "she's right. Why didn't I think of that?"

"Oh, I'm sorry. It was presumptuous of me to expect you to risk your life putting my plan to the test."

"No, Amy, it wasn't at all. I love all that bravery stuff and as for risking my life, I'm also careful. I was looking at you like that because you've just thought of something that should have been so obvious to me."

"Oh, in that case I'm glad you liked the plan."

"Yes, it's excellent." Steven then activated his blade and rushed towards the cat demon.

"Okay, stupid animal, prepare to fall victim to Pixie and Dixie's great plan," he said, staring straight at the cat demon. The he leapt on top of it and skinned all but its tail.

"Now I'm going to skin your extremely long tail." Steven finished the job and the cat demon froze to death, losing the third of its nine lives.

"That was a brilliant idea, Amy. How about another one to vanquish it for the fourth time?"

"What about this, then? I have just thought of pushing it off the roof of High Close Youth Hostel."

"Amy, that's another good idea and it might just work."

The cat demon was back. Amy and Steven then ran to High Close Youth Hostel knowing that cat demon would chase after them. It did, preparing to hurl a fur ball at them.

Steven looked at Amy as they ran. "The voice in my head tells me that there is another fur ball coming at us."

"So let's get out of its line of fire." Amy swerved towards some trees that were part of the forest, away from the cat demon's line of fire. Steven followed her and they both hid behind different trees.

The fur ball exploded some distance away from where Amy and Steven were hiding, and they began to run again.

"Come on," said Steven. Let's finish our journey to High Close."

The cat demon spotted them and chased after them.

Steven and Amy reached High Close and went up the stairs. They went out onto the balcony and from there, climbed up onto the roof.

The cat demon looked up at Steven and Amy who were standing on the roof and licked its lips as if it were going to eat them when it reached the top. It climbed up the front of the building, using the balcony banisters to lever itself up. When it came close enough to the roof, it leapt onto it. The beast looked around for Amy and Steven but it could not see them. That was because Steven and Amy went part way down the building, clinging onto the ledge with their fingers while the cat demon was climbing up on to the roof.

"Amy," Steven whispered, "the voice in my head has just told me that the cat demon is on the opposite side of the roof, so lets see if our plan works."

While the cat demon was still on the opposite side of the roof, Steven and Amy climbed quietly and carefully back to the top of the roof. Together, they ran at the cat demon and pushed it off the roof, just stopping themselves from going over with it.

The cat demon fell heavily to the ground and experienced its fourth death.

They go back downstairs.

"Steven, couldn't we just repeatedly attract the cat demon up onto the roof of the youth hostel and keep throwing it off until it is permanently vanquished?"

"No, I'm afraid not. The voice in my head has just told me that we have to kill the cat demon five more times but by a different method from the four we have used already."

"Right, well I'll have to think of a way to vanquish its fifth life."

Amy sat down quietly for a few moments, trying to gather her thoughts. Killing this monster was proving to to be harder than they had imagined. To kill it once hadn't been easy; to manage it four times up to now had seemed to be a miracle, but the cat demon had another five lives still to be eliminated... and they couldn't afford to hang about.

She jumped up. "I know, Steven." She pointed ahead of her. "There are two big guard dogs at that house. If we run over there, the cat demon will follow us and the dogs will attack it. Surely they will kill it between them?"

Steven looked anxious. "They won't attack us as well, will they?"

"No, not when they have the cat demon to deal with."

"Okay, but come on, the damn thing's come to life again."

They set off, running towards the house. As expected, the cat demon pursued them. They slowed down as they reached the gates and opened them quietly.

"Nice doggies," Steven said softly. "Here comes the cat with Basil Brush hanging off its tail, kill, boys!"

Amy turned round; the cat demon was almost upon them.

"Quick, Steven, push the gates wide open and then step aside!"

As they both jumped to the side, the cat demon shot through the gates, propelling itself straight into the path of two massive, hungry rottweilers.

It was all over very quickly and Steven and Amy hurriedly left the scene as the dogs sorted out the bones.

"I don't suppose you have any thoughts about vanquishing its sixth life, Amy?"

"As a matter of fact, I have. Yeah, my family's cat hates being put into its crate; I think it gets claustrophobia. So, if we can trap it in a small, confined space, that might work. What do you think?"

"Worth a try," Steven agreed, "but what can we use to trap the cat demon?" They began to look around for a suitable place to entrap the cat demon.

"Hey, what about that tiny garrett right at the top of High Close?"

"Yeah, it's small enough, and the cat demon won't be able to get out of there. I'll have to do a bit of vandalizing, though..."

"Yeah, but it's justifiable, Steven, to take another life from that creature." "Okay, time to run, here it comes!"

They ran to the stairs of High Close with the cat demon in hot pursuit. They made it to the balcony and were quickly up onto the roof. Steven then activated his blade.

"Okay, here goes," he said, using the blade to cut a hole big enough to admit the cat demon into the small attic.

He surveyed his handiwork. "Oh dear, look at that. I can no longer call myself Mr Sensible."

Amy laughed, then put a warning finger to her lips. "Here it comes!"

As the cat demon clawed its way onto the roof, Steven leapt on its back to restrain it while Amy forced it through the hole using her telekinesis powers. Steven jumped clear just before the cat demon went flying into the attic, knocking itself out. Before it had a chance to escape, Amy touched a slate next to the hole and incanted a spell.

"Make this slate cover up the hole in the roof, so the cat demon will suffer from claustrophobia and go poof."

The slate then expanded, completely filling the hole in the roof.

The cat demon woke up to find itself trapped in a dark, stuffy attic and immediately went into a violent, trembling, claustrophobic panic. It could not breathe and its sixth life was successfully snuffed out.

"Six lives down," Steven said, sharing a high five with Amy.

"Yeah, only three to go and I think I know of a seventh way to kill the cat demon."

"Really?"

"My family's cat climbs up trees, but seems to be afraid of heights. So if we can find somewhere really high to put it, the cat demon will probably be too afraid to come down and it will be vanquished."

"That's a good one. But we have to find a place high enough to scare it." Steven looked around for something suitable. "How about a pylon?"

"Yeah, that should work perfectly, but how are we going to get it to go up there?"

"Hm. We have to find a way, and quickly."

They both racked their brains for a few moments and then Steven smiled broadly at Amy.

"What?" she asked.

"How do you fancy climbing up the pylon pole?"

"Me?"

"Both of us."

"Sounds okay."

"Right we'll need some mountaineering ropes from High Close. Come on."

Amy followed Steven into High Close and they came out with two ropes apiece.

"We'll have to get on with it before anyone misses them," Steven said.

When they reached the pole, Steven and Amy turned the ropes into lassoes by making loops at the ends and tying triple knots at the end of the loops to make sure they wouldn't come undone with pressure. Then they each threw one lasso over the top of the pylon and began to climb up it, stopping near the top.

"Okay, now we wait for the cat demon to appear," Steven said.

They did not have to wait long.

"Hey, cat demon! Come and get us," they both shouted.

The cat demon growled at them menacingly and ran towards the pole. Just as it was about to climb up the pole Amy threw her lasso around the back end of the cat demon and Steven did likewise around its chest. They then used the ropes to hoist the beast right up onto the top of the pole. Steven and Amy then descended quickly to ensure that it could not use them as human stepping-stones.

They looked up at the cat demon from the bottom of the pole to see that it was indeed scared of heights and had been literally frightened to death. That meant it had now lost seven of its nine lives.

Amy had already thought of a method to rid the cat demon of its penultimate life.

"When we take the ropes back to High Close, we borrow a couple of vacuum cleaners; cats are scared to death of those as well!"

Steven laughed. "Scaredy cats, then, you could say? Okay, you get the vacuum cleaners while I return the ropes."

They were fortunate to smuggle the ropes back in and the vacuum cleaners out without being seen. When they came out of High Close the cat demon was patiently waiting for them and directed a fur ball towards Amy. Quick off the mark, she put the vacuum cleaner down and deflected the fur ball into a nearby tree, destroying it instantly.

"Amy?"

"Yeah?"

"This may sound like a minor detail, but how do you plan to get the vacuums to work without electricity?"

Amy glanced carefully around her. "Listen very carefully; I will say this only once," she said, in a French accent.

Steven grinned confidently, knowing she had something clever in mind to vanquish the cat demon's eighth life.

Amy touched the vacuum cleaners. "Make all of these vacuums come to life to take away the cat demon's second last life and stop it from causing any more strife," she said.

When Amy removed her hand from the vacuums, they came to life and again, the cat demon was literally scared to death. Now it had only one life left.

"We could get the White Lady to scare the cat demon to death for the last time," Amy suggested.

"Yeah; why don't we do that... oh..." Steven looks deflated. "Oh no!"

"What's the voice in your head saying?"

"Well there is an awkward twist. Apparently the only way we can kill the cat demon's ninth life and therefore vanquish it for good, is to kill it on the exact stroke of nine o'clock. Luckily we can do that at AM or PM time, so we won't have too long to wait.

"Perhaps I'll change my watch to AM/PM time, then," joked Amy.

Steven laughed but then the grotesque cat demon appeared.

"Come on, let's run somewhere until nine o'clock," Steven said.

Steven and Amy ran away from the cat demon and lost it by going down Dead Man's Drop where they each hid behind a tree.

"What shall we do, wait here until half past eight and then go back to High Close so we've got time to get the White Lady to scare the cat demon to death?" Amy asked.

"Yeah, that's about right. Oh, I'm just getting a message from the voice in my head that it's all clear for us to run to High Close."

"So let's go."

As Steven and Amy approached High Close, the cat demon had his back turned to them, but turned around in time to see them going inside. It chased after them and waited outside for them to come out.

In High Close, Steven and Amy were carefully searching for the White Lady. When they spotted her, Steven captured her attention.

"Hey! Come and get me, you ugly white witch," he called out to her.

The White Lady turned round, looking angrily at Steven, and floated after him. Just before she reached him Amy stepped in front of him, halting the White Lady's progress.

"Look, please don't hurt Steven. I know he's a bit of an idiot a sometimes but he's a good guy as well," she explained.

"Yeah," Steven pleaded. "Amy's right, I am a good guy and I'm sorry for that hurtful comment. You are a nice looking woman."

"Apology accepted. Although you were right about me being a white witch."

"Really?"

"Yes, you were right because I was a good witch when I was alive, but now I'm dead I'm just a cranky old woman. However, I still like to think of myself as a witch," she said, leaning towards Steven.

Steven smiled at the White Lady. "Well, the reason I wanted to get your attention was because Amy and I wanted to ask you if you could scare the cat demon to death?"

"That's right," Amy agreed.

"Yes, I will help you because you seem like nice people, but what demon?"

"The one just outside. Here, come with me," Steven said.

She followed him to the balcony and Amy brought up the rear.

Steven pointed down to the ground near the staircase. "There." He did a double take, looking bemused. "That's odd. How could a thing that big just disappear?" he asked, turning round to Amy and the White Lady.

"Could you use your special power to find it?" Amy asked.

"Good idea. I could try asking the voice in my head if it knows where the cat demon is. I've never tried that before but hopefully it will work." He closed his eyes and bowed his head.

The White Lady gave Steven a pitiful glance. "Did he just say what I thought he said?" she asked Amy, clearly suspecting that Steven was mad.

"Yeah, and I know it sounds like he's mad, but he really does hear a voice in his head. It's a special power he has."

Steven looked up. "The voice in my head has just told me that the cat demon is round the corner of the building so do you both want to come with me to get ready to surprise it?"

"What are we waiting for?" said Amy.

The White Lady was keen to see this demon creature they had talked of and was ready to go with them.

"Okay, I'll just check my watch. Oh, its only eight forty-five and we have to do it at nine on the dot."

The White Lady looked from Steven to Amy, still somewhat puzzled by it all. "Well, do you want to wait here for fourteen minutes and then go downstairs to where the cat demon is, to start the vanquishing process?"

"Yeah, great. That should give us time to get down the stairs and vanquish the cat demon and... if I just look at my watch, we've now only got thirteen minutes to wait. So I'll just clear my mind ready for any unexpected messages from the voice in my head until its time to go downstairs." He began to meditate.

Amy and the white lady laughed; he did look rather strange... as if in a trance.

After nearly thirteen minutes Steven looked at his watch. "Okay," he said, "let's go."

They went downstairs to get ready to surprise the cat demon.

"Now, I'll distract the cat demon so that it will concentrate only on me and won't be able to shimmer off somewhere before you float into it from behind in about twenty seconds. I want you to wait ten seconds and then use your full frightening powers to scare it to death... that's after exactly ten seconds. Okay?"

"Okay," the White Lady replied.

Steven then appeared to the cat demon from round the corner.

"Hey, Deputy Dawg's enemy, come and kill me," he taunted it.

The cat demon tried to attack Steven, thinking that Steven would kill it in self-defence before the nine o'clock deadline. Steven of course had other ideas and jumped on top of the cat demon. Then he turned it away from Amy and the White Lady so that, as there had now been a twenty seconds interval since Steven instructed the White Lady, she could float into it from behind.

She did just that and Steven jumped off the cat demon as his work was done. Ten seconds after floating into the cat demon the White Lady then literally scared the living daylights out of it with her full frightening powers. However, that was not the end of the cat demon because just after it appeared to be vanquished it reappeared, although it was motionless.

"What's gone wrong?" the White Lady asked, "Why didn't I kill it?"

"I don't know; you've rendered it unable to do anything whatsoever, but for some unknown reason you weren't able to erase it from existence," Steven replied, mystified.

They all looked bemused. Steven's face went blank and then quickly returned to normal.

"Ah, now I know why the cat demon hasn't been erased from existence yet. The voice in my head has just told me that it is because Amy and I have to sing a song. That is the final part of the vanquishing process of all the advanced demons sent after us by an unknown being. It's a shame we don't have Greg because he's good at writing songs, but he's currently possessed by evil so Amy and I will just have to write the song. It shouldn't be too hard; after all we've already had to fight and kill a stronger demon without Greg." He sighed. "The combined powers of Greg and Oddball would have made it much easier to vanquish it."

"Do we have to kill it?" Amy asked. "Couldn't we just leave it there to rest in peace? I mean it is no longer doing us any harm."

"Amy, I admire your new-found magnanimity, but I want to kill it," declared Steven.

"You're cruel, you know," she retorted.

"I know and I'm sure I'll go to hell for it some day. Although, to be honest, I've been there and done that."

Amy and the White Lady laughed and he grinned back at them.

"Are you sure we have to kill it, though?" Amy asked him.

"Positive, because the voice in my head said if we don't kill it, it will come back in nine years time and start killing people indiscriminately."

"Oh, I see. And do we have to write the song together?"

"I am being told that's not necessary, so I can write it myself if you want me to?"

"Er, it might be fun to write it together, though?"

"Sure, we'll write it together, then."

"Well, I have to go now," said the White Lady. "Byee."

"Why do you have to go?" Steven asked.

"Because I have to attend a Dead People's Convention which is being held by Jesus."

Amy and Steven laughed. "What's that?" Amy asked.

"Well, the Dead People's Convention is basically a meeting between all of the dead people in heaven and, of course, God. At our meetings God assigns us tasks. In fact, one of my earlier tasks was to help you two, so I was waiting for you to come to me in High Close."

"Really? So you weren't actually angry with me and you weren't going to hurt me?" Steven asked.

"Not quite right! *Yes*, I was angry with you, but *no*, I wasn't going to hurt you."

"Oh. Then I apologise once again for what I said to you."

"Thank you. Now I'm off to the Bahamas in the sky," the White Lady said as she began to float upward in her ascent to heaven.

Steven and Amy waved until she was out of sight.

"Okay should we find something to write the lyrics on for the bad kitty rap?"

"Yeah... and that's a good name for the song. Now if we can only find something to write on," Steven said, looking around. Then he projected a holographic piece of paper in mid air.

"Wow! How did you do that?" Amy asked.

"I don't know exactly. I wished for something that we could write the lyrics on and in doing that I must have activated a new power."

"Cool."

"Right, let's think about the lyrics. You can do the first part of the song and I'll do the second part and the chorus, okay?"

"Okay."

They concentrated quietly for a few minutes.

"How are you doing?" Steven asked Amy. "I've got my lyrics all ready to put onto the holographic paper."

"Yeah, I've got mine as well," she replied.

"Good, Now, if I think of the lyrics they should appear on the holographic paper, right? So if you can think of your lyrics as I touch your head with my hand, they should be transported to my brain so that I can see them and they will then appear on the holographic paper."

Amy closed her eyes and thought of her lyrics.

Steven placed his hand on Amy's head and her lyrics were psychically placed on the holographic paper. He removed his hand and then transmitted his own lyrics.

"The song is written," Steven said with a smile. "Are you ready to sing?" "You bet."

Reading the lyrics from the holographic paper, they sang *Bad Kitty Rap.*

> # *You've been a bad kitty and we can't tell a lie,*
> *we will finish you off so you will finally die.*
> *Your death will be nasty, messy and explosive*
> *The world will rejoice and be happy as Mary and Joseph.*
>
> *(Chorus) Bad kitty, bad kitty you are very, very bad*
> *and now you'll be vanquished, you sick, delinquent lad.*
>
> *Thanks to us you will never ever hurt anyone*
> *you and your killing ways will soon be gone.*
> *You won't be going to a beautiful land,*
> *You'll be forgotten as fast as the worst boy band.*
>
> *(Chorus)*
>
> *You will be done for, grounded forever*

and as for doing more evil, that will be never.
And nobody will give a damn or an atom
So here's a sharp kick right up your bottom.

(Chorus)

Because you are stuffed full of nothing but waste
is why you'll be vanquished with indecent haste.
Your stink will then disappear at last
and you won't even be a thing of the past.

(Chorus)

You're going out with a big, bad bang
Or, if you like, we can leave you to hang.
You have to admit that we've passed your test
because you are nothing and we are, simply, the best.

(Chorus)

When Steven and Amy stopped singing, the cat demon was then vanquished from existence but it was not as they thought. All of the cats that were used to make the cat demon ascended up to heaven, leaving Amy and Steven looking up to the sky with mixed feelings.

"Oh no, I didn't expect that," Amy said, gazing skywards sympathetically.

"Yeah, you know, it makes me feel guilty about saying the cat demon was full of waste when in fact it was full of innocent cats."

Amy made a valid comment. "I know we were guilty for saying the cat demon was full of waste, but we still did the right thing in getting rid of it once and for all because it was evil. We've also managed to free those innocent cats."

Steven cheered up. "D'you know what? We did do the right thing. Yeah."

In Adrian's laboratory in Romania Adrian, Greg and Christopher the Idiot were preparing to make another animal demon.

"This time, we'll summon a hundred stray dogs to make Domon, which of course is a dog demon. So I'll write a spell and show it to you both," Adrian told Greg and Christopher the Idiot.

Adrian produced the spell and gave it to Greg and Christopher the Idiot to read.

"Okay, have you read it?"

Greg and Christopher the Idiot both said they had.

"Then let's commence," said Adrian.

"Commence what?" said Christopher the Idiot who didn't have a clue about what Adrian said.

"Say the spell, dummy," Greg said impatiently.

Christopher the Idiot looked at Greg with hatred, but recited the spell together with him and Adrian.

"Send us one hundred dogs here today and turn them into Domon so it can blow a lot of people away."

Then one hundred dogs magically appeared in Adrian's laboratory and formed a ten-foot dog demon, or Domon, as Adrian called it.

"Listen up, these are your orders," Adrian told Domon. "I want you to kill as many people as possible. These people include two superheroes; one of them wearing green, the other blue. Make sure you that you try harder to kill them than the cat demon did, which was to just attack them as it knew that they would think it was trying to kill them. Then they would have to kill it nine times; which is what it wanted because it knew that if they killed it nine times before the nine o'clock deadline then it would become impossible to vanquish. However, its selfish ways didn't come to anything because your targets managed to find out that killing the cat demon at the exact stroke of nine o'clock would vanquish it forever and of course that's exactly what they did. So I suggest you surprise them from behind and strike when the iron is hot so that you will have a good chance of killing them. Oh, and just in case you are thinking of doing what the cat demon did... and if you somehow succeed, then I will vanquish you with a special chemical potion that I made earlier. Don't imagine that it is not powerful enough to destroy you; it has the power to vanquish a demon ten times your size. So that's an incentive to try hard to kill the superheroes along with all the people in the world as well, if you can. Now, locate their position on the magically enhanced television and then go all out to kill them."

Domon studied the television screen and then left on his mission to kill Steven, Amy and all the people in the world.

In the Lake District, Steven has been forewarned by the voice in his head that Domon was about to attack.

"Amy! When I say 'now' step back a yard from where you are. Domon is about to pay us a visit. Then use your power to keep throwing him up in the air until I can improvise a bed of nails for him to fall on and be vanquished."

"Okay, will do," she replied.

"Ready, steady... now!"

At the precise moment that Domon arrived in the Lake District and was about to bite Amy, she stepped back a yard and instead of biting her flesh, he tore only at fresh air. While Steven went to find some sharp objects, Amy threw Domon up in the air and somehow managed to throw him into the overhead power line, therefore vanquishing the dog's first life.

"Wow, that was lucky," she said, surprised at what she had done.

"Yeah, your powers advanced at the right time, just as I was struggling to think of original ways to kill it, based on what is available to us," Steven agreed.

Amy laughed. "We might be able to beat the demon in seconds rather than hours."

Steven laughed with her. "Now, I've just thought of how we can get rid of Domon's second life or the second of his *ten* lives, as the voice in my head has just informed me. You use your new power to throw Domon all the way into the sun and therefore incinerate it."

Amy looked at Steven with wide eyes. "Yeah? Okay, then. I think I could do that."

When Domon reappeared, Amy immediately used her power to send Domon into the sun, therefore incinerating him.

"Now, here's the third way to kill Domon. You could send him into Pluto so he will freeze to death."

"Cool, yeah?" she joked.

Steven grinned, watching as Domon reappeared and Amy sent him to Pluto where he froze to death.

"Well done," he said. "This time, death number four, will involve sending Domon into the atmosphere of space. It will be difficult to breathe and he will suffocate."

When Domon reappeared, Amy swiftly sent him into space where he struggled to breathe and suffocated to death.

"And for the fifth way to vanquish Domon, you could try throwing it really hard into that mountain in the distance," Steven said, pointing towards Scafell Pike.

"Yeah I'm sure I can do that."

When Domon arrived, Amy sent him crashing into the mountain, therefore destroying his fifth life.

"To take his sixth life, you could try propelling it all the way into a Dutch windmill. Head first."

"Okay; I'll try. Now where's Holland?"

"Over there," Steven replied, waving an arm in a south-easterly direction.

When Domon reappeared, Amy propelled him head first into a Dutch windmill, decapitating him and therefore vanquishing his sixth life.

The windmill death had given Amy inspiration.

"Steven, I've thought of four ways to vanquish Domon once and for all. I could drop him into the Grand Canyon by using just enough force to put it over the giant chasm and he will hopefully fall to the bottom and die for the sixth time. Then I could hurl him into the cables used to power the San Francisco cable cars and strangle him to death. Next I will send him into a war zone where soldiers with firearms will kill him and last, but not least, how about if I send him into the kitchen of a New York restaurant where angry chefs will kill it? Obviously I will only do the last one on the exact stroke of ten o'clock... I think that's right?"

"That's exactly what the voice in my head has just told me," Steven confirmed.

"Okay, I'm ready for him."

When Domon reappeared Amy plunged the monster to the bottom of the Grand Canyon just as she promised and Domon fell to his seventh death.

The eighth came when she successfully cast Domon into the San Francisco power cables and strangled him.

As soon as Domon reappeared Amy sent him into a dangerous war zone where he was immediately shot dead. Nine lives destroyed; one more to go.

"What do you think? Should we go and hide in that field over there until it's time to vanquish Domon once and for all?" she asked Steven.

"Good idea. Come on."

They were lying flat in the field so that Domon would not be able to see them. Steven moved his head slightly and noticed a house nearby. In fact, it was close enough for him to be able to see its occupants.

"Amy, I think there's a problem."

"What's the problem?"

"Well, we're in somebody's back garden."

Amy looked around in shock and then sprang to her feet and ran from the garden.

"Wait for me!" Steven shouted, running out of the garden behind her.

They ran to a clump of trees and hid behind a couple of broad trunks, panting from their exertions.

"I think I'll wait until just before ten o'clock to start the process of vanquishing Domon once and for all," Amy suggested.

"Yeah, I'll wait here as well to make sure that Domon doesn't surprise you from behind," Steven replied. "Oh, I'm just hearing from the voice in my head that it's all clear for you to go out into the open space and finish off Domon once for and all."

Amy came out from behind her tree and saw Domon with his back towards her. Using her powers for the tenth time, she sent him to the kitchen of a busy New York restaurant.

In the restaurant, the angry head chef had his knife pointing in the direction of one his chefs.

"That's it, and if you make one more mistake, I'll kill you!" he yelled at the unfortunate chef.

As luck would have it, on the exact stroke of ten o'clock, Domon came hurtling through the restaurant, narrowly missing the diners, into the kitchen and straight into the sharp, pointed end of the knife. He was vanquished.

"Okay, Amy, well done. I've just received a message from the voice in my head that Domon has been vanquished and is being magically transported here, so we will have to sing a song to see it permanently vanquished," Steven said.

He made the holographic piece of paper appear. Then, with Amy, he wrote the song down.

"Right, let's sing," he said.

The Domon will be Dead rap

Domon will be dead soon
and we will be over the moon.
When Domon is dead its blood will be shed
And with it, we'll paint the town red.

(Chorus) Domon will be dead, Domon will be dead

and our hunger for peace will finally be fed.
Domon will not be any threat to human society
nor will it be a threat to other beings' hierarchy.
So all good beings will be safe from this beast
Who is evil and sick, at the very least.
We will do our best to be rid of the obscenity
That threatened the lives of all humanity.

(Chorus)

In a short while evil Domon will be no more
and the innocent dogs inside him will be freed;
they are nothing like him, he is rotten to the core;
and the world will rejoice at our good deed.

(Chorus)

Domon was then vanquished from existence, leaving the town painted red and Steven made the holographic paper disappear.

Amy had the last word. "Clean up this town up of all the red blood, so everything looks as as fresh as a sweet rose bud."

In Adrian's laboratory in Romania, Adrian, Greg and Christopher the Idiot have just received Domon's powers.

"Okay, I'll write down a spell to summon one hundred black widows to make Blawemon; a black widow demon," said Adrian to Greg and Christopher the Idiot. He then wrote down a spell and showed it to them.

"When you have read it, we will say it," he told them.

The three of them incanted the spell together: "Send us one hundred black widows to make Blawemon here today, to kill a lot of people and make them go away."

Then one hundred black widows magically arrived in the laboratory and formed Blawemon.

"Your instructions are as follows," Adrian told Blawemon, "you are to try and kill as many people as possible, including two superheroes, one of whom is wearing green and the other is wearing blue. Look at the magically enhanced wide screen television to see where they are and then go to try and kill them."

Blawemon looked at the magically enhanced wide screen television and then went out to try to kill Amy and Steven and as many people as possible.

Steven has received a message from the voice in his head.

"Amy, we must move out of the way; a monster spider called Blawemon is coming to the Lake District."

As he spoke, Blawemon appeared and immediately cast a demonic spider's web at them. Because of the warning message, they jumped out of the way and the spider's web went into a tree instead. The web burnt a hole through the middle of the trunk, causing the tree to crash to the ground.

"Wow, that is one feisty spider," Steven exclaimed.

"Sure is. Okay, I'll send it into the black hole of Calcutta," Amy replied, and before Blawemon could throw another web, she used her power to send it into the black hole of Calcutta, where it was vanquished for the first time.

"That's good," Stephen said. "Now, how about sending Blawemon just outside the earth's atmosphere so that when it reappears it will be burned up?"

When Blawemon reappeared from Calcutta, Amy used her power to send it just outside the earth's atmosphere, where it was burned up. The second of Blawemon's lives was therefore vanquished.

"What if I end its third life by making a giant plug hole in the ground and drowning it?" Amy asked.

"Great."

Amy closed her eyes. "Make a giant plug hole in the ground, so that when Blawemon reappears I can put the demon in to be drowned."

A giant plughole appeared in the ground and when Blawemon arrived

Amy used her power to send it into the plughole. Blawemon drowned, and its third life was vanquished.

"When it reappears, I'll use my power to send it up to God, who can smite it to death."

"Yeah, go for it," Steven agreed.

As soon as Blawemon returned, Amy used her power to send it up to God who smote it and vanquished for the fourth time.

Steven gave Amy a thumbs-up signal. "God is on our side; Blawemon is vanquished again."

"So far, so good," she said. "This time I'll send it to a stingray fish in Australia."

"Yeah, that sounds good treatment for it."

Blawemon was sent to a stingray fish in Australia and killed by it, vanquishing the monster for the fifth time.

Again, Steven gave Amy the thumbs-up.

"Okay. How about if I send it to the centre of the Earth's core?"

"Ooh yeah, cremate it," he grinned.

As soon as Blawemon reappeared Amy used her power to send it to the centre of the Earth's core where it was burnt to a cinder.

"Six lives down," Steven confirmed.

"I'll try sending it to Orlando, Florida, now."

"You're not going to let it loose at Disneyland?" he joked.

"No. It is still night time there and I think an electric storm will kill it."

"Go ahead if you think it will work, then."

Amy soon despatched Blawemon to Orlando, where a bolt of lightning killed it outright.

"Good one, Amy; vanquish number seven complete!"

"Right, now what do you think of this one? I could say a spell to summon some plutonium..."

"Whoa, steady on, that might be a danger to us, as well?"

Amy gave Steven a scornful look. "I am not stupid; it will be securely contained and then disguised as a fly proportionate to the size of Blawemon. It will most likely think it is some sort of specially modified fly for it to eat. Once it swallows the fly, Blawemon will begin to melt from the inside."

"Send us some safely contained plutonium disguised as a fly to tempt Blawemon and leave no traces or else we will go down with the demon," she recited.

Some safely contained plutonium disguised as a large fly appeared on the grass.

"I'd better say a spell to protect us from any possible spray from Blawemon's jaws," Amy said.

"That would be good, yeah."

She again closed her eyes. "Surround Steven and me with an invisible protective bubble so Blawemon can't cause us any trouble."

A protective bubble magically surrounded Amy and Steven and then became invisible.

"Okay, now we wait for Blawemon to take the bait." Amy said.

When Blawemon arrived it tried to kill Amy and Steven by casting its acidic web at them but of course, the protective bubble protected them. The spider's web rebounded off the bubble and headed towards Blawemon, who dived out of the way, leaving it to destroy a nearby tree. Blawemon then noticed the plutonium disguised as a fly and greedily devoured it.

The plutonium melted Blawemon from the inside, leaving a black, viscid mess, but not a trace of plutonium. The monster spider had now been vanquished eight times.

"Remove this invisible protective bubble because to us there is no more trouble." said Amy and they were freed.

"I thought for the ninth way of killing Blawemon I could poison it with carbon monoxide. Do you know any place that has some CO?"

The voice in Steven's head told him where such a place was. He pointed to his right. "Yeah, there's a warehouse full of it, just over there."

"Great, thanks."

So when Blawemon reappeared, Amy used her power to send Blawemon to the warehouse containing carbon monoxide. When it choked to death on the poisonous fumes it was vanquished for the ninth time.

"Only two more to go, Amy. I've just thought of a way to vanquish Blawemon for the tenth time. Could you summon the Ebola virus, safely contained, of course, to the exact spot I point to? According to the voice in my head, that is where Blawemon will arrive next, and it will stand on the container and release the Ebola virus upon itself."

"Okay, I will say a spell." Amy closed her eyes tightly. "Send us the Ebola virus, safely contained, for Blawemon to stand on and cause it great pain."

The Ebola virus appeared at the spot where Steven had previously pointed, Amy said the invisible protective spell and the bubble immediately enveloped her and Steven.

Blawemon was set down at the exact place Steven had indicated and unknowingly stood on the container, releasing the Ebola virus upon itself. Thus it was vanquished for the tenth time.

Amy then cast the spell to remove the invisible protective bubble from around her and Steven.

"I've just thought of the eleventh way to kill Blawemon and therefore render it inactive,"Amy said. "I could send it into a place infected with anthrax at eleven o'clock."

"Oh, that's a good one and the voice in my head has just told me that there is a place like that in that direction." Steven pointed straight ahead.

They waited behind a tree until Blawemon reappeared, just before eleven o'clock. At eleven o'clock precisely, Amy sent Blawemon to the place infected with anthrax and it was poisoned by the anthrax spores.

Steven confirmed that Blawemon had been vanquished for the eleventh time.

Blawemon then appeared in a suspended state.

Steven made his holographic piece of paper appear again and he and Amy spoke their lyrics, which were psychically transferred to the holographic paper.

"So are you ready to sing?" Steven asked.

"I'm ready."

Blawemon will be Splattered

*# Blawemon's going to get a bashing
and we will jump up and down on it to give it a mashing.
This demon was very, very bad
and this is why, when it is gone, we won't be sad.*

(Chorus) Blawemon will be battered,
Blawemon will be shattered
and then afterwards, well and truly splattered.

When your eight legs have been removed,
your head will be then moved.
As it leaves your gross body
you will look extremely shoddy.

(Chorus)

The poison will be sucked out of your vile body
and placed on the ground, nowhere near anybody.
All of this will be before you are battered
and the whole world knows you never mattered.

(Chorus)

When Blawemon's life is over we'll all be thrilled
To know for certain that the monster's been killed.
Your web of poison will be destroyed,
making all the good people feel overjoyed.

(Chorus)

When at last you are gone
you will be the unknown one,
You won't be the devil because he can come back
But you won't have the means for a future attack.

(Chorus)

Blawemon was then magically bashed against a mountain; first its legs were removed from its shattered body, and then its head was moved away. After that, its venom was sucked from its body and placed on the ground away from everybody, where it could cause no harm. What remained of Blawemon was then splattered against the ground.

"Wow, it got what we wanted it to," said Steven.

"Yeah, our powers must be growing, but it hasn't yet been permanently vanquished... why is that?" Amy asked.

"Must be something we haven't done."

Steven and Amy tried to think what it was that they had overlooked.

"Oh, I know," Steven suddenly exclaimed, "we haven't jumped up and down on its soft body parts yet."

Amy pulled a face. "Ugh, well I suppose we'd better do that, then."

"Come on," said Steven, "it won't take long."

Amy and Steven went and and jumped up and down on Blawemon's soft body parts and it was finally vanquished.

But in the laboratory in Romania, Adrian, Greg and Christopher the Idiot were preparing to conjure up another animal demon.

"This time, I've decided we are going to make an animal demon out of two sets of animals. I've thought of one; a chameleon. Can either of you think of another?" Adrian asked.

Christopher the Idiot looked blank. "I can't think of anything."

"You do surprise me!" Greg said sarcastically.

Christopher the Idiot stared at Greg with narrowed eyes; he was getting fed up with his snide remarks.

Greg was unmoved. "Unlike Christopher, I do have an animal in mind; the Australian jellyfish that is supposed to be able to kill animals far greater than its own size. So a demonic version should be able to kill people and superheroes."

"Good suggestion. Okay, I'll write a spell to summon fifty chameleons and fifty Australian jellyfish and have them turned into Chamajellmon," Adrian said.

When Adrian had finished writing out the spell, he showed it to Greg and Christopher the Idiot who read it.

"If you have finished reading the spell," Adrian said, "we will say it together."

"Send us fifty chameleons and fifty Australian jellyfish here today, then turn them into Chamajellmon, who will able to blow many people away," they recited.

Chamajellmon magically appeared in Adrian's laboratory.

"Your orders are to kill as many people as possible and two superheroes. Look at the television to find out where they are," Adrian told it.

Chamajellmon looked at the television screen and then left, ready to try and kill its targets.

It arrived in the Lake District but could not be seen.

"Amy, we must keep an eye out for when Chamajellmon arrives," Steven said.

"Chamajellmon? That's a strange name."

"That's what I thought when the voice in my head told me its name. Although I don't know why it didn't tell me when, or where Chamajellmon is coming to."

"That is strange; we'll just have to keep our eyes peeled." Amy replied, walking about and looking around to see if the monster had arrived yet.

Steven was looking around as well. When he looked down at the ground, he noticed there were no daisies on the patch of grass that Amy was about to walk on, even though the rest of the grass was covered in them.

"Amy, stop!"

She stopped dead. "What's wrong?"

"Well, there are no daisies on the patch of grass in front of you, so at a guess I would say that it is not a patch of grass at all, but the demon in camouflage."

Amy looked down at the patch of grass and then used her power to send camouflaged Chamajellmon to Mercury, where it was vanquished for the first time.

"Okay, the voice in my head has told me that Chamajellmon has been vanquished. So now we need to think of a new way to vanquish it," Steven said.

"I know, when Chamajellmon reappears I'll use my power to send it to the top of the Eiffel tower."

"Okay, Amy. Go ahead."

Amy waited for it to reappear and immediately sent it to the top of the Eiffel tower; where it was spiked and vanquished for the second time.

Steven listened to the voice in his head and nodded to Amy. "Okay, the demon has been vanquished again."

"Now, what if I send it smashing into the Taj Mahal at extreme velocity?"

"Ooh, painful! Yes, do it."

When Chamajellmon reappeared, Amy used her power and sent it into the Taj Mahal at extreme velocity. Chamajellmon was therefore vanquished for the third time.

"Yes," said Steven, listening to the voice in his head, "the third vanquish has been accomplished."

"Next time, I'll send it to Mars."

As it reappeared, Amy dispatched Chamajellmon directly to Mars, where it could not breathe and died from suffocation.

"Yes," said Steven, nodding. The fourth vanquish is complete."

"I'll try Saturn next time, then; hopefully it will be vanquished for the fifth time?"

"Yeah, go for it, Amy."

Being unable to withstand the atmosphere, Chamajellmon withered and died on Saturn and Steven confirmed that it had been vanquished for the fifth time.

"And when it reappears, I shall send it to Jupiter," Amy declared.

Again, Chamajellmon could not tolerate the atmosphere and was vanquished by the violent turbulence around Jupiter's surface.

"The voice in my head has just told me that the sixth vanquish is complete," Steven said.

"When Chamajellmon reappears this time, I'll send it onto the goalposts at Kingston Park Rugby Stadium," Amy told him.

Steven laughed. "The goal posts? What will they do to it?"

"Impale it through its black heart!" she cried, using her power to send it onto the goalposts at Kingston Park.

It was indeed impaled through the heart and died instantly.

"Oh, well done. The seventh vanquish is complete," congratulated Steven.

"Top of Blackpool tower next."

"Okay," Steven said, "carry on."

When Chamajellmon emerged, Amy used her power to send it onto the top of Blackpool tower where it was again spiked and vanquished for the eighth time.

"The voice is confirming that the eighth vanquish is now complete."

"That's good. What about ICI in Middlesbrough... can the fumes kill it?" Amy asked.

"Undoubtedly. Send it there."

When Chamajellmon reappeared Amy's power sent it to ICI in Middlesbrough where it suffocated from the fumes. That was the ninth time it had been vanquished and Steven confirmed that the voice in his head was telling him so.

"That's good and now I'll send it into the path of a big road truck."

Crushed to death by a massive 16-wheeler, Chamajellmon was vanquished for the tenth time.

"The voice in my head has just told me that it has been destroyed for the tenth time." Steven said.

"Great. Have you got any ideas about how to vanquish it for the eleventh time?"

"Yeah, actually, I have just thought of a way to shock it to death. You could send it to the shooting range in North Wales that Greg and I once attended with the RAF cadets. The noise will kill it," Steven suggested.

"Really? Noise?"

"Undoubtedly. If you ever heard it, you would agree."

"Okay. Can you point in the direction of the shooting range?"

Steven pointed. "Sure, it's over there."

When Chamajellmon reappeared, Amy used her power again to send it to the shooting range in North Wales, where it did indeed die of shock at the sound of numerous guns being fired simultaneously.

"The voice in my head has just told me that it has been vanquished for the eleventh time," Steven said. "Now, can you think of a twelfth way to vanquish Chamajellmon?"

"Well, I'd have to say no," Amy replied.

"I see," said Steven, looking suspiciously at Amy. He then looked down and saw that she was preparing to use her power on him. Luckily, he jumped out of the way so that Amy, or at least what appeared to be Amy, couldn't send him to his death.

"Rape the Virgin Mary!" he exclaimed, shocked at what had just happened.

"If that's your way of saying it's not possible that I'm in Amy's body, then you're sadly mistaken," said Chamajellmon in Amy's body, using her voice.

Then Chamajellmon again prepared to use Amy's power to send Steven to his death, but Steven was quick to notice and dodged out of Chamajellmon's way. He ran away, losing Chamjellmon in the process, and hid behind a tree.

Steven communicated with the voice in his head. "Okay, so Chamajellmon must have somehow worked out how to camouflage itself before it was magically transported here, so that Amy or myself could not see it, and then it must have used some sort of demonic Chameleon power to switch bodies with Amy. So if you, the voice in my head, could tell me how to get Amy back into her body and vanquish Chamajellmon, that would be very kind? Oh, and by the way, if you're in contact with the Virgin Mary could you say that I meant no offence by my earlier rape the Virgin Mary remark? It was just my own figure of speech, meaning it couldn't be possible."

The voice in Steven's head complied with his requests.

"Thank you, and now to put your plan to the test," he replied. He checked his watch. "Ah, that's lucky, it's a minute before twelve o'clock. So I've got enough time to have Chamajellmon chase me to the house with the garden where Amy and I trespassed earlier."

Steven emerged from behind the tree and ran in front of the house he mentioned.

Chamajellmon, who was still inside Amy's body, then chased after him and when it arrived at the house it prepared to use Amy's power on him.

Steven then moved out Chamajellmon's line of fire and the power it was about to unleash on him at the last second before twelve o'clock. Naturally, the power missed Steven and rebounded off the house directly at Chamajellmon. Then, at exactly twelve o'clock, Chamajellmon turned back into his normal state as Amy appeared from behind a tree and Chamajellmon was vanquished for the twelfth time.

Steven looked at Amy.

"Its nice to see you... well, the real you."

Amy laughed. "Thanks for saving me."

"Oh, I didn't do much; the voice in my head came up with the plan and all I did was execute it."

"You still deserve credit for what you did."

Steven smiled at her.

"I didn't know that my own power could be used against me. I'll have to be careful in future," Amy said.

"Well, actually, the voice in my head has just told me that because you were technically a part of Chamajellmon, albeit its camouflaged body, and it was a part of you, you have inherited one of its traits, which is immunity from a vanquish which killed it."

Amy was relieved. "Well that's good."

"Good for you, yeah, but all the more reason why we must get rid of Chamajellmon once and for all."

Chamajellmon was then magically transported to the Lake District and placed on the grass in a suspended state.

"Okay, Amy, are you ready to sing away all our troubles, or to be more precise, are you ready to sing Chamajellmon away?"

"You bet."

Steven then makes his holographic piece of paper appear. Amy tells him her lyrics and he psychically writes them down as well as his own.

"Ready to sing?"

Amy nodded. "Ready."

Chamajellmon will be Obliterated

 # Chamajellmon will be obliterated
because it tried to make people feel ill fated.
It's got a very stupid name
and for what it has done is now motionless as well as tame.

(Chorus) Chamajellmon will be obliterated

because it so hated.
It will also be blown up beyond hell
because it's worse than a really bad spell.
Chamajellmon is worse than sick pond life
That's dumb and deaf and lost its sight
It is exactly like a diseased worm;
It's evil brain is just like a germ.

(Chorus)

Chamajellmon has brought too much grief to this place
and that is why it is nothing but a disgrace.
But when it is finally blasted
all will be glad that it never lasted.

(Chorus)

When Chamajellmon is gone everyone will be free,
as ecstatic as a songbird in a tree.
When it is gone we'll all be delirious
for the whole thing has been just too serious.

(Chorus)

Chamajellmon is then obliterated beyond hell and therefore vanquished for good.

"Okay, it is vanquished. Now we can go back to Newcastle to try and find Greg. We have to stop him, Christopher and the person responsible for putting Greg under the spell from doing anything stupid," Amy said.

"Okay, what are we waiting for?"

"Hold my hand while I say a spell to take us back to Newcastle."

As Steven held her hand, Amy incanted the words: "Take us back to Newcastle so we can try and find certain people to stop them being delinquents and causing all this hassle."

"Now we're back in Newcastle, let's think where Greg and his soon to be ex-friends might be," Amy said, but while she and Steven were doing that, Greg, Adrian and Christopher the Idiot were discussing something in Romania.

"We have enough powers from the animal demons to go with the powers that Christopher and I acquired from the other demons to perform the next part of my plan," Adrian was saying to Christopher the Idiot and Greg.

"Okay, but I don't see why we had to wait for the superheroes to kill the animal demons when surely we could have killed them ourselves?" Greg queried.

"Actually, first point: we were waiting for the superheroes to be killed, and second point: we couldn't have killed the animal demons because they could only be killed, directly or indirectly, by good beings," Adrian told him. "Do you see?"

Whether he did or not, Greg nodded.

"Now then, we have to go a wide open space because what I have in mind requires more space than there is in this laboratory. Can either of you think of such a place?"

"Sure, the town moor in Newcastle," Greg suggested.

"Right, then let's teleport ourselves to the town moor in Newcastle."

Greg used his teleportation power to take him to the town moor in Newcastle.

Christopher the Idiot then repeated three times the sentence, 'there is no place like the town moor.' Then he thought of the town moor in Newcastle and used his teleportation power that he picked up from the Emperors of the Sun to teleport himself there.

"God, he's an idiot," Christopher murmured, thinking the words, 'town moor in Newcastle' and using his teleportation power that he picked up from the Ku Klux Klan to teleport himself to the town moor in Newcastle.

"I will now write a song that will begin the process of bringing my dead back," Adrian told Greg and Christopher the Idiot. He took pen and paper from his pocket, wrote the song down and showed it to them.

In another part of Newcastle, Steven and Amy still can't think where Greg, Adrian and Christopher the Idiot might be.

Then Steven has quite a prolonged premonition.

"Amy, I've just had a premonition. In it, I saw a vision of the past and a vision of the future. In the vision of the past, Greg appeared to kill someone and in the vision of the future I saw Greg, the idiot and the person who put Greg under a spell bringing back dead people, therefore inadvertently ending the world. I assume Greg had to make a kill to bind him magically to the other killers, who resurrected demons to kill innocent people. And they may have made other kills; I foresaw the resurrection of the dead taking place at the town moor."

Amy frowned. "I can't understand why Greg did what he did."

"Well, he's under a spell."

"Yeah, so you keep saying, but Greg has shown he has a violent side before. Although I am grateful to him for beating that idiot up, nevertheless his violent side might be the reason he was eligible to be put under a spell."

"You don't really believe that, do you?" Steven asked her.

"Yes. Anyway, let's go to the town moor to stop Greg and the others from carrying out their plan."

Steven held Amy's hand. "Okay, and hopefully we can get Greg back on our side."

Just then they heard a couple of passers-by talking.

"That was a terrible thing to happen to that person who lost a lung just because he was a smoker," said one of them.

"Yes, I know; he's lucky to be alive after being stabbed by an evil-looking alien," the other replied.

Steven raised an eyebrow. "Did you hear that? They must have been talking about Greg in alien format. So Greg is still good and the evil ones can't do what they've planned."

"Greg still did a bad thing, though, and might finish the job if he somehow finds out he didn't kill the smoker. So we've got to get to town moor before he finds out... and we have to kill the three evil stooges."

"I hope you change your mind, Amy."

"Don't count on it." Amy concentrated her thoughts on the town moor in Newcastle and then incanted a spell. "Take us to the town moor first, so we can stop the three evil stooges from doing their worst."

Amy and Steven were then magically transported to the town moor in Newcastle. They crouched down behind some cows, out of sight from Adrian, Christopher the Idiot and Greg. They moved carefully between the cows so they could see what was going on.

Greg, Christopher the Idiot and Adrian were about to sing:

Bringing my Dead Back

(Adrian sings the first verse)

Bringing my dead back is what I am going to do
so I can have a great day.
I am the greatest person in the world and what I do is so great.

(Adrian sings the Chorus) Bringing my dead back to life is what I want.
Bringing my dead back to life is what I will do.

(Greg sings the second verse)

Bringing my dead back to life is absolutely necessary
to correct God's mistake of letting them get away from me.
I am better than God who is nothing to me.

(Greg sings the Chorus)

(Christopher the Idiot sings the third verse)

Bringing my dead back might make God angry
but I will feel joyous and absolutely powerful.

(Christopher the Idiot sings the Chorus)

"That was interesting," Amy remarked.

"Yeah, Greg singing heavy metal is like Newcastle United winning the FA cup."

Amy laughed. "What should we do now?"

"Just wait for them to look clueless after realizing their plan has failed."

"Okay, I'll think of a spell that is more powerful than any of my others to vanquish the evil before us."

Steven nodded. "Yeah, and hopefully we can get Greg back on our side to say the spell with us."

"That would be good," Amy agreed.

Adrian was instructing Greg and Christopher the Idiot. "Now when I do an 'A' shape I want both of you to make a 'D' shape with your hands."

Amy and Steven watched as they formed the letters.

"ADD? What's all that about?" whispered Amy.

"Search me; maybe Greg has turned them into maths geeks."

Amy laughed.

Then a black, supernatural circle appeared above the heads of Adrian, Christopher the Idiot and Greg. This was followed by the sound of thunder as the ground began to rumble ominously.

"Whoa! How is their plan working when Greg hasn't killed anyone good?" Amy wondered.

"Greg may not have killed anyone good but he did kill a part of a good person; a lung, to be exact. So technically he has made a kill."

"I see, so Greg's evil forever?"

Steven shook his head. "Not necessarily, because as I said, Greg only made a kill technically speaking. I don't think technicalities are very important in life, so if we can convince him that he is good, then hopefully the technical kill won't matter in the eyes of God, and we will be allowed to turn Greg back to the side of good."

Amy looked hopeful. "That might work."

Steven stood up. "Greg, stop what you're doing!" he shouted.

Greg looked at Steven, but carried on with what he was doing and when Adrian ordered him to ignore Steven, he looked away.

"Well, Amy, you and I are going to have talk Greg into rejoining our side," Steven said.

"Why should I, after what he's done?" Amy asked.

"Well for one thing, the world's about to end and for another... you loved him once and love doesn't die that quickly, so you must be still in love with him."

"Yeah, you're right; the world is about to end," she replied, getting up and walking towards Adrian, Christopher the Idiot and Greg.

Steven was amused by Amy's reluctance to admit she was still in love with Greg. Catching her up, he walked beside her. They stopped when they reached Greg, Adrian and Christopher the Idiot.

"Okay, Greg, stop being an idiot," Amy said.

Greg ignored her.

"Amy's right, Greg," Steven added.

Greg ignored Steven also.

Steven tried again. "Greg, would you please look at me, or at least look at Amy, because you still love her even if you are too stubborn to admit it, just like she is."

After a few seconds, Greg looked at Amy and stopped making the 'D' sign with his hands, therefore ceasing to help Adrian and Christopher the Idiot to inadvertently end the world.

Steven and Amy breathed huge sighs of relief that there was no apparent danger of the world being inadvertently ended.

"I do still love you, Amy," Greg said.

"Ditto," Amy answered, with some reluctance.

Steven smiled, pleased that Greg and Amy had at least admitted they were in love with each other.

Adrian was annoyed and decided to try and kill Greg using the fireball power he picked up from the Ku Klux Klan because, of course, if he killed Greg he would bring his dead back that way.

Fortunately, Amy realised this and used her power to deflect the fireball into Adrian's body, but the fireball didn't kill him because his body magically absorbed it.

"Well, lucky me, it looks like I'm indestructible," Adrian said with a sarcastic grin at Amy, Greg and Steven.

"Actually, according to the voice in my head, you're only immune to individual powers, but what you are not immune to is the Destroyer, which is the overall power of good, not just us," Steven informed him.

Greg and Amy looked interested in Steven's revelations.

Adrian looked gobsmacked.

"Hm," Adrian mused silently. "So killing Greg won't make my plan happen. Although I could use my body switching power that I got from Chamajellmon to switch bodies with Greg, and by doing that, I could have Amy and Steven inadvertently kill Greg, because he will be in my body so they will think he's me. That might make my plan of destroying the Destroyer work because if part of the Destroyer goes against his own kind, then surely the Destroyer will cease to exist as he will have done the opposite of what the Destroyer stands for."

After these thoughts, Adrian used his body switching power to switch bodies with Greg. Steven and Amy didn't even notice. He then looked smugly at his body with Greg in it.

Greg is shocked at what Adrian has done.

"Oh no! Adrian must have used his body switching power to swap bodies with me," Greg thought, in Adrian's body. He froze with fear of what might happen to him.

"Have you got a spell in mind, Amy?" Steven asked.

"Yeah." She began to say the spell.

Then Steven looked at Greg's body with Adrian in it; he was smiling in an evil way.

"Amy, stop saying the spell!"

"Why?"

Steven activated his blade and jabbed it into the heart of Greg's body.

Amy looked horrified.

"Steven! Why did you just do that?" she shrieked.

"Well because Adrian is in Greg's body and now I've stabbed it, he should return to his own body."

Greg relaxed. "Phew," he thought, "Steven figured out what Adrian was doing."

"Are you sure?" Amy asked.

"I'm positive."

Adrian then held Greg's heart to try and stop the blood pouring out of it. This was an attempt to prolong his life, because if he were forced back into his own body, Amy, Steven and Greg would vanquish him once Oddball had healed Greg's body.

He then tried to use Greg's transportation power to transport himself back to his laboratory to make a potion to heal Greg's heart so that he could kill a good person and therefore try to trick God into thinking Greg had killed a good person, going against everything the Destroyer stood for. Then God might end the Destroyer, which would possibly enable Adrian's plan to work. However, Adrian was too weak to use Greg's transportation power and do what he wanted.

"So, is Greg in Adrian's body?" asked Amy.

Steven looked from Greg to Amy. "Either that, or a mental patient is Adrian's body."

Amy looked at Greg and burst out laughing. Greg was dancing on his tiptoes.

"Okay, come to me Oddball," Greg said, looking at his body.

Oddball came out of Greg's body and went into his hand. Greg was still dancing on his tiptoes.

"Say hello to Oddball," he said in a Cuban accent. "Now start dying," he said in his usual Geordie accent. He then threw Oddball into his own body in an attempt to force a weak yet stubborn Adrian out of his body.

Adrian was then weakened further and his hand slipped off Greg's heart. He was then forced out of Greg's body and, at the same time, Greg was forced out of Adrian's body.

Before Adrian and Greg returned to their original bodies, Oddball went into Greg's heart and healed it. Adrian tried to use his powers but he couldn't because his soul had been weakened by the impact of Oddball.

Amy and Steven smiled at Greg, glad to have him back in his own body.

"Well, should I think of a song to help vanquish Adrian and Christopher the Idiot now?" Greg asked.

"Actually," Steven replied, "I don't think Christopher should be killed, because deep down he's just a scared little boy who can barely think for himself. I mean, he could have killed us at any time while we were dealing with Adrian but he didn't as he finds it hard to make decisions without someone telling him what to do. As for thinking of the song we can all do that and I'll psychically put it on my holographic piece of paper."

"I'll say a spell to weaken Adrian completely and to stop him from regaining his strength," Amy said.

"Render Adrian weak and inactive like someone who has overdosed on fibre and laxative," Amy incanted, looking at Adrian.

Adrian was then rendered inactive.

"Okay, now before we think of a song I want Oddball to take away all the powers from the Christopher the Idiot," Greg said.

Oddball appeared and entered Christopher the Idiot's body, taking away all his powers.

"Now, Oddball, take this unintelligent loser into a derelict building and magically turn it into a magical prison that has magical beings working there to re-educate Christopher the Idiot, as well as to feed him nothing but bread and water until he's a reformed criminal."

"Okay, and I'll call it Oddball's Prison for Dummies," Oddball replied.

Greg, Steven and Amy all laughed.

"Yeah, very good," said Greg.

"Whoa! I am not a dummy because I made up a couple of poems after I murdered your friend," Christopher the Idiot pointed out.

"Oh, my God! How stupid are you? Here we are, trying to give you the opportunity to turn your life around and you're trying to prove you are an intelligent killer so you can go dead pie in the sky... well, to hell, to be more precise. One of those poems was terrible though, and even if it wasn't they could only be a couple of examples of your intelligence. So you need one more."

"Okay, how about the fact that I got into sixth form with 'A' grade passes?" Christopher the Idiot asked Greg.

"Fine. Look, I'll kill you if you want."

"Actually, Greg, the voice in my head has just told me that Christopher switched all his test papers with the most intelligent person in the class, Paul Renoir, and changed Renoir's name to his. He wrote Renoir's on his paper. Christopher's actual papers didn't even get graded."

Greg looked at Christopher the Idiot with a smug look on his face.

"Well, it looks like you're still a dummy so, unfortunately, I won't get to kill you. Anyway, all joking aside, what did you want to be when you were nipper, Christopher?"

"A journalist. Not that it matters because as Adrian said to me, bullies get nowhere in life."

"Well Adrian was right there. Bullies get nowhere in life, because he was a bully, and the worst kind as he didn't know he was a bully and now he is literally a useless statue. So he's going nowhere in life. If you are willing to change your ways and accept a re-educating process to make you a fully qualified journalist, you will not go the same way as Adrian as you will not be a bully. So are you willing to turn your life around?" Greg asked him.

"Yes. I am."

"Okay, Oddball, take Christopher to his destiny. Make sure you switch the names of Paul Renoir's and Christopher's test papers, but first of all I want you to strip Christopher's powers and vanquish the bad souls that he got the powers from."

Oddball performed his stripping and vanquishing and then took Christopher to a derelict building. He then came out of Christopher and turned the building into a prison that would magically lock him in. Then Oddball created magical beings to re-educate Christopher and finally, wrote 'Oddball's Prison for Dummies' on the top of the prison. He then left the prison to go to Christopher's old school, where he swapped the names round on the test papers and left them on a desk ready for someone to notice them. Then Oddball returned to Greg.

"Okay, I've made the prison and locked Christopher inside it. I've also rightfully switched the names on the test papers," Oddball told Greg.

"That's good, and while you were away we told our lyrics to Steven and he put them and his own lyrics on his holographic piece of paper after he'd activated it using his psychic powers."

Oddball looked pleased. "Oh that's good, and I could add music to it."

"So that's another secret power that you possess?"

Oddball winked cheekily at Greg. Then he looked at the holographic piece of paper and memorised the lyrics off by heart to enable him to set the lyrics to music.

Greg, Steven and Amy smiled at Oddball.

"Right, I'm ready to play the music. Are you three ready to sing the lyrics?" he asked.

As Oddball played the music, Greg, Amy and Steven began to sing.

Adrian's Plan has Failed

 # Trying to bring the dead back can never work,
so Adrian's plan would have brought an end to the world
as it would have made God berserk.

(Chorus) Adrian's plan has miserably failed
and all the good people who grieve must be hailed.
Adrian's plan could never go ahead
because God would simply have made the world dead.

Beings on this planet should be treasured for
what's inside, not outside them.
The moment a person is treasured for their body
is the moment when the world becomes unGodly.

(Chorus)

When the world becomes ungodly, we all know
That nothing any good can ever grow
so we won't make the apocalypse real,
but we will stop it happening... that's the deal.

(Chorus)

If we remember that no one really dies
And not to treat them like a bingo prize
Then we will all live happily ever after
Pursuing kindness, love and laughter.

(Chorus)

Then Adrian was vanquished from existence along with all the bad souls whose powers he had used to try and bring back his dead, along with help from Christopher the Idiot and Greg. The bad souls' powers were vanquished from existence as well.

"Now that Adrian's gone," Greg said, "I think I have to apologise for everything I have put you both through."

"No, that's not necessary," Amy and Steven replied.

"Well, I think it is necessary. So sorry to both of you."

"Apology accepted, then."

Greg was smiling at them both. "Thank you."

"And now I've got my apology out of the way, I feel I should come up with a saying to remind me not to hurt good beings. So here goes: Arrogance shown towards good beings will destroy me, whereas if I only show arrogance towards bad beings or to demonstrate my good abilities, then destiny will lead me to my true greatness."

"I like that saying," Amy said.

Steven nodded. "Yeah, me too."

"It's good that you both like it, especially you, Amy, because it means I'm well and truly back in your good books."

Before she could respond, Greg knelt on one knee in front of her. "Amy, will you marry me?"

"Yes," said Amy with a winning smile, "I will marry you, Greg."

Greg smiled back at her, but then suddenly frowned in annoyance. "Oh, I forgot about the engagement ring. Oddball, can you turn into an engagement ring?" He held his hand out.

Oddball went into Greg's hand and turned into a sparkling engagement ring.

"May I place this ring, courtesy of Oddball, on your finger?" Greg asked his bride to be.

"You may," she replied, grinning broadly.

Greg slid the ring onto Amy's marriage finger and they all admired it.

Looks like I'm going beat you to getting married, Steven," Greg joked.

Steven smiled knowingly. "Aha, you're wrong there, mate. I'm off to see my wife now."

Amy looked pleasantly surprised, but Greg was completely gobsmacked at Steven's breaking news.

"Well jigger me sideways! When did you get married, then?" Greg asked.

"Well, after that nightclub incident I went on my journey to see Jessica and I realised how much I loved her. So I decided to go and buy an engagement ring... very similar to that one, actually," he said, pointing to Amy's finger. Then I went and asked Jessica to marry me and she said yes. One of her sisters had just been ordained as an Internet minister and agreed to marry us. So our respective parents were invited to meet up with us in Jessica's back garden and then her sister married us."

"But where did you meet Jessica?" Greg asked.

"I thought you might be wondering. I met her at the night club we went to after you met Amy."

"Oh right. Well, congratulations, mate."

"Yeah, I'm really pleased for you too, Steven," Amy added.

"Thanks. I'll be off, then."

Greg looked at Amy and took hold of her hand. "Okay, fiancée, do you want to go back to my place? Or mine and Steven's place to be precise."

"Yeah," she agreed. "Let's go."

The next morning Greg went to see the bouncer whose nose he broke and apologised for what he did and then thanked him for not pressing charges. Greg then went to a jewellery store to buy an engagement ring. On his way to see Amy, Greg then received a phone call from Jack Clarke asking him, Steven and Amy to perform in a concert at Clarkesville; which was the name of the stadium that Jack Clarke took over from Greg, Steven and Amy.

Greg agreed to do the concert and agreed to try and persuade the witch and the psychic to do it. He then told Jack Clarke to look at the signature 'the Destroyer' and delete the word 'the' from the form the superheroes signed.

"Why is that?" Jack wanted to know.

"Because I am just a Destroyer, not *the* Destroyer."

He called Amy first, and then Steven to ask if they would do the concert. They both agreed. Greg went to see Amy to give her the engagement he bought. Oddball returned to its normal form.

A few days later, Greg, Amy and Steven, all in their superheroes costumes, went along to the sold out Clarkesville stadium to perform in the concert, having learnt the lyrics they wrote together beforehand. Oddball made some music to go with the lyrics.

They went out onto the specially built platform.

"All right, you awesome people, are you ready for the time of your lives?" Greg shouted to the crowd.

"YEAH!" the crowd screamed back.

"All right, the first song is called *The Destroyer of Evil*," he announced.

Oddball appeared and began playing the music.

The Destroyer of Evil

 # The Destroyer of evil is a very good thing,
because it makes everybody happy enough to smile cheekily and sing.

(Chorus) The Destroyer of evil is a very good thing, it has a good ring
and the feeling of being part of it is better than anything.

The Destroyer of evil has so much power
and more good feeling than a pub's happy hour
The Destroyer of evil is more than all right;
the Destroyer of evil is full of light.

The crowd applauded with great enthusiasm and only stopped when Greg raised his hands.

"Thank you so much. The next song is called *Acting out of Revenge is Wrong*. The music, Oddball, please."

To Oddball's backing, the trio begin to sing:

 # If you think acting out of revenge is right,

your future won't be all that bright.
So if bullies have hurt someone close to you,
you must only stop the bullies from winning through
and not take revenge, though you really want to.

(Chorus) Revenge is not the best
and if you do it you'll eventually be laid to rest.
However you won't rest in peace in the good place,
you'll go to the bad place and be a disgrace.
Revenge is just a scalding hot dish
that will not grant any victim's wish.
Acting out of revenge is selfish, too
We don't want more bullies and neither do you.

(Chorus)

Acting out of revenge has more venom than a snake.
And it's easy to do, in fact a piece of cake,
but acting out of revenge is not clever
it just hurts good people and scars them forever.

(Chorus)

Acting out of revenge is wrong
That is our point in singing this song
So think hard before you commit a wrong act
Taking revenge is wrong and that is pure fact.

(Chorus)

The crowd erupted into rapturous applause and Greg waited for it to die down before introducing their next number.

"Thank you. Our next song is called *Bullies Become the Bullied*. The thinking behind it is the fact that I was a bully and I was bullied myself because I was placed under a spell and then forced to do certain things against my own will. It was definitely for my own good, although if I hadn't used such appalling arrogance towards good people... like for example, calling homosexuals 'poofs' then I probably would have been strong enough to overcome the spell much sooner than I did. And I would not have done the terrible things the bullies forced me to do. Anyway, I hope you enjoy this anti-bullying song. Thank you, Oddball..."

The Bullies Become the Bullied

The bullies who think they can carry on cruising
Are in for a beating, an awful bruising.

(Chorus) The bullies become the bullied, the bullies become the bullied,
the Bullies are going to get chased out of town
and they are going down, down, down.

Bullies who don't accept punishment are cowards
who don't give a damn who they hurt,
but what they don't realise is good people are clever and always alert.
So if all good people start pulling together
we can kick the bullies out of the world forever.

(Chorus)

A world without the bullies is worth thinking about
so good people can happily laugh, sing and shout.

The crowd showed their appreciation by whistling as they applauded.

Greg smiled at them. "I thought you might like that one. This next song is called *Smokers are Chokers*, which is a song to make people realise what harm they're doing not only to themselves but also other people."

Smokers are Chokers

 # People that smoke think they're big and clever
but they're not, they're as bad as awful weather.
Smokers kill themselves and others with what they do,
so what they do is evil and they're also a bit cuckoo.

(Chorus) Smokers are chokers; that's what they are

and if they continue to smoke they won't go far.
Smokers pollute this beautiful earth
Smelling like sewers, that's all they're worth.
So they're wasting their money on zero, or nothing
and will be laid prematurely in their coffin.

(Chorus)

Causing illness like heart disease, emphysema and cancer
It's just not worth being a weak-minded chancer
so smokers should choose to give up the habit
before it's too late and then you've had it.

(Chorus)

So give up tobacco and don't be like a prick,
a fool at the end of a little white stick.
Then you can look forward to a long happy life
instead of a brief one that's filled with strife.

After more deafening applause, Steven announced the next song.

"Thank you very much. The next song is called *Taking the Mick*. The Rolling Stones might sing this if Mick Jagger died but, hey, it's just a bit of fun so please, don't any of you be offended."

Oddball played the intro and Steven, Amy and Greg came in on cue.

Taking the Mick

We're not going to give up just because Mickey's dead,
No, we're going to keep the party of life going by singing and dancing.

(Chorus) Mickey's dead, Mickey's dead, but we're not going to quit,
we're going to on and have lots of fun. Yeah! Yeah! Yeah! Yeah!

Mickey might be gone, but he's not gone completely
and with his spirit we're going to rock and roll.

(Chorus)

We're keeping the party of life going
because that's the meaning of life no matter how much pain there is.

(Chorus)

Mickey's death doesn't change anything;
he was only a walking skeleton, walking dead.

(Chorus)

The crowd applauded, quietening down only when Amy spoke into the mic.

"You're a wonderful audience, thank you. This next song is called *No One Really Dies*, which is dedicated to anybody who has suffered a bereavement."

No One Really Dies.

\# *Everyone lives forever in memory and spirit*
if their soul has had love and hope in it.
The memories of someone are why no one really dies
and the spirit of someone goes to one of the many dreamlike skies.

(Chorus) No one really dies through spirit and memory
if they have been exemplary.
And no one really dies
if they do the good things before claiming a prize.
A soul of someone is important and if sins against the heart are committed
then no one can be forgiven nor are they benefited.
But if someone shares lots love and laughter
then they will pass beyond earth to be happy ever after.

(Chorus)

Love is an important thing in a person's heart
and if they have that they will never truly depart.
The ability of someone to always show love
Will bring them such peace from the angels above.

(Chorus)

All these things are why no one really dies
And after death the souls of good people always rise
and if we all have or want these things, then it's no surprise
when we end up forever in our home in the skies.

(Chorus)

Steven waited for the applause to die down before introducing their next number, *Spread the Hope, Heed the Love.*

Hope and Love

 # Hope, they say, springs eternal
and love is like writing the most powerful journal.
So if we put them both together,
we'll feel like we can literally live forever.

(Chorus)

Spread the hope, heed the love
and then we can fly like a big white dove.
Hope and love are what we need to do well in life
then we will forget about any confidence strife.
Hope and love both are special things
and if we embrace them we'll see what good destiny brings.

(Chorus)

Hope and love can take us a long way
and they can help us live for every moment each day.
Hope and love together can bring so much warmth to our heart
and that is why we must not let them drift apart.

(Chorus)

If we need a companion just hope for someone to come along
and then love will be sent to us like a beautiful song.
After love has been found it'll last forever,

so as for losing, that will be never.

When the applause for that finally died down, Steven announced their final number.

"Thank you. Our final song tonight is a really fun song which should encourage everyone here to believe we are capable of doing anything, and it's called *We are Gods to God.*

"We are Gods to God," Greg, Amy and Steven said in unison as Oddball played the intro.

We are Gods to God

\# *We should each try to be the best we possibly can*
because we each have the ability to be better than superman.
We just have to chase a dream of ours
and eventually, like seeds, it will grow into
something beautiful like flowers.

(Chorus) We are Gods to God,

so we don't have to bow down and nod.
We can take God in the good way
but we should never take God in a bad way.

We should all try to get whatever good we want
and not let people tell us that we can't.
We should all try to chase our goals
for each of us has important roles.

(Chorus)

We can build a legacy for ourselves
so that we are not left sitting on dusty old shelves.

We should try and outweigh the bad things in life
And bring goodness back where sinning is rife.

(Chorus)

We are God's children so we should all rejoice
that we are trying to listen to God's righteous voice.
As we look up to him he will proudly look down
On us, his people, spreading goodness around.

(Chorus)

If we do all this then we make ourselves great.
meaning we can rid this planet of all its hate.
We should all try harder to find our true calling,
so that when we are needed, we will not be caught falling.

The crowd then went wild, giving Greg, Amy and Steven a standing ovation. Some stamped their feet, others whistled, nearly all demanded "MORE! MORE!"

The superheroes obliged with a repeat of the last verse and chorus and then took their bows, each thanking the crowd in turn.

"Thank you very much," from Greg.

"Thanks for all your support," Amy said.

"You've been a brilliant audience; thanks a lot," Steven completed.

Over the next five years Greg, Amy and Steven went to university after each gaining the necessary AS level results. Paul Renoir, the unlucky victim of Christopher the Idiot's cheating was allowed into sixth firm as he rightfully deserved and did well, gaining a place at university. He did very well there and afterwards landed himself a good job.

Greg, Amy and Steven also did well at university, becoming an accountant, doctor and psychologist respectively.

Christopher the Idiot also did well in his re-education process in Oddball's prison for dummies. He was tutored by the magical beings in the prison to learn several necessary GCSE subjects and passed them all. AS level subjects followed and he passed all those as well. He then studied for a degree in journalism and passed that, too. So Christopher is no longer an idiot and in ten years' time, when he has finished his fifteen-year sentence for murder, he will be able to get a job as a journalist.

Amy, Steven and Greg did well in their jobs and soon saved enough money to buy the flat they had rented out of their grant money. Steven told his wife, Jessica, that he was a superhero and introduced her to his fellow superheroes.

Suitably impressed, Jessica was more than happy to move into the flat with them and so was Amy.

And they were all able to buy classy cars as well.

****

Greg drove to his work place, parked his car and left it, listening to that satisfying 'clunk' as he shut the door, the clunk of quality.

"# I've been driving in my car; it's better than a jaguar," Greg sang. He then locked his red Porsche and went into his work place.

Amy drove to work in her silver Mercedes convertible. That also made a satisfying 'clunk' when she shut the door.

Steven drove to work in his small, black Fiesta Ghia. He parked it outside the hospital and left it, singing: "# I've been driving my jet-black car; it's much better than a jaguar."

Eight hours later, Greg left his work place and drove off towards home. Halfway through his journey, Greg sensed evil, stopped the car, left the vehicle and locked it.

"Hm, I can sense evil from that man in front of me," Greg thought, and automatically changed into his orange superhero costume.

"Okay, Oddball, can you go into the man's briefcase and look for any evidence that he has three forms of intelligence?"

Oddball materialised and went into the man's briefcase unnoticed.

Greg walked behind the man with the briefcase.

After looking in the briefcase, Oddball emerged and went to Greg.

"He's a lawyer, Greg, and has been working as one for ten years."

Greg was still walking behind the man. "Wonderful! So he's obviously shown at least three forms of intelligence in passing five GCSE subjects and the required AS levels. Obviously he acquired a law degree. The fact that he has worked for ten years as a lawyer proves that he is genuinely intelligent in at least three forms, so he can't have cheated in gaining his qualifications. So he is eligible to have his pretty brains removed by us."

"Yeah," Oddball agrees.

Greg then takes Oddball. "Hey, case head; defend this," he shouted to the man in front of him.

The man with the briefcase turned round with an astonished look on his face.

"Yeah, you," said Greg, staring furiously at the man and then throwing Oddball into his head, rendering the man inactive.

"Now I'll have to sing, which I enjoy even if I do have to sing a song to vanquish evil doers due to Adrian Domescu's evil powers being left behind on earth after he was vanquished. Anyway, Oddball, do you want to play some music inside the man's head?"

"Love to."

Greg thought of a song and told the lyrics to Oddball in the man's head. Oddball then played the music while Greg sang the lyrics to *Mr Lawman's Going Down*.

> # Mr lawman, you're going down,
> yes you're going to get kicked out of town.
> When you're gone every good person will be ecstatic
> like someone playing trains upstairs in the attic.
>
> (Chorus) Mr lawman you're going down town
> so you can't make any more people miserable or frown.
> Mr lawman every good person hates you dearly
> and when you're dead your victims can walk around freely.
>
> Mr lawman, you've got nothing left to live for,
> because you are evil and evil is the one great bore.
> Evil people in the world make stories for the news
> but we don't want to see them in TV interviews.
>
> (Chorus)
>
> Mr lawman, you're a nasty man
> and you remind me of an old trash can.
> You're ugly, too, and that is bad;
> the definition of ugly is being evil and sad.
>
> (Chorus)
>
> You're head will explode like a fizzy beer can
> and your brains will resemble a bloodied flan.
> Then the rest of you will soon be gone
> and you will literally be no one.

(Chorus)

Oddball stopped playing the music and then the man with the briefcase had his head blown off magically and was vanquished. Oddball went back into Greg, who then drove off, continuing his journey home, unaware that a peeping tom had caught the whole vanquishing episode on camera.

The peeping tom hot-footed it to the BBC studio in Newcastle and handed the footage of the vanquishing episode in to the person in charge of the news.

Greg arrived back home and was greeted by Steven, Jessica and his fiancée, Amy.

"Hi, guys... hi, Amy," he greeted them, giving Amy a kiss.

Steven had just turned the television on.

"We break our programme to bring you a newsflash..."

All eyes turned to the TV screen.

"Good evening, this is Kenneth Clarke. Reports of a shocking incident are coming in. Just fifteen minutes ago, a man walking in the street was murdered. Before the killer carried out this cold-blooded attack, he automatically changed into a bright orange superhero costume. The police are trying to establish who the killer is. A passer by filmed footage of the events coming up. We must warn viewers of a nervous disposition that they may find this footage extremely distressing. Anyone who knows the identity of the killer should contact the number which we will show at the end of this newsflash."

The footage filmed by the peeping tom appeared on the screen and Steven switched the television off and turned to Greg.

"Greg, please tell me that the man you killed was evil?"

"Yes, of course. I sensed evil from the man before I killed him. So I definitely didn't kill an innocent man, even if it looks that way."

"Okay. Well, that's good."

Greg was looking serious. "Yeah. I think I did the right thing, but the police probably won't think so."

Five minutes later, there was a knock on the door and Amy went to answer it.

Two police officers stood in the doorway.

"Good evening," said one. "Is Greg Carter here?"

Greg went to the door. "I'm Greg Carter."

"Greg Carter, I am arresting you for the murder of Anthony Reed," said the police officer, who went on to caution Greg while the other officer handcuffed him. They then took him out to the police car where one of them sat in the back with him and the other drove to the police station.

Steven, Amy and Jessica looked at each other in shock at what had just taken place.

Amy took out her phone. "I will phone my lawyer to defend Greg for the trial."

As Greg was being locked up in the police cell, Amy had just finished explaining Greg's actions to her lawyer.

"Well, if I can prove that Greg was acting in self-defence I may be able to get a not guilty verdict," he told her. "I will go to the police station now to get his version of events."

Amy thanked him. "Please do your best for him," she urged.

After talking to Greg, the lawyer realised that he was going to find it difficult to find evidence that Greg had acted in self-defence.

Greg was remanded in custody while the prosecution and defence lawyers prepared their case and eventually the date of the trial was announced.

Amy, Steven and Jessica went to the court proceedings, anxious to support Greg as much as possible.

Greg's barrister was already present, his briefcase bulging with important documents relating to the case, and the courtroom was slowly filling up with various officials, press and members of the public. Amy, Steven and Jessica made their way to the public gallery to watch the proceedings and the victim's family sat uncomfortably close. The clerk of the court was checking his papers, the jury was sworn in and seated and the scene was complete, apart from the judge and the defendant.

A door was heard to open beneath the courtroom and then Greg climbed the stairs into the courtroom, flanked by two prison officers.

"Court rise!" a voice ordered and everyone stood as the judge entered and gave a brief bow to the court before being seated.

Two charges of attempted murder and murder were read out and Greg pleaded not guilty to both. The judge asked the prosecuting counsel to open the proceedings and the trial commenced.

Replying to the prosecuting barrister, Greg's counsel insisted that his client had been wrongly charged because he had simply taken an individual out of the world whom he knew to be an evil man, thus saving countless lives by his commendable actions. As soon as Greg's lawyer sat down, the prosecution lawyer again rose to his feet.

"You said the man your client killed was evil, but what evidence do you have to prove what you said is right?"

"Do you have any evidence?" asked the judge.

Greg's lawyer stood up again. He held a bundle of papers in his hand. "Well, your honour, I have here copies of a document proving that the man my client killed had a criminal record for murder."

Copies of the document were shown to the judge, the jury and the prosecution lawyer, who immediately rose to his feet.

"With respect, your honour, this criminal record does not prove that the man the defendant killed was evil; I put it to you that the man's moment of evil was in the past and the document also shows that he served eighteen years in prison for his crime. Therefore he had already been punished for what he did before the defendant killed him, proving that he was, effectively, innocent. He had wiped the slate clean."

He stared at Greg for a moment before proceeding. "The defendant is also guilty of attempted murder but hasn't been punished for trying to kill a man who was smoking a cigarette because, until now, no one knew the man who turned into the alien the victim had talked about to local journalists. Now of course we do know that he was the man in the dock, one Greg Carter."

He then produced a document detailing what happened to the man who had been smoking a cigarette. A copy was handed to the judge and then passed round the jury.

"Your honour," said Greg's lawyer, "I would like to ask my learned friend what proof he has that my client was the man who turned into an alien and then attempted to kill the man with the cigarette?"

The answer was swift and convincing,

"Your honour, members of the jury, in the video footage taken a week ago the defendant was clearly seen automatically changing into an orange costume, proving beyond doubt that he is more than a human. And it is clear from the video that the ball is also an alien ball because the defendant was able to literally throw it into the head of the deceased man. The ball seen coming out of the defendant was definitely part of him and he is clearly an alien. There cannot be any other aliens in Newcastle, which proves that he is the man who attempted to kill the man with the cigarette."

The judge then ordered the footage to be shown to the court and a DVD was produced, supporting everything the prosecuting counsel had said.

Greg then took the stand, but was not questioned by the prosecution lawyer, who instead addressed the court.

"Your honour, members of the jury, what you have just seen proves that the defendant here is guilty of attempted murder as well as the murder of an innocent man. I have no need to cross examine the accused, your honour."

Greg protested. "I didn't kill an innocent man! I did what any decent..."

"Silence!" bellowed the judge. He turned to Greg's counsel. "Any further questions?"

Greg's lawyer stood up. "Mr Carter, please explain to the court in your own words what actually happened in the video we have just seen."

"I sensed evil," Greg said, "which proved he was on his way to kill someone. All I did was to destroy a killer, thus preventing him from hurting anyone in the future. The bible states that it's okay to bully bullies and kill killers, and I simply felt I was carrying out God's work."

Greg's lawyer sat down and the prosecuting lawyer rose to his feet.

"Will you please tell the court whether you are qualified or indeed authorised to take it upon yourself to... carry out God's work?"

"No," Greg replied, "but I'm a catholic mathematician..."

This remark provoked a faint ripple of amusement and the prosecutor smiled in a pathetic way at Greg. "No further questions, your honour."

The judge cleared his throat and asked if there were any further witnesses or evidence and then turned his attention to the jury.

"Remember," he said, as he concluded his summing up, "that when reaching your verdict, you must be certain in your minds that the accused is either not guilty or guilty beyond reasonable doubt and your verdict in this case must be unanimous. You will now retire to consider your verdicts on the first count of attempted murder and on the second count of murder."

"Court rise!" commanded the court bailiff as the judge rose from the bench, the jury filed out and Greg was escorted down the steps back to the cell to await his fate.

Less than an hour later, Greg was brought back up to the courtroom where he stood in the dock between his two guards.

"Will the foreman of the jury please stand?" a voice commanded.

A neatly dressed woman of about forty rose to her feet.

"Please answer yes or no. Has the jury reached a verdict?"

"Yes."

"Again, please answer yes or no. Is your verdict unanimous?"

"Yes."

Greg could feel his heart pounding in his chest. There was no way they could have found him guilty. Surely?"

"On the first count, that of attempted murder, do you find the accused guilty or not guilty?"

"Guilty."

A buzz went round the court as people in the public gallery murmured amongst themselves.

"Silence in court! On the second count, that of murder, do you find the accused guilty or not guilty.

"Guilty."

Greg was devastated and couldn't believe what he was hearing as the judge pronounced sentence.

"... to pay your debt to society for these despicable acts you will be detained at Her Majesty's pleasure for fifteen years for attempted murder. You will also serve a concurrent life sentence for murder. I am making a recommendation that you go to prison for a minimum of thirty-five years." He banged his gavel down decisively. "Take him down."

Before Greg was escorted down the steps to await transportation in a prison van, he turned to look at his friends, helplessly.

Amy was in tears and Steven and Jessica were gobsmacked. None of them had expected this outcome.

A few days later, Amy, Steven and Jessica went to visit Greg in prison.

They were all very subdued as they sat round a table under the watchful eye of a couple of prison wardens.

"Our lawyer has lodged an appeal, Greg," Amy told him. "I'm sure you'll be out of here soon."

They asked him the usual questions about prison food, what was his cell like and did he want anything, and it was soon time to leave.

"We'll come and see you again soon, Greg," Amy said. She kissed him. "Try to keep positive."

After lunch in the prison canteen, an inmate sitting next to Greg became involved in an altercation with the person next to him.

"Hey dickhead," Greg warned, "stop picking on him and start acting like a decent human being instead of an idiot from *Big Brother*."

The man glared at Greg. "Oh yeah, and what are you going to do to make me?"

"This." Greg immediately grabbed the man and slammed him head first into the lunch table, holding him there.

A security guard was about to stop Greg's actions when a more senior security guard stepped in.

"Ratner, don't bother stopping Carter from bullying Boulder because, unlike some of the prisoners in here, Boulder hasn't seen the error of his ways and therefore deserves a bit of bullying."

"Yeah, Bobbit, you're right," said Ratner, and stood back.

"Okay, say sorry to your victim," Greg instructed Boulder whom he was holding face down across the table.

"No!"

Greg then twisted Boulder's arm, causing him to scream in pain.

"Aaaarrgh! Okay, sorry, Daniels."

Daniels waved a hand briefly. "Apology accepted, Boulder."

Only then did Greg let go of Boulder.

"Okay, let that be a lesson to any of you who think you can get away with bullying innocent people. Now, can I have a 'lesson learnt Carter, no bullying allowed, Carter,' quote, please!" he said, looking round at his fellow inmates.

"Lesson learnt Carter, no bullying allowed, Carter," the group chorused.

"Right, now with the permission of the security guards, I'd like to organise a tournament consisting of four games: darts, table football, basketball and last but not least... wrestling. I'll be the referee when one is required. So who's in?"

All the inmates shouted, "Me!"

Greg looked at the security guards. "Could you guys get us the necessary supplies?"

"Sure," Ratner agreed.

"Absolutely, it should be interesting to see all you slimy little maggots doing something worthwhile for once in your lives, especially you, Boulder," Bobbit added.

"Well, not the words I would use," Greg said, "but I understand why you do, because all of us inmates have done bad things and therefore don't have enough goodness in our lives. However by the end of the tournament I am organising with your help, Bobbit and Ratner, we will all have the feeling of playing so many games in a hard but fair way... or good duties as they could be called, that we hopefully won't want to do bad things ever again."

Ratner and Bobbit nodded their approval and went away to find the necessary supplies, returning half an hour later with their arms full.

"There's the dartboard and one hundred darts, so everyone can get to play," Said Bobbit, handing them over to Greg.

"And there's the table football set," Ratner said, putting it down on the floor. "The basketball posts are arranged accordingly in the yard,and you can wrestle in here."

Greg was pleased. "Okay, thanks. Now then, there's a hundred people in here, right? So that makes two teams of fifty for the game of darts, then the winning team will play off head to head against each other in twenty five table football matches, with the twenty-five winners splitting into five teams of five for basketball group stages. The winners of the group stages will then play off against each other in a five way wrestling match to see who is the winner of the overall tournament."

"It all sounds exciting, I'm looking forward to it," Ratner said.

"Thanks for the compliment," Greg said. "I'll get everyone organised." He turned to face the inmates who had all gathered around to hear more.

"Okay everyone, listen up. There are one hundred of you, right? So for the first game you'll be split into two teams of fifty with the winning team going on to play off against each other in twenty-five table football matches. The twenty-five winners will be placed into five teams of five for the basketball group stage. The group stage winners will play off against each other in a five way-wrestling match with the winner crowned champion of the overall tournament, or as I have just mentally named it, *The Good to do Good Tournament*. Cheer if you like the tournament I've created for you."

Greg's fellow inmates cheered with approval.

He smiled. "Thanks. Now, first all I'll draw out of a hat, or my shoe, since there isn't a hat around here. This way is fair, unlike the way my PE teacher used to do things, because there'll be no favouritism from bullies by picking their mates first and leaving the so called weaklings like Steven and me to be picked last. My way means all you bully-boy bad guys will have to play along with the nice bad boys and everyone will have to co-operate with each other. Anyone have a problem with that?"

"No, Carter!"

Ratner gave Greg a pen and some notepaper from his pocket.

"I'm going to pass this pen and paper round and I expect each of you to write your surname on the paper," he continued, passing the pen and paper to the nearest inmate.

When they had all written down their names, Greg removed his shoe, tore off the strips of paper containing the names, folded them in half and placed them in his shoe.

Shuffling the names around his shoe, he said, "I'll will now make the draw," and proceeded to draw the strips of paper from his shoe, calling the names out.

"Team one: Paul, Regnard, Adjugatsi, Ratini, Outhwaite, Stoddart, Bellamy, Lowery, Hunter, Dodds, Stasson, Soulsby, Foley, Tripsato, Lee, Gerrard, Hamilton, Drake, Torley, Mcfall, Woods, Guigeous, Craig, Sharp, Kitchen, Lyons, Dove, Kelly, Wills, Westgate, Joyce, Peters, Campbell, Henchoz, Carragher, Owen, Mann, Michaels Sutcliffe, Offiong, Ankers, Henderson, Steele, Milne, Boulder, Plimpson, Daniels, Glass, Corbit and... Barker.

"Team two will be Smith, Jones, Jack, Perry, Carey, Kodak, Maccano, Liverfool, Newhassle, Lonron, Birmingbacon, Coke, Boatlisle, Kane, Katona, McDonald, Westwood, Andrews, Murphy, Gray, Aranalde, Billy, Piper, Lumsden, Holmes, Harper, Lucas, Williams, Hayward, Tomlinson, Keach, Bailey, May, Wilkinson, Thomas, Armstrong, Cooper, Duffy, Ruane, Hodgkinson, Monahan, Wade, Dickinson, Schofield, Read, Bateman, Green, Flynn, Tate and, last one... Carrey. Now if you would all get into your teams in order, I would like to ask Ratner to toss a coin."

As the men shuffled around, getting into order, Ratner tossed a coin, covering it with his palm.

"Heads or tails, Paul?"

"Heads," Paul shouted, watching Ratner.

Ratner revealed the coin which had fallen heads up.

"It is heads," Ratner confirmed.

"So Paul, you will start the *Good to do Good* tournament for team one and then Smith will start for Team Two. Then the next player from team one will throw his dart and so on. I think we're ready to start," declared Greg.

Ratner grinned. "Apart from the fact that the dartboard hasn't been put up yet."

"Oh, yeah... well that would be a big help, like," one inmate sniggered.

Bobbit ran off to fetch a nail and hammer and five minutes later, the dartboard was in position.

"Thanks Bobbit," said Greg, distributing one dart to each inmate.

"In case anyone doesn't know the rules, each of you will have to try and accumulate the best score possible to help your team become first to reach zero exactly. You'll be playing down from five hundred and one and throwing from the marker, which is my shoe."

Putting his shoe down, Greg told Paul to open the tournament by throwing the first dart.

When all but two inmates had thrown their darts, Team One were down to a score of three and Team Two had a score of six. Barker was trying to win the game before Carrey and threw his dart at treble one, but hit treble two instead.. Disappointed, he yanked his dart from the board and stood on the side with the rest of his team to watch his opponent.

Carrey had a good chance to win the game. He aimed at double three, but missed completely, hitting the outer edge of the dartboard and scoring nothing.

With all the inmates now having thrown a dart each, Paul threw again. He confidently strode up to Greg's shoe and aimed at the figure one, hitting the mark. So team one had beaten Team Two and Paul clenched his fist, delighted that he had helped his team to beat Team Two.

"Well done, Team One," Greg said, putting his shoe back on. "You will now go to the table football set and play off head to head in the order your names were drawn out of my shoe. The first player to score wins through to the next round. Team Two will now be supporters of the winning team."

Team Two started cheering Team One and Team One acknowledged their good gamesmanship.

After an hour of table football, the winners were all confirmed and Greg read out the results.

"Regnard beat Paul. Adjugatsi beat Ratini. Stoddart beat Outhwaite. Bellamy beat Lowery. Hunter beat Dodds. Stasson beat Soulsby. Foley beat Tripsato. Lee beat Gerrard. Hamilton beat Drake. Torley beat Mcfall. Guigeous beat Woods. Sharp beat Craig. Lyons beat Kitchen. Kelly beat Dove. Westgate beat Wills. Joyce beat Peters. Campbell beat Henchoz. Carragher beat Owen. Mann beat Michaels. Offiong beat Sutcliffe. Ankers beat Henderson. Milne beat Steele. Boulder beat Plimpson. Daniels beat Glass. Barker beat Corbit."

Amidst the buzz going round all the inmates as they discussed the winners and losers, Greg wrote the winners' names on a piece of paper and tore it up into strips. Off came his shoe and in went the folded strips of paper. Shuffling the names around, he drew the names to make up the five teams for the next event.

"Hamilton, Offiong, Milne, Barker and Campbell will be Team One; Ankers, Lyons, Sharp, Hunter and Bellamy will be Team Two; Kelly, Carragher, Westgate, Mann and Joyce will be Team Three; Adjugatsi, Guigeous, Regnard, Boulder and Daniels will be team Four, and Foley, Lee, Torley, Stasson and Stoddart will make up Team Five. You will play each other for points and whichever team ends up with the most points will be the winner. A win is worth three points; a draw is worth one point and zero for a defeat. In the case of a tie, basket points difference will decide who wins the group."

The remaining *Good to do Good* tournament contestants assembled into their respective teams.

"Ready, you lot? Okay, lets go in to the yard," said Bobbit, leading them out to where the basketball posts were sited at either end of the yard.

"Each team will play four games, each game lasting ten minutes. I want hard but fair play from every team and I will referee all the games to make sure you play them in a good manner," Greg announced.

After three hours and twenty minutes, all the teams had finished playing and the group was decided. Team Three finished bottom of the group with zero points and a basket points difference of minus seven; Team One finished fourth with three points and a basket points difference of minus nine; Team Two finished third with six points and a basket points difference of plus one; Team Five finished second with ten points and a basket points difference of plus seven. Team four-finished top with the same number of points as team five but with a higher basket points difference of plus eight.

"Congratulations, Team Four, you have won the group and now you will have a five way wrestling match," said Greg.

"Come on, lads! Back inside for the wrestling," Bobbit ordered and they all reluctantly trooped back into the prison after the relative freedom of the yard.

Back within the prison walls, they arranged themselves accordingly; a circular gallery of seventy-five inmates with the wrestling candidates, Adjugatsi, Boulder, Regnard, Daniels, and Guigeous in the middle of them.

"I want good clean fights here, guys; lets get ready to rumble!" Greg declared.

Daniels wrestled Adjugatsi to the ground and held him there for three seconds. Adjugatsi was therefore out of the tournament and went to join the other defeated contestants. At the same as Adjugatsi was wrestled to the ground, Guigeous wrestled Regnard to the ground and held him there for two seconds. Then Boulder pulled Guigeous off of Regnard and pinned Guigeous to the floor, holding him there for three seconds. Guigeous was therefore out of the tournament.

Regnard wrestled Daniels to the floor and held him for only a second before Boulder hauled Regnard off Daniels and wrestled him to the floor. Boulder held Regnard there for three seconds, putting him out of the tournament. Boulder then wrestled Daniels to the ground and helds him for two seconds but Daniels kicked his right leg in the air. Then Daniels wrestled Boulder to the ground and held him there for two seconds, but Boulder also raised his right leg. Boulder then wrestled Daniels to the ground again and held him there for three seconds. Boulder therefore won the *Good to do Good* tournament.

"So the *Good to do Good* tournament winner is Boulder. A big round of applause for him, please?" said Greg to all the inmates as he shook hands with Boulder.

Boulder's fellow inmates applauded him and cheered.

"Congratulations, Boulder," said Greg, "well done."

"Thanks, Carter."

"I hope you are only going to do good things from now on?"

"Yeah, of course. I was actually an accountant before I committed murder. I don't think I'll go back to accountancy, though. I'd like to start a games club as I really enjoyed the games in the *Good to do Good* tournament and my accounting experience will come in handy to help me run it properly."

"That sounds good," Greg said. "I wish you well." Then turning to the rest of them, he said, "Well done to all of you. I hope you only do good from now on."

"Thanks Carter! We will only do good in future!"

"That's good to hear." Greg then left his fellow inmates and headed for the toilets, returning about ten minutes later.

"I must warn you now... if anyone wants to go to the toilet, hold your noses because I've just let Badolf Shitler out of my gas chamber.

There was a roar of laughter from all the inmates.

"Alright you've had your fun," Bobbit said. "Now you must all return to your cells; lights out in twenty minutes."

Greg and his fellow inmates went back into their cells. There was no bullying, shoving or threatening and Bobbit and Ratner exchanged looks of amazement as they locked up for the night.

Sweet dreams, guys," Ratner said, grinning at Bobbit.

In the defence lawyer's office, Steven Jessica and Amy had been discussing ways of gaining Greg's freedom. The lawyer was on the phone and from what they could hear from the conversation, it sounded a bit more positive.

"Yes," said the lawyer, "I am in my office now if you have the time... yes, that will be fine... in ten minutes, then? Goodbye."

He put the phone down and addressed the three. "The ex-girlfriend of the deceased man is coming to my office. She can hopefully give me some information that should prove Greg did not kill an innocent man."

"We'll go, then," said Amy.

"Alright. I'll be in touch," he replied.

Ten minutes later, the ex-girlfriend of the deceased man entered the lawyer's office. She had ominous looking facial bruises.

One week later, Jessica, Steven and Amy went to the court to see the appeal against Greg's convictions for murder and attempted murder. Before they entered the courtroom, the defence lawyer spoke to Amy.

"I have coached my witness and told Greg to say he was hypnotised by Adrian Domescu to make a kill. This won't be lying under oath because hypnotism is basically the same as being put under a spell," he said.

"Alright; hopefully you'll win Greg's freedom," Amy replied.

"Yes, I hope so, too. Keep your fingers crossed."

Steven, Amy and Jessica went and found seats at the back of the courtroom just as a prison guard was bringing Greg up the steps into the dock. He glanced across at them, and Amy gave him a brief wave.

"Court rise!"

The judge took his place and nodded to the court and everyone sat down except Greg.

Legal and technical formalities were dealt with and the appeal commenced.

Instead of the prosecution lawyer opening the proceedings, the judge spoke first to Greg's lawyer.

"I believe you have some new, vital evidence which is of great significance in this case?

Greg's lawyer rose to his feet. "Yes, your honour. My client has revealed that when his crimes were committed he was under the influence of an hypnotic spell."

"Really? Any why was this not made apparent at the trial?"

"The relevant questions were either not asked, or were asked but dismissed, your honour."

"Very well. Counsel for the prosecution will bear with the court whilst we hear the defendant's evidence."

"With respect, your honour," the prosecutor rose indignantly to his feet, "but I object to..."

The judge cut him off smartly. "Objection overruled. Please sit down. This court sits at my jurisdiction and I *will* hear the defendant's evidence now. Counsel for the defence, please continue."

"Thank you, your honour. Greg Carter, will you please tell the court why you stabbed a man," said his lawyer.

"I was hypnotised by Adrian Domescu specifically to become evil," Greg answered.

"And were you hypnotised willingly or unwillingly?"

"Unwillingly."

"No further questions, your honour."

"Prosecuting counsel, do you wish to cross examine the defendant?"

"No, your honour, but if I may call a witness to the stand?" he asked.

"You may call your witness."

"I call Johnny Jones."

Johnny Jones came to the witness stand and took the oath.

"You are Johnny Jones?"

"Yessir."

"You are the man who was stabbed while smoking a cigarette?"

"Yessir."

And can you confirm that the man in the dock, Greg Carter, was the man that stabbed you?"

"Yessir."

"Will you please tell the court why you are so certain?"

"Because after seeing the news story of Greg Carter killing a man, I remembered that the man who stabbed me was wearing the same Orange superhero costume that was worn by Greg Carter in the news footage before he turned into a ten-foot alien and used his hand in the form of a spike to stab me. So it must have been Greg Carter who stabbed me, sir."

"Alright; I just have one more question to ask you. Do you think the man who we now believe to be Greg Carter was under an hypnotic spell?"

Johnny shrugged. "Maybe, but he seemed to have an arrogant streak that he was using against me, which according to his statement was nothing to do with him being hypnotised."

"Thank you, Mr Jones, but will you please answer the question: Do you think he was under an hypnotic spell?"

"Yessir. But I believe the hypnotism merely exaggerated his arrogance and even if he wasn't hypnotised, I believe he would still have tried to kill me."

"No further questions."

Greg's lawyer then rose to his feet.

"Mr Jones, despite the defendant's arrogant frame of mind, do you think that subconsciously he may have missed your heart so that he didn't kill you?"

Johnny shrugged again. "Maybe, but I still think that would mean he intended to hurt me?"

"No further questions, your honour."

"Do any of you have any more witnesses to call?" the judge asked the prosecutor.

"No, your honour."

"And for the defence?"

"Yes, your honour. I would like to call Cindy Banford."

Cindy Banford was called to the witness stand and took the oath. Her facial bruises were noted by the jury and the judge spent some time peering at her over the top of his spectacles.

"You are Cindy Banford?" Greg's lawyer asked her.

"Yes," she replied softly.

"And you are the ex-girlfriend of the man who was killed by the defendant?"

"Yes."

"Please speak up Miss Banford so that we can all hear you," boomed the judge.

"Yes," she repeated.

"Miss Banford, did the man that my client killed threaten to kill you?"

"Yes. He said he would kill me if I told anyone that he had beaten me up."

"Thank you. Your honour, my witness's statement proves that my client, Greg Carter, did not kill an innocent man and therefore is only guilty of killing a bad and sinful man. I therefore put it to the jury that the murder sentence be reduced to that for manslaughter. I rest my case."

The judge addressed the jury. "You will now retire to the jury room to consider whether the new evidence we have heard at this appeal today is sufficient to convince you that the defendant is guilty of manslaughter, but not guilty of murder. Court adjourned."

"Court rise!"

It was about three hours later when the jury returned and took their places in the court.

"Will the foreman of the jury please stand?" the clerk commanded.

A thin man in glasses stood up.

"Have you reached a verdict?"

"Yes, sir."

"Is it a unanimous verdict?"

"No, sir."

"Is it a majority verdict of at least ten?"

"Yes, sir."

"Foreman of the jury, on appeal, do you find the defendant guilty or not guilty of attempted murder?"

"Not guilty."

"And on the count of actual bodily harm, do you find the defendant guilty or not guilty?"

"Guilty."

"On appeal, on the count of murder by killing an innocent, do you find the defendant guilty or not guilty?"

"Not guilty."

"And do you find the defendant guilty or not guilty of the manslaughter of a sinful man?"

"Guilty."

The court began to buzz as people in the public gallery discussed the verdicts.

"SILENCE IN COURT!"

"When the judge could hear a pin drop, he addressed Greg in the dock.

"Greg Carter, you have heard the verdicts of this court on your appeal against your convictions and I now hand down the following sentences, to run concurrently: you will serve six months in prison for actual bodily harm and you will serve three years in prison for manslaughter. The length of time already served by you will be taken into account."

"Court rise!"

Two years and three months later, Amy, Steven and Jessica waited outside the prison for Greg to be released. He had finally completed his three and a half year combined sentence, less the time he had already spent in prison and with some time deducted for good behaviour.

The huge, impenetrable doors slowly swung open and Greg appeared, carrying a plastic bag that held his belongings. He spotted his friends and hurried towards them, first kissing Amy and then hugging the others.

"So, Amy, what have you and Steven been up to? Anything naughty? Only kidding, Jessica. Steven wouldn't cheat on you. Amy might cheat on me though."

They all laughed, pleased that Greg had not lost his sense of humour.

"Well, Greg, all joking aside, we've erased evil doers from this beautiful world by sending all the demons that we encountered straight to hell with a supernatural smack down."

"Really? Go on, Amy."

First of all, I used my newly expanded power to magically smack them to hell, and then I thought of a spell to supernaturally lock them down there and we both said it to send them there. Then, at various points over the last two years, we enlisted Oddball's help when we were visiting you in prison by saying that we wished Oddball could help us send some bullies that Steven and I had been warned about in the form of Steven's newly enhanced power; a psychically projected holographic premonition. Steven had other premonitions of the same kind. Oddball kindly obliged and obviously heard us when he was in your body and organised a personal prison break to see us. We then described the bullies that we saw in Steven's premonitions to Oddball and asked the special ball if the cute one could take them to 'Oddball's prison for dummies'. Oddball did as we asked and took the bullies to the prison. Other than those things, we've been working in our jobs," Amy informed him.

"That all sounds good and you've obviously been working too hard today and the previous two years as well as three months. However, now that I'm out of prison I will be able to help you out with the workload that the Destroyer demands. In case you're wondering, I didn't get a newly enhanced power while I was in prison but I don't mind if I never get a newly enhanced power from the Destroyer because I have made too many mistakes in life and I have been rightly punished by not getting it.

"All I really need anyway are my current powers; most important is the power of my love for you, Amy, Steven, Jessica and Oddball.

"Huh, I feel a Greg-style speech coming on. We all have to go our own way in life regardless of whether anyone else thinks it's left or right."

"And if we do that then we will find out if our future's bright," said Amy.

Steven nodded his approval.

"Sure, and if it is not bright then we will be motivated to try something different by a feeling similar to the one that Satan felt when he was being punished by God's smite," Greg suggested, raising smiles from Amy and Steven.

Suddenly a bright, white light shone on all four of them.

"Wow!" exclaimed Jessica. "What was that light?"

"The voice in my head has just told me that it was the Destroyer magically binding us together so that we have to abide by our earlier promise. So that's what the white light was that bathed Amy, Greg and me before we got our supernatural powers. It was the Destroyer giving us those powers which will keep growing, including yours, Greg, one way or the other, even though you haven't received any of late," said Steven.

The others looked at Steven with interest.

"Oh, right. It doesn't seem right that I have to abide by your promise even though I don't have any powers to punish demons with. Although I am promising to swear by your promise," Jessica said to him.

He smiled. "Well actually, although you weren't blessed with any supernatural powers by the Destroyer, it has already blessed you with natural powers, like the power of love, job skills as well as others, and in the future you will blessed with other natural powers."

"True enough," she replied.

Oddball then came out of Greg's body.

"Hey, Greg, do you want to hear the song we made up while you were in prison and when I wasn't in your body?"

"Of course, Oddball."

Oddball then played the music to *We're the Chipmunks*.

"Amy, Jesse and Stevie J," he sang.

"We're the Oddballs," sang Amy, Jessica and Steven.

Do, Do, Do, Do, Do, Do," # Sang Amy, Jessica, Steven and Greg.

"Hey, that was fun," laughed Greg.

"Yeah, it's really good to make up a song when we want to, as opposed to when we had to, when we used to vanquish bullies and demons before we made our promise not to use true standards of bullies," Amy said.

"So, Greg and Amy, are you finally going to get married? Because it's about time you did as people haven't lived as long as the time you've been engaged," joked Steven.

Amy and Greg smiled at Steven and then at each other.

"Yeah. Eight and a half years is a long time to be engaged. Do you want to get married as soon as possible, Amy?" asked Greg.

"Yeah, a quick immediate-family-plus-close-friends wedding at Gretna Green would be best because a wedding is one of the most important things in life; purely and simply a bond of trust and should not be turned into a costly, glorified party," Amy answered.

"Okay, well let's get married in Jock land," Greg said.

Over the next twenty-four hours Amy and Greg organised their wedding in Gretna Green with Oddball's help and they also organised their honeymoon in the Bahamas. They chose wedding rings for each other and gave them to Jessica and Steven.

They went to Gretna Green with Steven, Jessica and their immediate families. A priest was waiting to marry them. Everyone gathered round the bride and groom, and the priest conducted the wedding ceremony.

Greg then prepared to sing a song for Amy.

"I'm going to sing a song for my new wife. It's called *Amy*," Greg declared.

Oddball then appeared from Greg's body and played the music for Greg to sing to.

Amy

 # I was not a strong man before I met you; Amy
but now I am and no one can ever again bring shame on me.
Hopefully you and I can make each other even stronger
so that we can stay healthy and live a lot longer.

(Chorus)

After I lost my way;
Amy you helped me find God's radar of destiny.
I hope we can create at least one more person
who can find God's radar of destiny
and I know we will be together, forever, amen.

You are a woman from heaven and I who was a man from hell
want to pick you up in my arms to make you feel extremely well.
When we're in that position we can touch each other
and feel lots of passion like red-hot lovers.

(Chorus)

I have found God with you, everyone here and all.
Now I can forever walk proudly, walk tall.

(Chorus)

When very soon on our Bahamas honeymoon
I'll be hoping to drink some rum
then you can fondle my lovely bum
Roses are red, sweet violets are blue
And in our hotel room, I'll make love to you.

(Chorus)

Everyone applauded Greg and Oddball. Greg then took Amy by the hand and together they left Gretna Green for their honeymoon in the Bahamas via Newcastle airport.

A week later, on a wet evening, they arrived back in Newcastle where Jessica and Steven were waiting for them.

"Welcome back to rainy old Geordie land, Mrs Carter," Greg said to Amy.

They smiled at each other and got into Steven's car.

Jessica drove them back to their flat.

"So what did you get up to while we were on honeymoon? Greg asked.

"Well," Steven replied, "when there were demons, Jessica, who wanted to do some evil doer fighting, and I just simply laughed at them which embarrassed them back to hell. They haven't been seen since so Satan must have felt their humiliation and vanquished them for failing to kill anyone. Then we saw a holographic premonition of mine that showed us some bullies and where they were from, about to be punished. We then called your body-dwelling friend, Oddball, in the Bahamas and asked him to take the bullies to Oddball's Prison for Dummies. We also told Oddball where they were from."

He grinned. "Oddball then said to us in a Caribbean accent, 'Yeah man,' and went to do as we asked. He came back to tell us that the bullies were locked away in Oddball's Prison for Dummies and then buggered off back to the Bahamas with you and Amy."

Greg was full of praise for Steven and Jessica. "That's impressive work you and Jessica have been doing, not to mention Oddball's work between going from and back to the Bahamas."

Then Oddball appeared. "It's all in a life's work for an alien ball," it said.

It was getting late and they all went to bed.

In the morning as they were having breakfast, there was a knock at the door. Greg went to answer it and opened the door to find a man standing there.

"Hi, Greg. I'm Manny, your biological father," said the man.

Greg was gob smacked for a moment but quickly composed himself.

"Sorry," he said, "I'm not buying that load of rubbish." He slammed the door shut.

"Greg! That was very rude of you," scolded Amy who went to the door and reopened it.

"Sorry for what Greg did. Come in, Manny," she said.

"Is that okay with you, Greg?" Manny asked.

"Yeah, come in estranged old man who neglected to father me when I was growing up and left someone else with the responsibility of being my dad. Trust me and come in to exchange niceties with me and my friends." He looked down his nose at Manny. "I am a trustworthy man, unlike you who can hardly live up to the first three letters of your name."

Manny entered the flat and closed the door behind him.

"I understand why you mocked me as I haven't been a good man but I've come here to make it up with you, Greg, and also to tell you and your friends something important. So here goes: Satan has just made demonic replicas of Greg, Steven and Amy from its demonic spawn. The reason Satan did this is because he has grown tired of you thwarting its evildoer's evil plans. So he thought the best way to stop you three doing any more of that was to create demonic replicas of you. Unfortunately, Satan used one of his spells to take your powers away from you and give them to its demonic replicas of you. So you don't have them any more to help you defeat your demonic replicas.

"In order to defeat them and get your powers back from them, therefore making them powerless, you will have to save their future victim or victims from dying or from having their body parts die. Otherwise, because you will not have done enough to save them − and therefore indirectly killed − you will then have technically broken part of your promise to the Destroyer. If that situation were to arise, the Destroyer would then vanquish you three and Jessica for failing to abide by your promise."

"That's bad, although I don't understand why I will be vanquished if that situation comes about," Jessica said.

"Well, because you made a promise to the Destroyer not to use true standards of bullics with Greg, Amy and Steven. So therefore you will break your promise if you also cannot do enough to save the evil trio's victim or victims. If you were wondering why the evil trio are immune from being vanquished, that's because they made no promise," Manny replied.

"I see."

"And in case you're all wondering where I got my information from, it was delivered to me in the form of a letter to my home planet by an unknown being or power of the universe that told me all the information I needed to know to tell you."

"Wow," exclaimed Jessica, and the other three were amazed by what Manny said.

"Yeah, that is good, but what I want to know is this; is Oddball gone until we beat Steven's, Amy's and my own annoying mirror world friends or not?" asked Greg.

"Oddball is the exception as it is more than just those things to you, it is also a friend to you," Manny replied.

"Oh right, so can we use Oddball to save the victims?"

"Yes, but only by having it turn into a medical supplies set, as you have to save the victim or victims as do Amy, Steven and Jessica also."

Greg looked thoughtful. "Right, well I've just got one more question to ask you. Did you have an Oddball?"

"I actually had your Oddball, so it's a living version of a family heirloom passed down to the next generation. So you won't be surprised to hear that it's immortal. So the Destroyer can't vanquish Oddball... unlike all of you who can get vanquished by the Destroyer, as you are mortal. "

"Oh right," said Greg. "I didn't know that."

"Manny, do you live forever, like Oddball?" asked Steven.

"Yes and that is that is why I couldn't father Greg when he was growing up as no one should outlive their child."

Steven was surprised by Manny's answer. "Really?"

"What a load of codswallop!" uttered Greg. "Just when I thought you were being a man as well."

"Greg..." Amy warned.

"Well, it's true, Amy, because when we have kids we will cherish all the memories they give us and their spirit. That way we will know that, one way or the other, we can't outlive our children." He turned to Manny. "No one can outlive their kids. So how do you like those apples, Daddy-o?"

"Yeah, I know and you're right. I should have had your wonderful attitude but all I can do now is say sorry, son, for not having it and for not being there for you when you were growing up."

"Apology accepted as you agree with my philosophy about having children."

Manny smiled at his son. "Does anyone have any more questions to ask me?"

"Yes, I have a few," Steven said. "Why didn't Satan just kill us himself or ask the evil versions of us that he created, to kill us instead of trying to get us to indirectly kill any part of their victims? Then there is this: how did Satan get his information about us to create demonic replicas of us?"

"Well, because they have been made with the powers of you three inside them. So they are therefore linked to you three, and technically, with your powers now inside them they are part of you, so they can't kill you, as they would die with you. Then they couldn't take over the world by getting rid of all the non-bullies in it, as Satan wants them to do. Satan himself can't kill you, as when God kicked him out of heaven He supernaturally locked him down in hell. Unfortunately God ensured that only Satan directly would be trapped in hell forever, so like Monty Python sang, every sperm is sacred; even Satan's evil spawn was seen by God as being potentially useful to his society.

"So any sort of Satan's demons can get out of hell, as they are indirect creations of Satan, not direct ones. That brings me to your final question and the answer is that Satan was told by demons, who were too afraid of taking you on because they knew you were hard to beat, that there were three superheroes with powers. When they informed Satan of those powers, he then vanquished the demons for failing to take you on, as he is not renowned for showing loyalty to beings that are afraid of hurting innocent people.

"Of course, from our point of view, less evildoers is a good thing as there's no doubt they would have hurt someone. We just don't want to be like Satan, that's all. Obviously I got my information about Satan from the letter I told you of earlier. I hope that answers your questions, Steven? "

"Thanks, Manny. Yeah, it does."

"Right, well goodbye to you all."

"Bye Manny," Steven, Jessica and Amy chorused.

"Bye, Pa," said Greg.

As Manny lifted off in his spaceship, heading for his home planet, Greg summoned Oddball.

"Oddball, can you go and see if there are any wounded?"

Off went Oddball, who spotted a wounded person and immediately returned. It stretched itself into Steven, Jessica, Amy and Greg and took them to the person. It then reverted to its usual shape.

"Thanks Oddball," Greg said.

Amy asked for a medical supplies set.

"I can do that, Amy." Oddball then turned into a medical supplies set.

"Right," said Amy, opening the medical kit. "Jessica, as a surgeon, I want you to perform the operation, please. I will give the anaesthetic. Steven, I want you to keep Jessica cool by mopping her brow, please and Greg, I want you to hand us the supplies we need. please."

Greg grinned. "So in other words, I get the crappy job."

Amy laughed. "Someone has to do it, Greg. Right, let's get to work now."

Greg handed a syringe and a bottle of anaesthetic to Amy. He passed needles and sutures to Jessica and a sponge to Steven.

Amy administered the anaesthetic and the wounded person went to sleep.

Jessica prepared to stitch the wound, but then noticed a coin lodged in the wounded person's chest.

"Tweezers, please, Greg."

Greg handed a pair of tweezers to Jessica.

Jessica removed the coin and laid it down on the ground as the others watched, astonished.

Jessica began to perspire, so Steven mopped her brow with the sponge.

Jessica then stitched the wounded person back together and left him to recover.

When the anaesthetic wore off, the wounded person regained consciousness.

"Make sure you get plenty of rest," said Amy.

"I will, and thanks to all of you for healing me." The person then got up and went home.

"Now, Oddball," said Steven, "can you go and search for another victim?" The evil me will no doubt have had a psychic vision that we have saved the last victim and will, with its friend's help, have wounded another person?"

Oddball reverted to its usual shape. "Yes Steven, I'll go now."

Oddball found another wounded person, stretched itself into Steven, Jessica, Amy and Greg, and took them to him. As before, it turned into a medical supplies set and the person was saved in the same way as the previous one. A coin was also found inside the person.

Over the next hour, Oddball found three more individually wounded people and they were saved in exactly the same way. Three more coins were found inside them.

Oddball had reverted to its normal state.

"Right, let's have a look at those five coins to see if there is anything special about them," said Greg to Amy.

Amy picked the coins up and studied them.

"They're marked with the numbers eighteen, one, twelve, twelve again and twenty- five."

"I see. Well, if I had to guess I would say that the evil threesome are trying to spell a word out to us using a numeric version of the alphabet and that word is rally," Greg suggested.

"Oh, right," said Steven, "so the three evil ones must have put the coins in the bodies of the wounded people in case we saved them to try and beat us in a rally. So as we've saved their victims we now have to find out where the rally is? I suppose the evil me had a psychic vision of where we are and wanted us to add the numbers up to find out the number of miles we have to travel from where we are?"

"Yeah, that makes sense. So that's eighteen, plus one, plus twelve, plus twelve, plus twenty-five... is sixty-eight." Greg answered.

"I'll turn into a map," announced Oddball, "so you can find out where to go to."

They studied the map and found the spot.

"That's private land," Steven said, "and I'm guessing the three evil ones robbed a bank after hours to buy it and then removed the surveillance tape so there is no evidence to connect them to the robbery."

"Come on; let's go to our cars," said Greg.

Oddball joined Greg in his car, Amy got into hers and Steven and Jessica followed in theirs. They all drove to the private land location where the demonic Greg, Steven and Amy were waiting to race against them in a rally. They stopped next to a Jaguar ready to drive on the road, where the demonic Greg wound down the window.

"The rules are simple. There aren't any, apart from that the winners of the race will keep their supernatural powers and weapons forever. The race is won when one of us drives past the chequered flag. Oh, and also, the losers must never come after the winners," demonic Greg said to original Greg."

"Okay, it's a deal," they all agreed, including Oddball.

Demonic Greg drove off in the Jaguar with demonic Steven and Amy as passengers and original Greg, Amy and Steven drove away in theirs.

When all the drivers were within a hundred yards of the finishing line, demonic Steven wound down the window, activated his blade and fired it towards one of Greg's front wheels.

Greg lost control and veered off the road, but managed to grind to a halt.

Demonic Steven then made his blade psychically return to him and he fired it at a front wheel of Amy's car.

Amy then lost control, skidded off the road, and managed to grind to a halt.

Again, demonic Steven psychically recalled his blade, but before he could fire it at Steven's car, Steven pressed a button on his steering wheel and sped past the fluttering chequered flag that evil Greg mentioned.

"Fucking hell! They've won the race. Right, well we're going to have to go with plan B; drive straight past the finishing line and don't stop," evil Greg ordered evil Amy and evil Steven.

But Steven and Jessica were out of the car with Oddball as a police tyre popper.

"So this is how Coyote feels when he's waiting for Roadrunner," Steven said with a grin.

Jessica laughed.

As evil Greg, evil Steven and evil Amy approached the finishing line in their Jaguar, original Steven threw the police tyre popper in front of the car. The car went out of control and evil Greg was forced to grind to a halt.

Oddball then reverted to its usual shape.

Steven approached the Jaguar. "Losers," he said arrogantly to evil Greg, evil Steven and evil Amy.

Evil Greg, evil Amy and evil Steven then automatically changed from wearing their superhero costumes to wearing nothing at all.

Original Steven changed into his superhero costume. "Ah," he declared, "it's good to be back in this, because I'm a hero. I deserve this. You never did and you certainly weren't superheroes but just masquerading as Amy, Greg and myself. So now I'll sing to you.

"I wear this best when you wear nothing at all," sang Steven to evil Greg, evil Amy and evil Steven.

Greg, wearing his superhero costume, then shimmered to Steven and Amy. Amy, wearing her superhero costume fell straight into his arms.

Evil Greg watched original Greg shimmering with Amy in his arms.

"Wait a minute... how the hell can they have their powers back when they didn't win the race?" he asked.

"Well, that's because they really did win the race as they are part of a team with Jessica and me. You see, we have the three musketeers' attitude whereby if any of us do something, we all do it," Steven explained to evil Greg.

"Oh." Evil Greg tried to do a runner.

Original Greg then rugby tackled evil Greg to the floor.

"Don't ever do that again," ordered Greg, pointing in an authoritarian manner at evil Greg.

"I can do what I want as soon as you release me, so go and disappear into some hole."

"Right, that's it." Original Greg pointed at evil Greg and then let out a high-pitched whining noise. Evil Greg disappeared into original Greg's mouth, leaving Greg looking pleasantly shocked.

"Well, I knew I had a big mouth but I didn't know it was that big," he joked.

Steven, Jessica and Amy laughed.

"How did you do that, Greg?" asked Amy. "Can Steven and I can get rid of our evil twins like that?"

"Sure. I just really bullied evil Greg by pointing in a authoritarian manner and then making a noise like a banshee. The rest, as they say is, history; evil Greg is rotting in a supernatural Alcatraz in my body."

Amy and Steven pointed with authority at their evil counterparts and made a high-pitched noise. Evil Amy went into original Amy's mouth but evil Steven didn't go into original Steven's mouth.

Steven frowned. "That's odd, I wonder why evil Steven didn't go in my mouth?"

Jessica thought she knew the answer. "Maybe that's because I have to have Steven go into my mouth, as I'm a superhero just like you three. The reason why I'm a superhero is based on the number twenty three theory. This particular number may be coming up in our lives because if you divide two by three, you get sixty seven percent; the numbers six and seven for sixty seven percent are significant because we have all got a sixth sense plus a seventh one. The latter; common sense, probably proves the existence of a supernatural sense as part of common sense is improvisation and that isn't something we can see, hear, smell, touch or find humorous, so, in the same way that our sense of humour is tied to our touch sense, our common sense is tied to our sixth sense, which is probably our supernatural sense.

"The fact that the sixth and seventh senses are tied together and the numbers of those senses make up the answer to two divided by three can't be a coincidence; it has to be more proof that we all have a sixth and seventh sense. So, if being in touch with my common sense to help others with a part of it like improvisation means I am a hero, then being in touch with my sixth sense, which is probably my supernatural sense, must mean that I am a supernatural hero or a superhero. Therefore, on top of the fact that I was blessed by the Destroyer along with you three, it means that if you, Steven, haven't got a supernatural Alcatraz then I must have."

The other three looked at her with some confusion, then Steven began to nod his understanding.

"Yeah, that makes sense," he said, finally.

Jessica pointed in an authoritarian manner at evil Steven and made a high-pitched noise.

Evil Steven then went into Jessica's mouth.

"I've just had a message from the voice in my head that we should use our supernatural Alcatrazes... and psychological Alcatraz in my case, to get all the supernatural demons and other bad supernatural beings as well as metaphorical demons into our bodies. Amy needs to come up with a spell for us to say before we can do that," Steven said.

"That sounds like a good plan," Greg said, and the others agreed.

"But before we perform that plan, Oddball can you take the Jag to a police car pound where it can be returned to its rightful owner, because as much as it would be fun to keep it and drive around in it singing, that would be dishonest. Besides, driving and singing in my Porsche is much better."

Oddball stretched itself into the jaguar and took it to the car pound, after which, it reverts to its normal state and returned to Greg, Amy, Steven and Jessica.

"Right Oddball, now we need you to say the spell with us. Are you ready to say the spell, 'the power of four shall end Satan's war' that Amy made up while you were away?" Greg asked.

Oddball made hands come out of its body and they all joined hands with each other.

"The power of Oddball plus four shall end Satan's war; the power of Oddball plus four shall end Satan's war; the power of

Oddball plus four shall end Satan's war; the power of Oddball plus four shall end Satan's war," they all chanted together.

Jessica, Greg, Steven and Amy then imagined Satan plus all his army of evil and used real bullying with authority to take Satan plus its evil army into their mouths. All the supernatural demons and other beings of Satan went into Amy's and Jessica's mouths respectively. All the metaphorical demons went into Stevens's mouth. Lastly, Satan went into Greg's mouth.

They let go of each other's hands and Oddball then reverted to its normal state.

"All the cancer of the universe is finally cured in every sense of the little 'c' word. I wonder if that means 'the overall power of good is no longer 'the Destroyer of evil' with no more evil in the world?'" Said Greg.

"The voice in my head said the the Destroyer will be known as the 'Destroyer of evil as it was known' as we with the blessings of the Destroyer didn't actually destroy evil, we just evolved it to destroy evil as it was known and therefore gave a whole new meaning to evil. So it's like you said, we have simply healed the evil of the world and therefore we have bettered beings, for example bullies, by turning them into good beings through taking away their personal demons like, for instance, fear of failure; the very fear that made them embrace the personal demon; anger when they experienced some kind of failure. This led them to take their frustration out on innocent beings and therefore they gave into their fear of being a non-bully, or non-bully phobia, as I prefer to call it. So, the world has been cured of evil as it was known, but it still exists in the world through our supernatural and psychological Alcatrazes," Steven explained.

"That sounds good enough to me. Well, in the name of the overall power of good, here's to the Destroyer of evil or the Destroyer, which sounds cooler," Greg said, holding his hand out in a high five position to Steven, Amy, Oddball and Jessica.

Oddball grows some hands then high fives Greg. Steven, Jessica and Amy all do the same and Oddball reverts to its normal state.

"Tell me something, Steven," said Greg, "how and why did you turn your car into a triple F and how will you cope with having all those personal demons inside of your psychological Alcatraz?"

"Well, before we lost our powers I got a message from the voice in my head which was: 'make your car as fast as possible as there will be a race for you to win.' Then I took my Fiesta to someone whom I knew could upgrade it to a fast and furious Fiesta. I will cope with my personal demons by telling myself what I told my psychology patients, which is that you must not use good to do bad but instead use bad to do things that are good. So I will have to find a proper vent for the things like anger and hatred inside my psychological Alcatraz. I was almost going to say I would be out of a job with no personal demons in the world any more, but there'll still be things like loss of confidence, which is just unlucky but still a psychological problem for me to help people with."

Greg nodded. "Now we know."

"Yeah, you do. Anyway, Greg, do I have your permission to use my bad stuff and then rugby tackle you to the ground?"

"Bring it on," Greg replied, gesturing with his hand to Steven.

Steven rushed at Greg and rugby tackled him to the ground.

"Wow, Steven you certainly know how to control your demons to play hard but fair rugby," Greg told him, getting up.

"Thanks, Greg. So how do you feel now you've got Satan inside you?"

"Hellish! So I feel the same."

Steven, Jessica, Amy and Oddball all laughed.

"Come on," said Steven, still grinning, "lets go and play golf because that's another way to relieve anger and hatred in a controlled manner."

"That sounds first class," Greg agreed on behalf of them all.

Over the next eighteen years, Amy, Greg, Steven and Jessica jointly bought a five bedroom house in the Lake District with their savings, as they planned to start families.

Amy and Greg conceived and raised twins called Claire and Robbie (after Father Robbie.)

Steven and Jessica produced a daughter called Felicity, whose boyfriend was a fire fighter called Sean 'Bashful' Yankee.

Claire, Sean, Felicity and Robbie all graduated from high school.

Sean gave Felicity, Claire and Robbie a lift home in a fire engine that he had permission to drive.

The Destroyer then supernaturally blessed Robbie, Claire, Felicity and Sean.

"Finally, I've been wondering when the Destroyer would do what our parents told us about." Said Robbie.

Robbie changed into his orange and green superhero costume and his muscles were instantly enhanced.

"Right, lets rock and roll. Turn the radio on will you, Bashful?" asked Robbie.

Sean flicked the switch.

"Oh no! Not another cover version of Ricky Gervais' classic, *Free Love Freeway*!' On second thoughts, turn it off, Bashful. I'll sing a song of my own for us."

"Oddball, can you go into my mind and read it and then play some music to my song, *We're Going to set the Universe on Fire*.

"Sure, Robbie." Oddball appeared from Robbie's body and went into his mind and then began playing the music.

We're Going to Set the Universe on Fire

We are the newly graduated
and that means we are very much appreciated.
We're going to show how proud we are of that
with fun things that make us feel we can fly like a bird or a bat.

(Chorus) we're going to set the universe on fire
to try and get what we desire.
So even in this peaceful time
we can still make the universe chime a greater chime.

What a feeling we have in our hands today,
with it we will go far away.
The universe is an oyster to be tried
and also a thrilling as well as everlasting ride.

(Chorus, which Robbie, Felicity, Claire and Sean all sing together.)

In the good way we're going to take the overall power of good on
so that we can switch ourselves on.
We hope that when we are fully spirited
we will achieve our dreams
and then enjoy a glass of something with spirits in it.

(Chorus, all sing together.)

When we have answered each and every one of our desires
our ability to dream will not be thrown on the fires.
This is because there is always a dream in life
As a bridegroom whispers to his new wife.

(Chorus, all sing together.)

Oddball stopped playing the music and went back into Robbie, who changed back into his original attire.

Sean stopped the fire engine outside the house of Steven, Jessica, Greg and Amy.

Robbie, Claire and Felicity all climbed down from the fire engine and went into the basement of the house and Sean drove the fire engine back to the fire station.

In the basement, Robbie was addressing Claire and Felicity.

"Right, you can both practice using your powers and I'll just finish fixing this time machine and attach it to the plane engine that I've built, enabling any plane to travel at three hundred and sixty."

"Yeah, okay." Claire imagines herself in a superhero costume and then automatically changes into a green and orange superhero costume.

"Wow! I look awesome," she said.

"My turn," said Felicity. She imagined herself in a superhero costume and, like Claire, automatically changed into a blue superhero costume.

"Woo, I did it!"

Sean then joined them in the basement.

"Hi, everybody," he said quietly. What did I miss?"

"Claire and Felicity just tried their powers out. Why don't you try yours out?" said Robbie.

"Okay, yeah, I will." Sean imagined himself in a superhero costume.

Nothing happened.

"That's odd. Why didn't you get your superhero costume?" Robbie asked him.

"I don't know, although I'm happy enough with my powers of love and hope for you as well as myself. I, like all of you, have Oddball to help me out as well."

"Yeah, well it's nice of you to say so, but I hope you discover an individual power like the ones we've got or I'm going to have to find a way to kick the Destroyer's infinitely large backside for not making us equal," Robbie joked.

They all laughed.

"Right, joking aside, I've finished fixing the time machine and attached it to the plane engine. So now I've just got to put it in a plane, as I plan to fly anticlockwise round this world at three hundred and sixty miles per hour," he explained.

"Oh right. Why three hundred and sixty miles per hour?" Felicity asked.

"Well because I reckon that if I fly backwards at the same speed as the number of degrees in this sphere shaped world, then hopefully I can get to this same world but in an earlier time. Unlike if I travelled at less than three hundred and sixty miles per hour; that would see me travel back in time to an incomplete alien world."

He looked at the others. "Oh, I've just realized that each of you didn't try your other powers. Like mine is the ability to make potions from my part alien/part witch blood."

"We don't know what they are, other than mine's some sort of psychic power and Claire's is some sort of witch power known as telekinesis. Our parents didn't tell us exactly what powers we've got," Felicity pointed out.

"That's true."

"I know what your powers are," Sean said quietly. "A voice in my head, which must be some sort of psychic power said to tell you, Claire, that your power is a form of the witch power telekinesis that allows you to move things and/or people including yourself with your mind, using your hands to direct where you want them to go. The alien part of you allows you to teleport things and/or people while you move them with your mind. You can use your combined witch and alien powers to move people or things through time as well. So it seems you and Robbie both have the power to time travel one way or the other. As for you, Felicity, you have the psychic power to communicate with the Gods to get them to produce a bolt of lightning in any place you want. So your nickname could be Felicity electricity."

"Really? Oh right," said Claire, smiling at Sean, "let's go and try our powers out then, Felicity."

Outside, Felicity was transferring her thoughts to the Gods.

"Gods, can you work your magic on the clouds to make lightning hit that drain," she thought, whilst looking at a nearby drain. She then looked at the sky anticipating the appearance of the Gods.

The Gods appeared in the sky, using their supernatural pitchforks to rub the clouds together. Then they stopped and used the supernatural pitchforks to point at the drain Felicity was looking at. A bolt of lightning struck the drain.

"Thanks," Felicity thought to the Gods.

"You're welcome," the Gods replied psychically and disappeared from sight.

Claire then thought of some shops and used her hands to direct her to them. Moving herself with her mind, she teleported herself to the shops and then went back home the same way.

"So where did you go?" asked Felicity.

"Just to some shops. I'll only use the time travel part of my combined alien and witch power when we're all ready to time travel."

Having tested their powers satisfactorily, they went back to the basement where Robbie and Sean were just about to leave.

"Hi, girls. We're just going out to buy a plane from Catterick airfield with our savings. Do you want to come?" Robbie asked.

"You bet!"

Robbie, Sean, Felicity and Claire went to RAF Leeming airfield and purchased a Bulldog plane.

"Okay, I'll replace the Bulldog engine with the combined plane engine and time machine so we'll be ready to go back in time," Robbie told them.

"We'll wait for you to do that, then," said Claire.

Robbie removed the Bulldog engine and replaced it with the combined plane engine and time machine.

He finally finished the job. "Do you all want to go back in time to see what happened in Jesus Christ's life between the ages of thirteen and twenty nine?" he asked the others.

"Yeah, great!" they enthused.

"Good. I'll just set the time on the digital time display monitor to when Jesus was thirteen." He twiddled a knob and pressed some buttons and turned to Sean.

"Right, Bashful, do you want to get in the passenger seat of the plane and play wingman to me, RC Maverick?"

"Great balls of fire, I do," said Sean in his quieter tone of voice. He opened the hatch and got into the plane.

"You said you're nickname was RC Maverick. I think a better one is RC Hole," Clare said mischievously.

"Why?"

"Why? Is there a hole in your intelligence that means you can't answer that for yourself? Anyway, never mind your intelligence, the reason I chose RC Hole as a nickname was because it sounds like arsehole and being my brother for all my life, you are naturally annoying. Therefore you are full of wind like an arsehole."

"Well in that case, I'd better not let you down on the annoying front, Sissy."

"Don't call me Sissy; just because my initials are CC, which sound like sissy."

"No, I think I'll continue with the German way of life and be annoying forever. So I'm going to keep calling you Sissy, and besides your initials sounding like sissy, the reason I'm going to keep calling you Sissy is..." Robbie pointed, "... look, Claire, there's a stain on your costume."

"Oh no! I won't look great anymore," moaned Claire, looking at her costume. Then she noticed there was nothing on her costume.

She looks annoyed with Robbie. "You tricked me."

"Yes, I told a white lie to prove a point, that your nickname should be Sissy. If you think you don't look great, you go all soft because you won't be able to be arrogant in terms of showing off how great you look. Although to be fair, I'm soft as well. So cheer up Sissy, It's not the end of the world."

Robbie climbed into the plane.

Claire was still annoyed, but kept smiling.

Sean and Robbie picked up their helmets from the floor and put them on.

"Oh," said Robbie, "I almost forgot. Felicity, can you ask the Gods to strike with lightning the piece of wire that is connected to the combined time machine and plane engine to enable the plane to be flown?"

"Felicity concentrated on the wire that was protruding from the plane and asked the Gods to strike it with lightning.

The Gods appeared to Felicity. Using their supernatural pitchforks to rub the clouds together, then they pointed at the piece of wire that Felicity was staring at and with a lightning flash, signalled to her that the job was done.

She gave the thumbs up to Robbie and thanked the Gods for their help,

"Are you ready to lock and load, Bashful?" Robbie asked.

"Yeah, Hole, lets put scientific time travel as a Sci-Fi concept in you like the waste of space it is," Sean replied.

"Hey, I like that, Bashful."

"Sean and Robbie closed the hatch of the plane and Robbie started the combined time machine and plane engine by pressing the ignition button. Robbie then taxied the Bulldog plane along the Catterick runway and took off into the sky.

"Do you want to try going back in time now, Felicity Electricity?" Claire asked.

"Yeah, Sister."

"That's better than Robbie's nickname for me," Claire said. She then thought of the year that Jesus was thirteen in Nazareth and waved her hand over Felicity and herself to move them through the air.

Felicity and Claire then moved through the air past the Bulldog plane containing Sean and Robbie. They then teleported back to when Jesus was thirteen.

"Were they birds? Were they planes?" Sean said quietly and with humour.

"No," Robbie answered with a giggle, "they were Felicity Electricity and Sissy."

The two boys burst out laughing.

Robbie then set the plane on course for the middle east and in a couple of hours they were flying over Israel.

"We are now cruising over Israel. I hope you enjoyed the flight," Robbie laughed, clearly enjoying himself.

Sean laughed with him. What's not to like, Hole?"

"Right, now listen up, Bashful, we'll be flying round the world and I will gradually increase the speed of the plane until we return to this point. The speed of the plane will then be exactly three hundred and sixty miles per hour. If my calculations are correct we should then time travel back to when Jesus was thirteen and therefore be able to land in Nazareth, Israel, in that particular time."

"All sounds good, Hole."

Robbie flew the Bulldog almost all the way round the world, gradually increasing the speed.

"Now, Bashful, the speed is at three hundred and fifty miles per hour. So the next ten miles per hour should be achieved when we fly over Israel."

"Right."

Robbie increased the speed and as predicted, the speed hit three hundred and sixty miles per hour as they flew over Israel. They had gone back in time to when Jesus was thirteen and Robbie landed the plane in his home town of Nazareth.

Robbie and Sean went to look for Claire and Felicity and found them waiting in the shade of some low, white buildings."

"Hi, girls. Everything okay?" Robbie asked.

"Yeah, fine," answered Claire. "And with you?"

"Never better. Great flight, wasn't it Bashful?"

Sean nodded, screwing up his eyes against the bright sunlight.

"Let's go and find Jesus, then."

The four of them followed a narrow street and asked some local people if they knew where Jesus was. They were told where he was most likely to be and they found him with some local youths, all of them dressed in long white robes and sandals, kicking a ball around a sandy courtyard.

"So Jesus was a rough and ready street soccer player," Robbie said.

"With some rough and ready sore toes, don't you think?" Sean remarked.

Jesus then scored.

"Yes! We've won the match five goals to three," said Jesus to his teammates who were none other than Matthew, Mark, Luke and John.

Jesus and his teammates then shook hands with the opposition they beat, who were captained by Judas Iscariot.

Sean, Robbie, Claire and Felicity applauded Jesus and his teammates and then went to talk to Jesus.

"Hi, we're admirerers of your, Jesus. We think you're a great competitor of life," Robbie said, as spokesman.

Jesus was delighted. "Oh wow, thank you, guys, I'll just go and get my team's autographs for you."

He came back with a small roll of papyrus upon which were inscribed the signatures of Jesus and his four team mates.

The four were stunned into silence until Robbie found his tongue.

He cleared his throat. "Thank you so much..."

"You are welcome," said Jesus, "but I must leave you now as the next match is due to begin."

"Perhaps we can watch the match before we leave for the next chapter in our exciting adventure of life?" said Claire.

"Of course," Jesus replied and then ran off to play the next game of street soccer.

"Claire?" said Robbie. "A word please?"

"What?"

"Claire, about moving on to the next chapter of our adventure. That's not going to happen and we won't be going home for seventeen years."

"Why not?" asked Sean, Claire and Felicity.

"Well, because we wanted to see Jesus' life between the ages of thirteen and twenty-nine, with the whole experience becoming a permanent record in our memories. You see, using time travel to have a time period that you haven't seen before as a permanent record in your memory is like wanting to watch a new television programme as well recording it at the same time on DVD."

The other three stared at him blankly.

"The point is, that in such a scenario you couldn't possibly skip to a new chapter as there wouldn't be any chapters created until you stop recording the new television programme. So what we are doing metaphorically is watching a new TV programme as well recording it, so we can't skip chapters until we have watched as well as recorded what we wanted. Understand?"

They still looked blank.

"So going home earlier than seventeen years can't happen until we have watched the metaphorical new television programme and made a metaphorical DVD."

"Oh, right," said Sean and Felicity.

Claire was annoyed. "Great! So we're going to have to stay here until Jesus turns twenty-nine. Well, thanks a lot, Robbie, for not mentioning that minor detail before leaving home."

"What can I say? I guess I was too busy enjoying myself thinking about what I had accomplished that it just slipped my mind."

Claire attempted to smile, but it turned into a grimace.

"The next game is about to start. Do you want to watch Jesus and his friends kick lumps out of the opposition team and vice versa?" Sean asked in a quiet voice.

"Yeah, let's do that," they agreed and gathered to watch Jesus and his friends play street soccer.

Jesus' team kicked off and within ten minutes the match ended five goals to four in favour of Jesus' team.

"Yes! We're through to the semi finals," said Jesus as he and his teammates shook hands with the beaten opposition.

Felicity, Sean, Robbie and Claire then applauded and congratulated Jesus and his team mates.

"Thank you. In a few minutes, we shall play the final.

The final got under way and in ten minutes, Jesus scored the volleyed winner to win the match by five goals to four.

"YES! We've won the street soccer cup," Jesus declared.

During the next year Robbie, Claire, Felicity and Sean watched Jesus play some more street soccer and win more street soccer trophies; they also discovered that he had a talent for musical street theatre.

"Come on," Robbie said, one evening. "Let's go and see Jesus and his girlfriend, Sandie, in the musical street play, *Life Lasts Forever.*"

The play opened with Jesus and Sandie made up to look elderly. An hour later, the finale was performed by Jesus and Sandie singing the title song.

Life lasts forever

*In knowing we have to face anatomical death we are long sufferers of life
but we just have to try to find ways to be happy and not to dwell
on that sort of strife. We've had a good innings and batted well
and with pride we can say that our life is swell.*

*(Chorus) Life lasts forever and death comes never.
Life lasts forever when there is true endeavour.*

*We have loved each other for so many years
and have memories worth more than crystal chandeliers.
We have had and now we hold
so many moments that are pure gold.*

(Chorus)

*We have shared so many walks through life together
That taught us to have faith that the truth lasts forever.
So we will go forward and stay strong
In the knowledge that life lasts forever long.*

(Chorus)

*We have shared so many memories that we can't tell them all
but of all of them we can wonderfully recall.
Our adventure is still ongoing and for us, there's more
So we wonder what for us God now has in store.*

*Chorus: (sung in an exaggerated weak tone of voice by a
smiling Jesus and Sandie as they pretend to die.)*

In the next three years, Robbie, Claire, Felicity and Sean watched Jesus continuing to win trophies in street soccer tournaments as well as perform in numerous street theatre plays such as: *We've Come so Far but We Still Make Mistakes*, *The Importance of Forgiveness* and *The World is Beautiful* with three new girlfriends, Andrea, Vicky and Louise.

A year after performing in those three plays Jesus was now approaching nineteen, with no girlfriend. He was a shepherd.

Robbie, Claire, Sean and Felicity went to see Jesus' sheep.

"Can we help you at all?" Robbie asked.

"Yes, you can. I'll go and get five camels so that they can carry us to those sheep over there, so we can guide them onto this hill," said Jesus, pointing into the distance.

Jesus returned with the camels, upon which they rode out to round up the sheep and brought them back to the hillside.

"Thank you," said Jesus. "Now would you like to play cowboys on camels?"

They all said they would love to.

Oddball appeared from Robbie. "I'll make five leather cowboy hats," it said and instantly produced them.

"Ready?" Jesus asked. "Right, let's play."

They all prepared to race and were about to start when Robbie said, "Hang about... Oddball, can you play Pato Banton's and Sting's song, *This Cowboy Song*?"

"Sure." Oddball played *This Cowboy Song*.

Robbie, Jesus, Sean, Felicity and Claire raced each other for one hundred metres.

Jesus won the race.

Oddball stopped playing the music and went back into Robbie.

"Wow, when the lyrics to the song are written in the future, they will be true. Jesus will strike you down, metaphorically speaking of course, for loving cowboys," Robbie said.

Sean, Claire and Felicity all laughed out loudly with Robbie.

"Yes. I guess I'm just too good for you, like Cristiano Ronaldo will be for opposition premier league defences," Jesus joked.

They all laughed again, enjoying the joke.

"Excuse me, while I return the camels whence they came."

In the next eleven years Jesus, Oddball, Claire, Robbie, Felicity and Sean built an ice hockey arena and Jesus met a woman called Mary Mags and arranged to marry her.

Robbie, Jesus, Claire, Oddball, Felicity and Sean all went to play ice hockey in the new stadium.

Jesus' team was himself, John the Baptist and three apostles; Robbie's team consisted of himself, Claire, Oddball, Sean and Felicity.

Paul was the referee and flipped a coin, landing it on the back of his hand. Covering it with his other hand, he called, "Heads or tails, Robbie?"

"Heads."

Paul uncovered the coin. "Heads it is," he said and blew his whistle to signal the start of the game.

Robbie started the game by passing the puck to Sean who scored.

"Yes, one nil to us," Robbie shouted.

Jesus' team faced off with John the Baptist, who passed the puck to Jesus who tried for a goal but Felicity saved it.

The minutes passed through the end of the first period, then the second and third with the score still one-nil.

"Yes, we've won. That was great fun," Robbie said and he and his team went to shake hands with Jesus and his team.

Jesus and Mary Mags went to the chapel to get married with Jesus' ice hockey team mates in attendance and Robbie, Oddball, Sean, Felicity and Claire were all invited to go with him as well.

They were married by John the Baptist and Robbie announced the wedding song.

"My friends and I, the only gay superhero in the superhero village, will now perform the wedding song entitled, This *is the Wedding of Mary Mags and Jesus.*"

Oddball started playing the music and Robbie, Sean, Claire and Felicity began to sing:

This is the Wedding of Mary Mags and Jesus

 # Mary Mags and Jesus have completed their bond of trust
and now they will go on to show lots of love as well as lust.
They have simple goals to treat each other with respect,
to help each other achieve their dreams and satisfy their souls.

(Chorus) this is the wedding of Jesus and Mary
Blessed by a rotund, singing fairy
Mary Mags has married God's son
A beautiful, faithful wife he's won.

Jesus and Mary Mags will go on in holy matrimony
to share a million memories.
They will go from strength to strength
and their happiness will have no end to its length.

(Chorus)

*There will be major sacrifices along the way
but there will also be creations and play.*

(Chorus)

As the music faded away, Robbie, Sean, Claire and Felicity stopped singing.

Jesus, Mary Mags and Jesus' ice hockey team mates then began to applaud Oddball, Robbie, Sean, Claire and Felicity.

"Thank you very much," said Robbie as the applause died down. "We're all now leaving for the next part of our journey through life."

As they left to climb back into the time machine plane, Jesus approached them.

Goodbye to all of you. I hope you have had a good time being here."

"Yeah," they said. "It's been great."

"I have a question for you," Robbie said. "What does your name, Jesus, stand for?"

"Well it stands for my first names which are: Justin Evolution Save Universal Souls."

"Wow! So does that serve as a message and tell us that we can escape evolution?"

"No. Everything is evolution, including living species that have passed away, in that their memories and spirits grow older everyday. So my name is a joke as well as a message to save souls and not to have them perish, even if its just through memory and spirit," Jesus explained.

Robbie, Sean, Claire, Felicity and Claire all laughed together.

"Does anyone else have any questions to ask me?" Jesus enquired.

"No," said Felicity and Oddball.

Sean said quietly, "I don't have one either, but I do have my greatest philosophy to share. It is this: shyness is greatness; when I'm proud of and happy with it, it gives me peace of mind and confidence at heart."

"Oh, that's a good philosopy. How did you think of it?" asked Jesus.

"Well as a shy person who was too shy, I wanted the bloody school psychologist I saw to prove that it wasn't my shyness that was the problem with me, but rather the way I was dealing with it. So I created that saying to prove that shyness is greatness and personally, I think everyone is shy as everyone has love and hope inside of themselves and love and hope are shy things in that hope is shy by way of being modest compared to confidence, and love is shy by way of being a quiet thing. We are also shy by way of being nervous as we all have a central nervous system, although I am obviously more nervous than most people, which is why my nickname is Bashful."

"I see," said Jesus, intrigued by Sean.

Claire spoke up. "I have a question for you. What is God and the soul?"

"Well the God is the truth about everyone and everything. We are all Gods though, as God can mean Idol and we are all idols to at least one living species like, for example, plants as we help them stay alive by feeding them with water and carbon dioxide. They are also idols to us as they help keep us alive by feeding us with oxygen. The soul is the truth about us individually."

"Oh right. Thanks," said Claire.

"Actually, I've just remembered, I do have a question to ask," Oddball said. "I remember that years ago, someone called Manny came here to earth and said that he had been sent a message. Who was that from?"

"That was from me, using my supernatural powers."

"Oh, was it? Right, thanks."

"So is the spirit the same as the soul?" Robbie asked Jesus.

"No. The spirit is our energy inside our bodies."

"Oh, I see. One more question?"

Jesus nodded.

"I know the Destroyer is the overall power of good in the world, but how does it dispense its powers?"

"Well, now, it dispenses its powers by listening to what the greater living species in evolution want, whether they say it verbally or otherwise, perhaps by thinking of what they want consciously or subconsciously, and it then grants them what they want. You see there's good in everyone so the good is always there to listen to us."

"Right. What about the light that we saw? What was that?"

"That was the sun. That is good and therefore part of the overall power of good blessing you, along with the good inside you, itself having been called to bless you."

"And what about all the religious books? How are they meant to be interpreted?"

"Well the books are written metaphorically, so they are not always meant to be taken literally."

"That's good to know. Thank you," Robbie said.

"Any more questions?" asked Jesus, looking around at them all.

"No," they said.

Apart from Robbie.

"Sorry, I have one more question to ask. What is the meaning of life?"

"It's about lots of things but most importantly its about embracing the thing that created us; God is the truth and as we are all evolved from it, therefore we are part of it. We all have to embrace each other, apart from the lesser species in evolution which have to be hurt and sacrificed from their bodies to be turned into food so that we, the greater living species are not sacrificed from our bodies. We should also have the philosophy that there is at least hope in every faith, religious and non-religious. We also need to experience moments that take our breath away. That's the important part of the meaning of the anatomic part of life. The memory and spiritual part of life is about all those things without exception and it is also about change because everything changes, even living species that have passed on grow older through memory and spirit."

"Thank you so much for that," said Robbie.

"You are most welcome."

"Goodbye, Jesus," said Sean, Robbie, Claire, Oddball and Felicity.

"Goodbye to you all," Jesus replied with a wave.

Sean, Robbie, Claire, Oddball and Felicity returned to the place where Robbie left his time machine plane.

Robbie and Sean opened the hatch of the plane, climbed in and closed the hatch.

"Right, Claire, throw me back home," said Felicity.

Claire threw Felicity back home using her supernatural power with her hand as a guide and then did the same thing to herself.

Oddball went into Robbie.

Robbie took off and flew himself and Sean back home.

Once home Sean, Robbie, Claire and Felicity went into their house.

"Hi Felicity," Steven said. "You don't have to explain where you have been as I had a premonition before you, Robbie, Oddball, Claire and Sean went time travelling, and I told everyone concerned where you were."

"Oh, did you? Right."

An hour later Greg, Amy, Oddball, Jessica, Steven, Sean, Robbie, Claire, and Felicity all went for a stroll. Just as they were nearing home, Greg made the mistake of stepping out into road without looking and a car inadvertently hit him.

They all rushed to his side.

"Goodbye, my loved and respected ones," he said, softly.

"Goodbye, Dad, we love and respect you too," Robbie and Claire whispered.

"Goodbye, Greg, and we all love and respect you too," said Amy, who spoke for Steven, Jessica, Oddball, Felicity and Sean.

Greg then passed away from his body.

Over the course of the following week, in accordance with the terms of Greg's will, his body was incinerated in an acid plant after some of his organs were removed for donor purposes. His brain was stored in a laboratory awaiting the time when scientists could link his brain to a machine.

Robbie, Amy, Claire, Felicity, Jessica, Steven, Oddball and Sean were all at their house. Steven was reading the paper.

"Oh, listen to this," he said, "here's a tribute to Greg by Christopher Burtwee; formally known as Christopher the Idiot. 'Greg Carter, a fine fighter of a man, passed away last week after he was involved in an accident. He was a superhero and we shall all feel the loss of not having him around in his body any more.'"

"That was a nice tribute by Christopher Burtwee," said Amy, wiping away a tear.

The next day Amy, Oddball, Steven, Robbie, Claire, Jessica, Sean and Felicity had arranged to perform a song dedicated to Greg at Clarkesville stadium.

Steven announced the song from the stage.

"Ladies and gentlemen, we will now sing *We've Come Full Circle*. This song is dedicated to Greg Carter who has been born again after he was lost from his body into my family's, friends' and my own natural heaven that is the mind as well the supernatural heaven.

We've Come Full Circle.

Our loved and respected one has gone
but he would want us to carry on.
Our loved and respected one want us to do
as much good as possible for all of you.

(Chorus) We've come full circle, we've loved, respected and lost,
now we must go on, make the most of ourselves and not count the cost.

We've learned so much from our loved and respected one,
and for that we give thanks from our hearts.
Our loved and respected one did so much
and we will pass on your good, kind touch.

(Chorus)

We now love and respect so many good people
Our love and respect towers over the steeple.
You've given us so many memories
and we'll cherish them fondly; they're our history.

(Chorus)

We've rolled into life and before we're rolled out,
we must not be afraid to laugh and to shout.

(Chorus)

There was a roar of applause from the crowd and a standing ovation for Amy, Steven, Oddball, Jessica, Robbie, Claire, Sean, and Felicity. They took their bows and eventually left the stage.

As they made their way back home, they all felt exhilarated by the crowd's reaction to their song.

But their happiness was, naturally, tinged with sadness.

THE DESTROYER 2: DESTROYER OF THE WORLD.

"We're sad about Dad's death, but there's plenty to cheer" said Robbie.

Meanwhile, in an evil planet outside the universe, so it's supernatural, there is an evil alien leave for Earth.

After a while he lands. He kills people, using his spike hand. He looks for more people to kill.

Where the Superheroes are, they are talking.

"It's nice, this peaceful time" said Jessica.

"Yeah it is" said Robbie JR.

"No more bullies" said Amy.

"No more world law breaking" said Steven.

"That's true" said Claire.

"Yeah it is" said Felicity.

"Okay" said Steven

"What?" said Jessica.

"I've had a prediction killing has happened" said Steven.

"How's that?" said Jessica.

"He's from outside the universe, so the spell doesn't apply to him" said Steven.

"Okay" said the other superheroes.

"Let's go and get him" said Steven.

"Yeah" said the other superheroes.

All the superheroes go to find the evil alien. He's moved from where Steven saw him on his premonition.

"Damn" said Robbie JR.

"Never mind, we'll catch him" said Steven

"We will" said Jessica.

"I agree" said Sean.

"Me, too" said Felicity

"We will catch him" said Claire.

"Yeah" said Amy

Where the evil alien is.

"This planet's so big, I'm going to need minions" said the evil alien.

He looks in the part of his mind that supernaturally sees the people on his planet and summons them using his powers. He gives them each orders.

"I don't know where he could be" said Steven.

"We'll find him" said Robbie Jr.

The first minion to be summoned by the evil alien is approaching people.

"I'm going to kill you!" said the first minion.

"Boo!" said Greg; now a ghost, who has just appeared behind the first minion.

The first minion turns and falls afters being accidently scared.

"I'm back!" said Greg.

"I've had a vision of where the villain's place is, also, Greg is back as a ghost" said Steven.

"Let's go!" said Robbie Jr.

"Yeah!" said the other superheroes.

After a while all the superheroes see the first minion and it tries to kill Robbie Jr.

He moves out the way and hits the first minion after getting out the way.

"Who do you think you are, Deadpool?" said the first minion.

"I'm not Deadpool, I'm worse" said Robbie Jr, he then opens his mouth and sucks the first minion into his supernatural Alcatraz.

"How about a song?" said Greg.

"Yeah!" said the other superheroes.

After a while the superheroes sing:

> *Your evil is beat, this song is our treat, we're*
> *action loving and you're extreme shoving.*

> *(Chorus: We kicked your ass, you're shattered like*
> *glass. No more you, you don't stick like glue)*

> *We'll keep beating the likes of you, you're pathetic are you.*
> *Bye, bye, you're way was like a lie*

> *(Chorus).*

> *We'll always beat your type, we may even smoke a pipe.*
> *Good stuff, we're not powder puff.*

> *(Chorus)*

> *We're victors again, we're ten out of ten.*
> *Life is messy, we'll mess you up and we'll win a cup.*

> *(Chorus)*

"Yeah!" said Greg.

"That was cool!" said Robbie Jr. He burps.

"That bad guy didn't agree with you" said Greg.

All the other superheroes laugh.

"It's good to see you again, Dad" said Robbie Jr.

"Don't you mean good to see through you, Robbie Jr!" said Greg.

All the superheroes laugh.

"Good response" said Greg.

"I don't know where the other being who's villainous is !" said Steven.

"Well wait for it" said Greg.

"Yeah we will" said Steven

"We probably all will" said Amy.

"Yeah!" said all the other superheroes.

"Okay" said Greg.

"Let's go home" said Steven.

"Yeah!" said the other superheroes.

All the superheroes go home.

"I beat you" said Greg.

"That's because you're a ghost" said Steven.

All the other superheroes laugh.

"Good" said Greg.

"It is" said Steven.

"There's nothing better than beating villains" said Greg.

"That's true" said Sean.

"It is" said Felicity.

"I agree" said Jessica.

"Me too" said Steven.

"Me as well" said Amy.

"I agree too" said Robbie Jr.

"I agree with you" said Claire.

"Okay" said Greg.

"Good" said Steven.

"We'll beat more" said Robbie Jr.

"We will" said Greg.

"That we will" said Jessica.

"Yeah!" said the other superheroes.

"I miss food, now I don't have my own body" said Greg.

"Okay" said Steven.

All the superheroes hug.

"That was nice" said Claire.

"It was" said Robbie Jr.

"I agree" said Steven.

"Me too" said Greg.

"Even though you could feel it" said Steven.

"Good one" said Greg.

"I felt it was a nice hug" said Amy.

"Me too" said Jessica.

"Me as well" said Felicity.

"I liked it" said Sean.

"Okay" said Greg.

"Let's get something to eat" said Steven.

After a while.

"Cheesy chips are delicious" said Steven.

"I remember them well" said Greg.

"They're nice" said Amy.

"They are" said Sean.

"Mine are nice with vinegar" said Felicity.

"They're nice" said Claire.

"They arc" said Jessica.

"Mine are too" said Robbie Jr.

"Okay" said Steven.

"Good" said Greg.

"Yeah it is" said Steven.

"Let's get something to drink" said Robbie Jr.

After a while.

"That's nice" said Steven.

"I can't drink, so I wet myself" said Greg.

"My drink is nice" said Claire.

"Mine too" said Robbie Jr.

"Mine's tasty" said Amy.

"Mine too" said Felicity.

"Mine as well" said Sean.

"Mine is too" said Jessica.

"Okay" said Steven

"It's good to have a drink after a meal" said Robbie Jr.

"It is" said Sean.

"Yeah it is" said Amy.

"It is" said Claire.

"I agree" said Jessica.

"Me too" said Felicity.

"Okay" said Greg.

"Let's go home" said Steven.

"Yeah" said all the other superheroes.

After a while.

"Home sweet home" said Greg.

"It is" said Steven.

"I agree" said Amy.

"Me too" said Jessica.

"Me as well" said Claire.

"Me too" said Felicity.

"I too agree" said Sean.

"It's good we don't kill any people or murderers anymore" said Greg.

"Yeah it is" said Robbie Jr.

"It is" said Amy.

"I agree" said Steven.

"Me too" said Sean.

"I do" said Jessica

"I do too" said Felicity

"Me as well" said Claire.

"Okay" said Greg.

"It is" said Steven.

"We're nice" said Greg.

"We are" said Steven.

"We are indeed" said Sean.

"That we are" said Robbie Jr.

"We are" said Amy.

"We are indeed" said Jessica.

"We'll keep being this way" said Felicity.

"We'll do that" said Claire.

"Okay" said Greg.

"Yeah it is" said Steven.

"We can do anything" said Greg.

"We can" said Steven.

"Yeah we can" said Robbie Jr.

"I agree" said Sean.

"Me too" said Felicity.

"Me as well" said Amy.

"I agree" said Claire.

"Me too" said Jessica.

"Okay" said Greg.

"It is" said Steven.

"Let's play footie" said Greg.

"Yeah!" said the other superheroes.

"Good" said Greg.

The superheroes start playing football.

"Man on!" said Greg.

"Thanks Coach" said Steven; he then side steps a tackle by Amy.

Sean's making coaching gestures.

Steven is still running, he scores past Robbie Jr.

"Yes!" said Steven.

"Well done" said Greg.

The superheroes on Steven's side celebrate with him.

"Let's stay focused" said Steven to his teammates, Jessica and Claire.

"Let's come back" said Felicity.

Amy kicks off.

"Pass!" said Sean.

"Okay" said Amy.

Amy passes the ball to Felicity.

"Thanks" said Felicity.

Felicity runs and shoots past Claire in goal.

"Yeah!" Said Sean, Felicity, Amy and Robbie Jr.

"Great stuff" said Sean.

"Yeah" said Felicity.

"Next goal wins" said Greg.

Steven kicks off. He plays it to Jessica.

"I'll run forwards now" said Steven.

Jessica finds Steven with a pass.

"Thanks" said Steven.

Steven runs forwards. He shoots and scores.

"Yes!" said Greg.

Greg runs down the touchline.

Claire, Greg, Steven and Jessica hug.

"Well don!" said Steven.

"Thanks mate!" said Greg.

Greg smiles. All the other superheroes smile big smiles.

"That was fun" said Greg.

"It was" said Steven.

"Yeah it was" said Jessica.

"It was" said Amy.

"It was indeed" said Sean.

"I agree" said Felicity.

"Me too" said Robbie Jr.

"Me as well" said Claire.

"Okay" said Greg.

"We'll have other fun" said Greg.

"Yeah we will" said Steven.

"We will" said Amy.

"That we will" said Jessica.

"We will" said Robbie Jr.

"We will do that" said Claire.

"That we will" said Felicity.

"We will" said Sean.

"Okay" said Greg.

"I agree" said Steven.

"Chocolate digestives are nice" said Amy.

"Ooh yeah, I remember them" said Greg.

"They are nice" said Steven.

"I enjoy them" said Jessica.

"Me too" said Robbie Jr.

"Me as well" said Sean.

"I like them" said Claire.

"Me too" said Felicity.

"Okay" said Greg.

"There'll be more nice things" said Steven.

"There will" said Claire.

"There will be" said Amy.

"I agree" said Greg.

"Me too" said Jessica.

"Me as well" said Felicity.

"I do think that" said Robbie Jr.

"I think that" said Sean.

"Okay" said Steven.

"We're all well" said Greg.

"Our world isn't fit in or get bullied, it's fit in or get challenged" said Amy.

"It is" said Greg.

"I agree" said Steven.

"Me as well" said Jessica.

"Me to" said Robbie Jr.

"I agree" said Sean.

"I think that" said Felicity.

"I too think that" said Claire.

"Okay" said Amy.

"We're better than Labour" said Greg.

"We are" said Amy.

"That we are" said Steven.

"We are" said Jessica.

"I agree" said Robbie Jr.

"Me too" said Claire.

"I think the same" said Sean.

"Me too" said Felicity.

"Okay" said Greg.

"Soup is nice" said Steven.

"Ooh yeah, prawn soup sounds nice" said Greg.

"Yeah it does" said Amy.

"It does" said Jessica.

"It does indeed" said Robbie Jr.

"I agree" said Steven.

"Me too" said Felicity.

"Me as well" said Claire.

"I do agree" said Sean.

"Okay" said Greg.

"Mental health is important" said Steven.

"It is" said Greg.

"I agree" said Amy.

"Me too" said Jessica.

"Yeah, the football mentioned it" said Sean.

"That's right, that's good" said Felicity.

"I agree" said Claire.

"Me too" said Robbie Jr

"Okay" said Steven.

"Good talk" said Greg.

"Yeah it was" said Steven.

"It was" said Amy.

"I agree" said Jessica.

"Me too" said Robbie Jr.

"Me as well" said Claire.

"Me too" said Sean.

"I agree" said Felicity.

"Okay" said Greg.

"It is" said Steven.

"Any news Steven?" said Amy.

"Yeah, I know" said Steven.

After a while the superheroes find and fight the murderer they're after.

"Time to go down" said Steven. He makes the murderer go down into his supernatural Alcatraz.

"Sickly" said Steven.

"Let's sing" said Greg.

We are good again and you are each a villain.
That's it, we can hit.
We are great, you are full of hate.

(Chorus: We beat you, that is what we do. We're ace and in your face).

Goodness, we're uniqueness.
We are, we'll go far.

(Chorus)

Our fate will be great.
Hear our hearts, they're better than farts.

(Chorus)

We're the best, we passed the test.
We'll keep winning to best your sinning.

"Great!" said Greg.

"It was" said Steven.

"I agree" said Amy.

"Me too" said Jessica.

"Yeah, me to" said Robbie Jr.

"Me as well" said Sean.

"Me too" said Felicity.

"I agree" said Claire.

"Okay" said Greg.

"It is" said Steven.

"We've done well" said Greg.

"We've certainly done that" said Steven.

"We are successful" said Amy.

"We are" said Jessica.

"I agree" said Robbie Jr.

"Me too" said Sean.

"Me as well" said Felicity.

"I agree" said Claire.

"Okay" said Greg.

"It is" said Steven.

"The e-premier league and e-world cup. Would be good to win" said Greg.

"Yeah!" said Steven.

"Well, I can't win it, all you can" said Greg.

"We will" said Amy.

"I agree" said Jessica.

"Me too" said Robbie Jr.

"We'll win" said Claire.

"We will" said Sean.

"I think the same" said Felicity.

"Okay" said Greg.

"It's good for hand-eye coordination" said Steven.

"Yeah it is" said Greg.

"I agree" said Amy.

"Me too" said Jessica.

"Me as well" said Robbie Jr.

"I think that" said Sean.

"Me as well" said Felicity.

"I agree too" said Claire.

"Okay" said Steven.

"It is" said Greg.

"We'll go to the pub" said Steven.

"Okay" said Greg.

"We will" said Amy.

"We will indeed" said Jessica.

"We will do that" said Robbie Jr.

"I agree" said Sean.

"Me as well" said Felicity.

"Me too" said Claire.

"Okay" said Steven.

"It is" said Greg.

The superheroes go to the pub.

"Ah, this beer is nice" said Steven.

"Yeah it is" said Amy.

"I feel that" said Jessica.

"Good" said Greg.

"Mine's good" said Robbie Jr.

"Mine too" said Sean.

"Mine as well" said Felicity.

"Good" said Steven.

"Let's go back" said Greg.

"Yeah!" said the other superheroes.

The superheroes go home.

"I'm tired" said Steven.

"Me too" said Amy.

"Are you still boycotting human stuff" said Steven.

"Ha!" said Greg.

"I'm tired" said Jessica.

"I'm tired too" said Robbie Jr.

"Me too" said Sean.

"I'm knackered" said Felicity.

"Me too" said Claire.

"Okay" said Steven.

"All the superheroes except Greg go to bed for hours.

"Ah, that was nice" said Steven.

"Good" said Amy.

"Was your sleep good" said Steven.

"Yes!" said Amy.

"Hi sleepless" said Steven to Greg.

"Okay sleepyhead" said Greg to Steven.

"Ha!" said Steven.

"My sleep was good" said Jessica.

"Mine too" said Robbie Jr.

"Mine as well" said Sean.

"My sleep was good" said Felicity.

"Mine too" said Claire.

"Good" said Greg.

"It is" said Steven.

"We're refreshed" said Amy.

"We needed it" said Steven.

"Good, you did" said Greg.

"We did" said Jessica.

"That we did" said Robbie Jr.

"I agree" said Sean.

"Me too" said Felicity.

"Me as well" said Claire.

"Good" said Greg.

"It is good" said Steven.

"We're the force of good with the rest of society" said Amy.

"We are" said Jessica.

"I think we are" said Robbie Jr.

"We are" said Sean.

"That we are" said Steven.

"I agree" said Greg.

"Me too" said Felicity.

"Me as well" said Claire.

"Okay" said Amy.

"It is" said Greg.

"We're good at passing challenges" said Steven.

"We are" said Greg.

"We are indeed" said Amy.

"That we are" said Jessica.

"We are" said Robbie Jr.

"I agree" said Sean.

"Me too" said Felicity.

"Me as well" said Claire.

"Okay" said Greg.

"There'll be many more" said Steven.

"There will" said Greg.

"I think that" said Amy.

"Me too" said Jessica.

"I agree" said Robbie Jr.

"Me too" said Sean.

"Me as well" said Felicity.

"Me too" said Claire.

"Okay" said Steven.

"We're good at singing" said Amy.

"We're that" said Jessica.

"That we are" said Robbie Jr.

"Okay" said Steven.

"It is okay" said Greg.

"There'll be more singing to do" said Amy.

"There will" said Greg.

"There will be" said Steven.

"I agree" said Jessica.

"Me too" said Robbie Jr.

"I do as well" said Sean.

"Me as well" said Felicity.

"Me too" said Claire.

"Okay" said Amy.

"It is" said Greg.

"That'll be fun" said Amy.

"It will" said Greg.

"It will be" said Jessica.

"I agree" said Steven.

"Me too" said Robbie Jr.

"Me as well" said Sean.

"I agree" said Felicity.

"I do" said Claire.

"Okay" said Amy.

"We're the best at having fun" said Greg.

"We are" said Steven.

"We are indeed" said Amy.

"I agree" said Jessica.

"I do too" said Robbie Jr.

"Me too" said Sean.

"Me as well" said Felicity.

"Me the same" said Claire.

"Okay" said Greg.

"We're great" said Steven.

"We are" said Amy.

"That we are" said Jessica.

"We are indeed" said Greg.

"I agree" said Robbie Jr.

"Me too" said Sean.

"Me as well" said Felicity.

"I agree" said Claire.

"Okay" said Steven.

"It is" said Greg.

"Let's go to the seaside" said Amy.

"I agree to that" said Steven.

"Me too" said Jessica.

"Me as well" said Greg.

"I'll do that" said Robbie Jr.

"I'll go" said Sean.

"I'll go there as well" said Felicity.

"I'll go there" said Claire.

"Good" said Amy.

The superheroes go to the seaside.

"I'm going to make a sandcastle" said Robbie Jr.

"Good" said Greg.

"It is" said Amy.

"I'll kick it, just kidding" said Sean.

"Good one Sean" said Robbie Jr.

"I'm lying down looking beautiful" said Claire.

"Me too Claire" said Felicity.

"Okay" said Amy.

"It's a beautiful day" said Steven.

"It is" said Jessica.

"Okay" said Steven.

"Let's go back" said Greg.

The superheroes go back home.

"That was good" said Greg.

"Yeah it was" said Steven.

"It was" said Amy.

"I agree" said Jessica.

"Me too" said Robbie Jr.

"I do" said Sean.

"It was brilliant" said Felicity.

"It was" said Claire.

"Okay" said Greg.

"It is" said Steven.

"It's good you think that" said Amy.

"We'll do it again" said Greg.

"We will do that" said Steven.

"We will" said Amy.

"I agree" said Jessica.

"Me too" said Robbie Jr.

"I agree" said Sean.

"I do" said Felicity.

"I think the same" said Claire.

"Okay" said Greg.

"It is" said Steven.

"Liar Liar is the joint best film" said Amy.

"It is fun" said Jessica.

"I agree" said Steven.

"I do too" said Greg.

"Me too" said Robbie Jr.

"Me as well" said Sean.

"I say it's good too" said Felicity.

"Me too" said Claire.

"Okay" said Greg.

"It is" said Amy.

"Twirl's are nice" said Greg.

"They are" said Amy.

"They are indeed" said Steven.

"I agree" said Jessica.

"Me too" said Robbie Jr.

"Me as well" said Sean.

"I agree" said Felicity.

"Me too" said Claire.

"Okay" said Greg.

"It is" said Steven.

"Singing is good, we could record an album" said Amy.

"I agree" said Steven.

"That would be good for you" said Greg.

"It would" said Jessica.

"We should do that" said Robbie Jr.

"I agree to that" said Sean.

"Me too" said Felicity.

"Me as well" said Claire.

"Good" said Amy.

"It is" said Greg.

"Making movies would be good" said Amy.

"It would for you" said Greg.

"Yeah it will" said Amy.

"I agree" said Steven.

"Me too" said Jessica.

"Me as well" said Robbie Jr.

"It would be good" said Sean.

"I feel that" said felicity.

"Me too" said Claire.

"Okay" said Amy.

"It is" said Greg.

"Sonic the hedgehog is good" said Steven.

"It is" said Jessica.

"I agree" said Greg.

"Me too" said Amy.

"He's cute" said Robbie Jr.

"Yeah, he's feisty" said Sean.

"I think those things" said Felicity

"Me as well" said Claire.

"Okay" said Steven.

"It is" said Greg.

"The game was good" said Steven.

"Yeah it was" said Greg.

"I agree" said Amy.

"Me too" said Jessica.

"I agree" said Robbie Jr.

"I do too" said Sean.

"Me as well" said Felicity.

"I'm the same" said Claire.

"Okay" said Steven.

"It is" said Greg.

"The Lion King is good" said Steven.

"Yeah, the game and the movie" said Greg.

"I think that" said Amy.

"I agree" said Jessica.

"Me too" said Robbie Jr.

"I feel that" said Sean.

"Me too" said Felicity.

"I'm the same" said Claire.

"Okay" said Steven.

"It is" said Greg.

"Johnny English is fun" said Steven.

"It is" said Amy.

"I agree" said Jessica.

"Me too" said Greg.

"Me as well" said Robbie Jr.

"It is good" said Sean.

"It is" said Felicity.

"Yeah it is" said Claire.

"Okay" said Steven.

"It is" said Greg.

"Spa orange zero is quite nice" said Amy.

"It is" said Steven.

"That it is" said Jessica.

"I agree" said Robbie Jr.

"Me too" said Sean.

"I as well agree" said Felicity.

"Me as well" said Claire.

"Okay" said Amy.

"It is" said Greg.

"Killers wont' win" said Steven.

"Yeah, there'll be less suffering" said Greg.

"I agree" said Amy.

"Me too" said Jessica.

"I as well think that" said Robbie Jr.

"Me too" said Sean.

"I agree" said Felicity.

"Me too" said Claire.

"Okay" said Steven.

"It is" said Greg.

"We're strong than them" said Steven.

"Yeah, we keep having selfless fun against adversity" said Greg.

"We do" said Amy.

"That we do" said Jessica.

"It's good we do" said Robbie Jr.

"Yeah we're good" said Sean.

"I agree" said Felicity.

"Me too" said Claire.

"Time to fight" said Steven.

"Yeah" said all the other superheroes.

The superheroes all go to a new villain. He's already killed a human.

"Stop!" said Greg.

The villain stops.

Claire sucks the new minion into the supernatural Alcatraz of her.

"Let's sing" said Greg.

Sung the superheroes.

We sucked you in for your sin.
You'll never win because only we are the thing that's in.

(Chorus: no more you, your stink is of poo.
This is our time, it's like a chime).

You're the worst, beating you quenches our thirst. We are
together and you'll be remembered badly forever.

(Chorus)

We struck back at your attack.
We love ourselves and people like you hate themselves.

(Chorus)

Our fight will go on until your kind has gone.
This is good and you felt our thud.

(Chorus)

"Now that was fun" said Greg.

"Yeah!" said Steven.

"It was" said Amy.

"Yeah it was" said Jessica.

"I agree" said Robbie Jr.

"Me too" said Sean.

"Me as well" said Felicity.

"It is enjoyable" said Claire.

"Okay" said Greg.

"It is" said Steven.

"Let's go home" said Greg.

"Yeah!" said the other superheroes.

The superheroes go home

"Beans are nice" said Steven.

"Yeah, especially baked beans" said Amy.

"I agree" said Jessica.

"Me too" said Robbie Jr.

"I as well think and feel that" said Sean.

"They are nice" said Felicity.

"True stuff" said Claire.

"Okay" said Greg.

"Let's have tea" said Steven.

"I'll have a cup" said Amy.

"Me too" said Jessica.

"I'll have some" said Robbie Jr.

"Me as well" said Sean.

"I want some" said Felicity.

"I'll have a cup" said Claire.

"Okay" said Greg.

Amy makes cups of tea for all the superheroes apart from Greg.

"That's nice" said Steven.

"Mine's nice" said Amy.

"Good" said Greg.

"It's good" said Jessica.

"Mine too" said Robbie Jr.

"I like me tea" said Sean.

"I like mine" said Felicity.

"Nice" said Claire.

"Okay" said Greg.

"It is" said Amy.

"I'll get us biscuits from the tin" said Steven.

"Yeah!" said all the other superheroes apart from Greg.

"Good" said Steven.

Steven gets biscuits.

"Nice" said Amy.

"It is" said Steven.

"It's tasty" said Jessica.

"Mine is" said Robbie Jr.

"It's delicious" said Sean.

"Mine too" said Felicity.

"Mine as well" said Claire.

"Good" said Greg.

"We're good at enjoying things" said Steven.

"We are" said Greg.

"That we are" said Steven.

"We are" said Amy.

"We are indeed" said Jessica.

"We're fun-loving" said Robbie Jr.

"I agree" said Sean.

"Me too" said Felicity.

"We are fun" said Claire.

"Okay" said Steven.

"Let's have a movie marathon" said Greg.

"Yeah!" said all the superheroes apart from Greg.

"Good" said Greg.

Steven picks a movie out and plays it. Everyone enjoys it, then more movies.

"That was fun" said Greg.

"It was" said Steven.

"It was for me" said Amy.

"Same" said Jessica.

"I loved it" said Robbie Jr.

"Me too" said Sean.

"Me as well" said Felicity.

"I enjoyed it" said Claire.

"Okay" said Greg.

"I'll do Sudoku with Oddball" said Greg.

Oddball appears from Robbie Jr. Greg tells him to turn into a digital Sudoku board, he tells him what squares to put one to nine in.

"That was fun" said Greg.

"Good" said Steven.

"It looked good" said Jessica.

"I agree" said Amy.

"Same here" said Robbie Jr.

"I agree" said Sean.

"Me too" said Felicity.

"Mc as wcll" said Claire.

"Okay" said Greg.

"I'm having chocolate, who wants some?" said Steven.

"Me!" said all the others apart from Greg.

"I'll get it" said Steven.

"Yey" said all the others apart from Greg.

Steven gets chocolate. He breaks it up and gives it to the people that want it. The people and Steven eat it.

"Nice" said Steven.

"Yeah!" said Amy.

"Delicious" said Jessica.

"Good stuff" said Robbie Jr.

"It is" said Sean.

"Mine too" said Felicity.

"Mine as well" said Claire.

"Okay" said Greg.

"Let's watch 'Friends'" said Steven.

"What episode?" said Greg.

"I don't know, my favourites 'the one with the bullies, what's yours?" said Steven.

"The one that could have been!" said Greg.

"Mine's 'the one with all the cheesecakes" said Amy.

"Mine's 'the one with the dance routine'" said Jessica.

"Mine's 'the last one'" said Robbie Jr.

"Mine's 'the one with Chandler's work laugh'" said Sean.

"Mine's where Ross gets hit" said Felicity.

"Mine's 'the one where Mr Heckles dies'" said Claire.

"Let's put all those in a hat" said Steven.

Steven writes the superheroes favourite 'Friends' episodes on bits of paper including his. He gets a hat and puts the bits of paper in it. He draws one.

"Bullies episode, let's watch it" said Steven.

"Yeah!" said all the superheroes.

The superheroes watch 'The one with the bullies'.

"That was good" said Greg.

"It was that" said Steven.

"I agree" said Amy.

"Me too" said Jessica.

"It was brilliant" said Robbie Jr.

"It was" said Sean.

"I agree" said Felicity.

"Me too" said Claire.

"Okay" said Steven.

"We'll do it again sometime" said Greg.

"Yeah we will" said Steven.

"That we will" said Amy.

"We will" said Jessica.

"I agree" said Robbie Jr.

"Me too" said Sean.

"We will do it again" said Felicity.

"Same here" said Claire.

"Okay" said Greg.

"Spending money is good" said Steven.

"It was for me" said Greg.

"It's good" said Amy.

"I agree" said Jessica.

"Me too" said Robbie Jr.

"Me as well" said Sean.

"I like it" said Felicity.

"Me too" said Claire.

"Okay" said Steven.

"Clearly fun is more important though" said Greg.

"It is" said Steven.

"I agree" said Amy.

"Me too" said Jessica.

"I think that" said Robbie Jr.

"It is the best" said Sean.

"Best indeed" said Felicity.

"The best" said Claire.

"Okay" said Greg.

"Writing is good" said Steven.

"Yeah it is" said Greg.

"It is, it's the most calming thing" said Amy.

"I agree" said Jessica.

"Me too" said Robbie Jr.

"I do" said Sean.

"Me as well" said Felicity.

"I feel the same" said Claire.

"Okay" said Steven.

"It's important having calmness" said Greg.

"It is" said Amy.

"Good it is" said Jessica.

"It is" said Robbie Jr.

"I agree" said Steven.

"Me too" said Sean.

"Me as well" said Felicity.

"It's good" said Claire.

"Okay" said Greg.

"I like the way pens feel in my hand" said Steven.

"I do too" said Greg.

"Okay" said Steven.

"Well, I did" said Greg.

"I like it" said Amy.

"Me too" said Jessica.

"It's nice" said Robbie Jr.

"It is nice" said Sean.

"It makes me feel good" said Felicity.

"I'm the same" said Claire.

"Okay" said Steven.

"Werder Bremen are fighting" said Greg.

"They are" said Steven.

"I agree" said Amy.

"Me too" said Jessica.

"Me as well" said Robbie Jr.

"They're admirable" said Sean.

"They are" said Felicity.

"I rate them" said Claire.

"Okay" said Greg.

"German footballs good" said Steven.

"It is" said Greg.

"Yeah it is" said Amy.

"It's good" said Jessica.

"It's class" said Robbie Jr.

"I agree" said Sean.

"Me too" said Claire.

"Me as well" said Felicity.

"Okay" said Steven.

"Lockdown was bad" said Greg.

"It was" said Amy.

"I agree" said Steven.

"Me too" said Jessica.

"Me as well" said Robbie Jr.

"I'm the same" said Sean.

"Me too" said Felicity.

"Me as well" said Claire.

"Okay" said Greg.

"Politicians aren't the best people" said Steven.

"That's right" said Greg.

"It is" said Amy.

"I agree" said Jessica.

"Me as well" said Robbie Jr.

"Me too" said Sean.

"It's right" said Felicity.

"Yeah it is" said Claire.

"Okay" said Greg.

"Discos are nice" said Steven.

"They are" said Amy.

"They are nice to eat" said Jessica.

"They were" said Greg.

"Good potato snacks" said Robbie Jr.

"I agree" said Sean.

"Me too" said Felicity.

"Nice" said Claire.

"Okay" said Steven.

"Happy shopper orange juice was nice" said Greg.

"It's nice" said Steven.

"It is" said Amy.

"It is nice" said Jessica.

"Okay" said Robbie Jr.

"It's delicious" said Sean.

"It tastes nice" said Felicity.

"It is" said Claire.

"Okay" said Greg.

"Something to look forward to" said Steven.

"Like hotdogs" said Amy.

"Yeah!" said Steven.

"They're tasty" said Jessica.

"They are" said Robbie Jr.

"I like them" said Sean.

"Me too" said Felicity.

"Me as well" said Claire.

"Okay" said Amy.

"It is that" said Greg.

"Mustard on them is nice" said Steven.

"Mustard is a good addition" said Amy.

"It is" said Jessica.

"I agree" said Robbie Jr.

"Me too" said Sean.

"Me as well" said Felicity.

"Me too" said Claire.

"My cat Foley used to get scared when I cried" said Greg.

"Cats must be sensitive" said Amy.

"Yeah they are" said Steven.

"They are" said Jessica.

All the other superheroes nod.

"I had a friend was killed by a fall, he jumped off a bridge" said Greg.

"Pizza crisps are nice" said Steven.

"They are" said Jessica.

"That they are" said Amy.

"I agree" said Robbie Jr.

"Me to" said Sean.

"Tasty" said Felicity.

"They are" said Claire.

"Okay" said Greg.

"Pepper cheese is nice" said Amy.

"It is" said Steven.

"Yeah it is" said Jessica.

"It's spicy" said Robbie Jr.

"Yeah and nice" said Sean.

"It is" said Felicity.

"Delicious it is" said Claire.

"Good" said Greg.

"Tennis is good" said Steven.

"Yeah it is" said Amy.

"It is" said Greg.

"I like it" said Jessica.

"I love it" said Robbie Jr.

"It's good" said Felicity.

"It is" said Sean.

"I agree" said Claire.

"Okay" said Steven.

"Football is the best" said Greg.

"It is" said Steven.

"Yeah it's got the most skill" said Amy.

"It does" said Jessica.

"I love it" said Robbie Jr.

"Me too" said Sean.

"Me as well" said Felicity.

"It's good" said Claire.

"Okay" said Greg.

"It is" said Steven.

"Cats are nice" said Amy.

"They are" said Greg.

"I agree" said Jessica.

"Me too" said Steven.

"They're cute" said Robbie Jr.

"They are" said Sean.

"That they are" said Felicity.

"Same here" said Claire.

"Okay" said Amy.

"It is" said Greg.

"Good" said Steven.

"Jelly babies are nice" said Jessica.

"Mmm! They are" said Amy.

"They are" said Steven.

"That they are" said Robbie Jr.

"Delicious" said Sean.

"Delicious they are" said Felicity.

"I agree" said Claire.

"Okay" said Greg.

"Whips are delicious" said Steven.

"Ooh, they are" said Amy.

"Yeah they are" said Jessica.

"They're delicious" said Robbie Jr.

"They are" said Sean.

"I like them" said Felicity.

"I love them" said Claire.

"Okay" said Greg.

"There's a killer to catch" said a disappointed Steven.

The superheroes go to where the killer is.

"Stop!" said Greg.

The killer stops.

Robbie Jr sucks the killer into his supernatural Alcatraz.

"Let's sing" said Robbie Jr.

"Yeah!" said all the other superheroes.

*"# We best another villainous one, it's good you've gone.
This is good as we pump our blood.*

*(Chorus: We'd dare to do, we're through with you.
This is who we are, we're like a well fuelled car).*

You are gone and you can't say you shone.

(Chorus)

*This is how we play; we say what we feel, hey, hey.
It's positive, not negative.*

(Chorus)

*Down with you, a mouth you went through.
Hip, hip, hooray, this is our day.*

(Chorus)

"That was fun" said Amy.
"Yeah it was" said Greg.
"It was" said Steven.
"I feel that" said Jessica.
"I do" said Robbie Jr.
"I do too" said Sean.
"Me as well" said Felicity.
"Me too" said Claire.
"A brilliant song" said Steven.
"It was" said Greg.
"I agree" said Amy.
"Me as well" said Jessica.
"Me too" said Robbie Jr.

"It was full of rhythm" said Sean.

"It was" said Felicity.

"Yeah it was" said Claire.

"Okay" said Steven.

"Let's go home" said Greg.

"Yeah!" said all the other superheroes.

The superheroes go home.

"That was good" said Greg.

"Yeah it was" said Amy.

"It was" said Steven.

"I agree" said Jessica.

"Me too" said Robbie Jr.

"Me thinks that" said Felicity.

"Me as well" said Claire.

"Okay" said Greg.

"It is" said Steven.

"It is good to gamble, just not with money" said Greg.

"It is" said Steven.

"Yeah it is" said Amy.

"I agree" said Jessica.

"What do you call a Newcastle Utd, pirate loving fan called Earl? Said Robbie Jr.

"Curse of the black and white Earl" said Sean.

"I like pirates" said Amy.

"Me too" said Greg.

"Me as well" said Jessica.

"I do like them" said Steven.

"Same here" said Robbie Jr.

"I love them" said Sean.

"Me too" said Felicity.

"They're good" said Claire.

"Okay" said Greg.

"It is" said Steven.

"They are great, the sword fights are the best thing" said Greg.

"True" said Amy.

"They are good" said Steven.

"I agree" said Jessica.

"Me too" said Robbie Jr.

"Me as well" said Sean.

"They're great fun" said Felicity.

"Same for me" said Claire.

"Okay" said Greg.

"We should have one" said Steven.

"We should" said Greg.

"We should do that" said Amy.

"I agree" said Jessica

"Me as well" said Robbie Jr.

"Me too" said Sean.

"It would be good" said Felicity.

"That it would" said Claire.

"Okay" said Steven.

"Cheese burgers with tomato sauce are nice" said Amy.

"They are" said Steven.

"That they are" said Jessica.

"I love them" said Robbie Jr.

"Me too" said Sean.

"I do too" said Felicity.

"Me as well" said Claire.

"Okay" said Greg.

"Gherkins are nice on them" said Amy.

"They are" said Steven.

"That they are" said Jessica.

"They're good stuff" said Robbie Jr.

"I agree" said Sean.

"Me too" said Felicity.

"Me as well" said Claire.

"Okay" said Greg.

"Draughts is good" said Steven.

"It is" said Greg.

"Yeah it is" said Amy.

"It is" said Robbie Jr.

"I like them" said Jessica.

"It's fun" said Sean.

"It is" said Robbie Jr.

"I like them" said Jessica.

"It's fun" said Sean.

"It is" said Felicity.

"I agree" said Claire.

"Okay" said Steven.

"It's a nice day" said Greg.

"It is" said Steven.

"Beautiful" said Jessica.

"Yeah it is" said Amy.

"It is good" said Robbie Jr.

"As Jim Carey says; b,e,a,utifal" said Sean.

"It is" said Felicity.

"I agree" said Claire.

"Okay" said Greg.

"Lots of midfielders in football is good" said Greg.

"True" said Steven.

"True indeed" said Amy.

"It is" said Jessica.

"I agree to that" said Robbie Jr.

"I agree" said Sean.

"It's positive" said Felicity.

"It is" said Claire.

"Okay" said Greg.

"It works on championship manager" said Steven.

"It does" said Greg.

"True" said Amy.

"True it is" said Jessica.

"I agree" said Robbie Jr.

"Me too" said Sean.

"Me as well" said Felicity.

"It's good" said Claire.

"Okay" said Greg.

"I love manager games" said Steven.

"Me too" said Greg.

"Me as well" said Amy.

"They're addictively fun" said Jessica.

"They are" said Robbie Jr.

"That they are" said Sean.

"I agree" said Felicity.

"Me too" said Claire.

"Okay" said Greg.

"Tennis games on consoles are good" said Steven.

"They are" said Greg.

"That they are" said Amy.

"I agree" said Jessica.

"Me too" said Robbie Jr.

"Me as well" said Sean.

"I as well think that" said Felicity.

"Me too" said Claire.

"Okay" said Steven.

"Good talk" said Greg.

"It was" said Steven.

"I agree" said Amy.

"Me too agrees" said Jessica.

"Me as well" said Robbie Jr.

"Good talks are refreshing" said Sean.

"They are" said Felicity.

"I feel that" said Claire.

"Okay" said Greg.

"Mulligatawny soup's nice" said Steven.

"Yeah, Ainsley Harriet's was" said Greg.

"Ooh yeah" said Amy.

"I agree" said Jessica.

"Same here" said Robbie Jr.

"It's nice" said Sean.

"It is" said Felicity.

"Yeah it is" said Claire.

"Okay" said Steven.

"Blackcurrant and apple juice is nice" said Robbie Jr.

"Yeah, it's refreshing" said Amy.

"It is" said Steven.

"Yeah it is" said Jessica.

"It's scrummy" said Sean.

"It is" said Felicity.

"I agree" said Claire.

"Okay" said Greg.

"Custard is nice" said Steven.

"It is" said Amy.

"Yeah it is" said Jessica.

"True" said Robbie Jr.

"It is" said Sean.

"Yeah it is" said Felicity.

"I agree" said Claire.

"Okay" said Greg.

"Dating agencies are good" said Steven.

"They are" said Greg.

"You can meet people is the reason" said Amy.

"I agree" said Jessica.

"Me to" said Robbie Jr.

"I agree too" said Sean.

"Me too" said Felicity.

"I'm the same" said Claire.

"Okay" said Greg.

"Facebook posts are good" said Steven.

"They are" said Greg.

"That they are" said Amy

"I agree" said Jessica.

"Me too" said Robbie Jr.

"I as well say that" said Sean.

"Me as well" said Felicity.

"Me too" said Claire.

"Okay" said Steven.

"It's a good way of speaking your mind" said Greg.

"It is" said Steven.

"Yeah it is" said Amy

"I agree" said Jessica.

"Me too" said Robbie Jr.

"Me as well" said Sean.

"It's good" said Felicity.

"It is" said Claire.

"Okay" said Greg.

"We'll do more" said Steven.

"We will" said Greg.

"That we will" said Amy.

"We will" said Jessica.

"We will do that" said Robbie Jr.

"I agree" said Sean.

"Me as well" said Felicity.

"Me too" said Claire.

"Okay" said Steven.

"Union Jack radio is good" said Greg.

"It is" said Steven.

"Yeah it is" said Amy

"It's decent" said Jessica.

"It is" said Robbie Jr.

"Good indeed" said Sean.

"True" said Felicity.

"True stuff" said Claire.

"Okay" said Greg.

"I like listening to people talk about sport" said Steven.

"I do" said Greg.

"Me too" said Amy.

"Me as well" said Jessica.

"Good stuff" said Robbie Jr.

"It is positive stuff" said Sean.

"It is" said Felicity.

"I agree" said Claire.

"Okay" said Steven.

"Football talk is best" said Steven.

"Yeah it is" said Greg.

"It is that" said Amy.

"I agree" said Jessica.

"Me too" said Robbie Jr.

"Me as well" said Sean.

"I agree" said Felicity.

"Yeah, it's lovely" said Claire.

"Okay" said Steven.

"Tony the tiger teddy is good" said Greg.

"Yeah it is" said Steven.

"Yeah, his neckerchief is good" said Amy.

"It is" said Jessica.

"Yeah it is" said Robbie Jr.

"I agree" said Sean.

"Me too" said Felicity.

"I agree" said Claire.

"Okay" said Greg.

"Slippers are nice" said Steven.

"I agree" said Amy.

"Me as well" said Greg.

"Me too" said Jessica.

"Me as well" said Robbie Jr.

"Same here" said Sean.

"Me too" said Felicity.

"They're comfy" said Claire.

"Okay" said Steven.

"Bubbles are good fun" said Greg.

"They are" said Steven.

"I agree" said Amy.

"Bubble-tastic" said Jessica.

"I agree" said Robbie Jr.

"Me as well" said Sean.

"Me too" said Felicity.

"They're good" said Claire.

"Okay" said Greg.

"Bags are good to carry things" said Steven.

"Yeah they are" said Greg.

"They are" said Amy.

"That they are" said Jessica.

"I agree" said Robbie Jr.

"Me as well" said Sean.

"Me too" said Felicity.

"They're useful" said Claire.

"Okay" said Steven.

"Rail holidays look nice but expensive" said Greg.

"I agree" said Steven.

"They do look nice" said Amy.

"Same here" said Jessica.

"Me too" said Robbie Jr.

"Me as well" said Sean.

"They're nice" said Felicity.

"I agree" said Claire.

"Okay" said Greg.

"Italian chocolate cakes are nice" said Steven.

"They are" said Amy.

"I agree" said Jessica.

"Me too" said Robbie Jr.

"I do" said Sean.

"Me too" said Felicity.

"Me as well" said Claire.

"Okay" said Steven.

"Good talk" said Greg.

"Yeah it was" said Steven.

"It was" said Amy

"I agree" said Jessica.

"Me as well" said Robbie Jr.

"Me too" said Sean.

"Me as well" said Felicity.

"I agree it was" said Claire.

"Okay" said Greg.

"Pencils are good to use" said Steven.

"That they are" said Jessica.

"They are" said Amy.

"Same here" said Robbie Jr.

"I think they're good" said Sean.

"Me too" said Felicity.

"Me as well" said Claire.

"Okay" said Steven.

"DVD books are goods" said Greg.

"They are" said Steven.

"That they are" said Amy.

"I agree" said Jessica.

"Me too" said Robbie Jr.

"Me as well" said Sean.

"I agree" said Felicity.

"Me too" said Claire.

"Okay" said Greg.

"Honesty is from the food chain, this is because demands all sorts, so we can do everything against various creatures, which is determined by the food chain" said Steven.

"That's true" said Greg.

"It is" said Amy.

"I agree" said Jessica.

"Me too" said Robbie Jr.

"I as well agree" said Sean.

"Me as well" said Felicity.

"Me too" said Claire.

"I am okay with that" said Steven.

"Good" said Greg.

"We're unique thinkers" said Steven.

"We are" said Greg.

"This we are" said Amy.

"We are" said Jessica.

"I agree too" said Robbie Jr.

"Me too" said Sean.

"Me as well" said Felicity.

"Me as well guys" said Claire.

"Okay" said Steven.

"Off-side should be a foot or more off-side to be off-side" said Amy.

"I agree" said Greg.

"Me too" said Steven.

"Me as well" said Jessica.

"I agree" said Robbie Jr.

"Same here" said Sean.

"Same" said Felicity.

"Same here" said Claire.

"Said well" said Amy.

"It was" said Greg.

"Psychologic evil is the only evil, as death is just pain, terrorists weren't loved" said Amy.

"That's true" said Greg.

"It is" said Steven.

"That it is" said Jessica.

"I agree" said Robbie Jr.

"Me too" said Sean.

"Me as well" said Felicity.

"Me too" said Claire.

"Okay" said Amy.

"Good" said Greg.

"Director twenty one is a good game" said Steven.

"It is" said Amy.

"I love it" said Greg.

"Me too" said Robbie Jr.

"Same here" said Sean.

"Same" said Felicity.

"Same here" said Claire.

"Okay" said Steven.

"Philips is a good maker" said Greg.

"It is" said Amy.

"Yeah it is" said Steven.

"I agree" said Jessica.

"Same here" said Robbie Jr.

"Same for me" said Sean.

"I agree too" said Felicity.

"Me too" said Claire.

"Okay" said Greg.

"It is" said Amy.

"Sony is good too" said Greg.

"It is" said Amy.

"Yeah it is" said Jessica.

"I agree" said Steven.

"Me too" said Robbie Jr.

"Me as well" said Sean.

"I'm the same" said Felicity.

"Me too" said Claire.

"Okay" said Greg.

"It is" said Amy.

"Mandy Moore's a good singer" said Jessica.

"She is" said Greg.

"I agree" said Amy.

"Me too" said Steven.

"Me as well" said Robbie Jr.

"I love her" said Sean.

"Me too" said Felicity.

"Me as well" said Claire.

"Okay" said Greg.

"Handling offences in football should only be punished with free kicks" said Amy.

"I agree" said Greg.

"Me too" said Steven.

"Me as well" said Jessica.

"Me too" said Robbie Jr.

"I agree" said Sean.

"I agree as well" said Felicity.

"Me too" said Claire.

"Okay" said Greg.

"We know our football" said Steven.

"Yeah!" said the other superheroes.

"Time to fight" said Steven.

All the superheroes go to a villain.

"Stop!" said Greg.

The villain stops.

Robbie Jr sucks the villain into his supernatural Alcatraz.

"Another one is beaten" said Robbie Jr.

"Yeah he is" said Greg.

"Same here" said Amy.

"I agree" said Jessica.

"Me too" said Steven.

"Me as well" said Sean.

"Me too" said Felicity.

"Me as well" said Claire.

"Honesty is often mad, it comes from the heart" said Greg.

"I agree" said Amy

"Yeah honesty is mad" said Steven.

"I agree" said Jessica.

"Me too" said Robbie Jr.

"I do too" said Sean.

"Me as well" said Felicity.

"Me too" said Claire.

"Okay" said Greg.

"Constipation's not good" said Steven.

"It's not" said Greg.

"I agree" said Amy

"Me too" said Jessica.

"I agree" said Robbie Jr.

"Me as well" said Sean.

"Yeah, it drains you" said Felicity.

"Yeah, let's sing" said Claire.

"Yeah!" said all the other superheroes.

"# You're frustrating like constipation and we beat you for the nation. Poo poo, like you.

(Chorus: thing to remember is you're not our member. Brilliant us, we're like a bus).

You're in us now, like a farmer's cow.
Good on us, no fuss.

(Chorus)

We're the best, you were a pest.
That's true, we do.

(Chorus)

We hate your behaviour, we're the saviour.
We're hot stuff, you were too rough.

(Chorus)

"That was fun" said Amy
"Yes it was" said Robbie Jr.
"That it was" said Greg.
"It was" said Steven.
"I agree" said Jessica
"Me as well" said Sean.
"Me too" said Felicity.
"Me as well" said Claire.
"Okay" said Greg.
"Let's go home" said Amy.
The superheroes all go home.
"String for cats is fun" said Greg.
"Yeah it is" said Amy.
"It is" said Steven.
"Yeah it is" said Jessica.
"I agree" said Robbie Jr.
"Me too" said Sean.
"Me as well" said Felicity.

"Me too" said Claire.

"Okay" said Greg.

"It is" said Steven.

"Lockdown was bad" said Greg.

"It was" said Steven".

"Yeah it was" said Jessica.

"That it was" said Amy.

"I feel that" said Robbie Jr.

"I agree" said Sean.

"Me too" said Felicity.

"Me as well" said Claire.

"Okay" said Greg.

"IPhones are good" said Steven.

"They are" said Greg.

"I think that" said Amy.

"I agree" said Jessica.

"Me too" said Robbie Jr.

"Me as well" said Sean.

"Me too" said Felicity.

"I say that" said Claire.

"Okay" said Greg.

"It is" said Steven.

"Blue cheese wrapped in toast is nice" said Greg.

"It is" said Steven.

"Yes it is" said Jessica.

"I agree" said Amy.

"Me as well" said Robbie Jr.

"Me too" said Sean.

"I love it" said Felicity.

"Me as well" said Claire.

"Okay" said Greg.

"It is" said Steven.

"Headphones are good" said Greg.

"They are" said Steven.

"True they are" said Amy.

"I agree" said Jessica.

"Me too" said Robbie Jr.

"Me as well" said Sean.

"Me too" said Felicity.

"I say the same" said Claire.

"Everything starts with invention, so everything's an opinion" said Greg.

"Yes popular opinion is the right way" said Steven.

"I agree" said Amy.

"I agree too" said Jessica.

"Me too" said Robbie Jr.

"That's right" said Sean.

"It is" said Felicity.

"Yeah it is" said Claire.

"Okay" said Greg.

"It is" said Steven.

"Masala nuts are nice" said Claire.

"They are" said Steven.

"I feel that" said Robbie Jr.

"Me too" said Sean.

"Me as well" said Felicity.

"Same here" said Amy.

"Same" said Jessica.

"Okay" said Greg.

"Sausage roll crisps are nice" said Steven.

"That they are" said Jessica.

"They are" said Amy.

"I feel that" said Robbie Jr.

"Me too" said Sean.

"Me as well" said Felicity.

"I'm the same" said Claire.

"Okay" said Greg.

"Hand sanitizer is good stuff" said Steven.

"It is" said Greg.

"Yeah it is" said Amy.

"That it is" said Jessica.

"I feel that" said Robbie Jr.

"Me as well" said Sean.

"Me too" said Felicity.

"Same" said Claire.

"Okay" said Greg.

"It is" said Steven.

"Tissues are good for a cold" said Greg.

"They are" said Steven.

"That they are" said Jessica.

"They are" said Amy.

"I agree they are" said Robbie Jr.

"Same here" said Sean.

"Me as well" said Felicity.

"Me too" said Claire.

"Okay" said Greg.

"It is" said Steven

"Anxiety isn't nice" said Steven.

"I agree" said Jessica.

"Me too" said Amy.

"Me as well" said Robbie Jr.

"I do feel that" said Sean.

"Me too" said Felicity.

"Same here" said Claire.

"Okay" said Greg.

"It is" said Steven.

"Stop watches are good" said Greg.

"They are" said Steven.

"Yeah they are" said Amy.

"That they are" said Jessica.

"I feel the same" said Robbie Jr.

"Same right here" said Sean.

"Me too" said Felicity.

"I as well say that" said Claire.

"Okay" said Greg.

"It is" said Steven.

"Come together is good" said Greg.

"Good song" said Steven.

"It is that" said Amy.

"I say the same thing" said Jessica.

"I agree" said Robbie Jr.

"Me as well" said Sean.

"Same" said Felicity.

"Same here" said Claire.

"Good" said Greg.

"It is" said Steven.

"What are you thinking" said Greg.

"People can talk to the dead through mediums" said Steven.

"True" said Greg.

"I agree" said Amy.

"Me too" said Jessica.

"Me as well" said Robbie Jr.

"Same" said Sean.

"Same here" said Felicity.

"I agree" said Claire.

"Okay" said Greg.

"That it is" said Steven.

"New five pound notes can slip out of pockets easily" said Amy.

"They can" said Steven.

"Yeah, I nearly lost a plastic note" said Jessica.

"Me too" said Robbie Jr.

"Me as well" said Sean.

"Same here" said Felicity.

"Same" said Claire.

"Okay" said Greg.

"It is that" said Steven.

"Samosas are nice in paper bags" said Amy.

"They are" said Steven.

"I agree" said Jessica.

"They are nice" said Robbie Jr.

"That they are" said Sean.

"They are nice things" said Felicity.

"Same here" said Claire.

"Okay" said Greg.

"It is" said Steven.

"Newcastle Utd fans should buy the club" said Greg.

"They should" said Steven.

"I agree" said Amy.

"Me too" said Jessica.

"Me as well" said Robbie Jr.

"Me too" said Sean.

"I agree" said Felicity.

"Me too" said Claire.

"Okay" said Greg.

"It is" said Steven.

"Erections are fun" said Sean.

"They are" said Steven.

"That they are" said Robbie Jr.

"Good" said Greg.

"It is" said Jessica.

"Yeah it is" said Amy.

"I agree" said Felicity.

"Me too" said Claire.

"I think only blatant handballs should be punished in football and flailing arms should be punished if the player has his eyes on the ball. All players should be punished if they have eyes on the ball and get the ball" said Greg.

"I agree" said Steven.

"Me as well" said Jessica.

"Me too" said Amy.

"Same here" said Robbie Jr.

"Same, okay" said Sean.

"I agree" said Felicity.

"I agree too" said Claire.

"Okay" said Greg.

"Stag chili is nice" said Steven.

"It is" said Amy.

"Yeah it is" said Jessica.

"I agree" said Robbie Jr.

"I feel that" said Sean.

"Same" said Felicity.

"Same here" said Claire.

"Good" said Greg.

"Sunpat peanut butter is nice" said Steven.

"It is" said Jessica.

"Yeah, I agree" said Amy.

"It's nice" said Robbie Jr.

"Nice" said Sean.

"Same" said Felicity"

"Same" said Claire.

"Good" said Greg.

"Scrambled eggs are nice" said Steven.

"That's how I feel" said Amy.

"Me too" said Jessica.

"Me as well" said Robbie Jr.

"Same here" said Sean.

"Me too" said Felicity

"Me as well" said Claire.

"Right, there are villains to fight" said Steven.

All the superheroes go to fight the latest villains.

Robbie Jr sucks one villain into his supernatural Alcatraz and Sean sucks the other into his.

"Let's sing" said Steven.

"# We won again, so long then.
We're top gun, we're fun.

(Chorus: we fight on, we fight on, we fight on as one)

Good times for us, you're like the back end of a bus.
That's right, we've got to fight.

(Chorus)

We're on fire, we've got the desire.
Yes, we go to good, you a dud.

(Chorus)

We are great, we'll best total hate.
This is our message now, we've eaten you like a cow.

(Chorus)

The superheroes go home.

"Rap music's good" said Greg.

"I don't like it" said Robbie Jr.

"I like it" said Amy

"Same" said Jessica.

"Same here" said Steven.

"It's good" said Sean.

"I feel that" said Felicity.

"Me too" said Claire.

"Good" said Greg.

"It is" said Steven.

"# We're top notch, like a stylish watch.
Yeah, yeah, we care.

(Chorus: We're awesome, we're not too dumb.
Yes we are, we're better than a car).

We've got drive, we thrive.
Good, we can give a thud

(Chorus)

We don't take nonsense, we make sense.
We do things, we have dealings.

(Chorus)

We're happy, evil is crappy.
That's true, we're good in this zoo.

(Chorus)
 # sung by the superheroes

"That was fun" said Greg.

"Yeah it was" said Amy.

"It was" said Jessica.

"I agree" said Steven.

"Me as well" said Robbie Jr.

"That was good" said Sean.

"It was" said Felicity.

"Yeah it was" said Claire.

"Okay" said Greg.

"It is" said Steven.

"Heron cheese is the best" said Greg.

"It is" said Steven.

"I feel that" said Jessica.

"Me too" said Amy.

"Me as well" said Robbie Jr.

"Same here" said Sean.

"Same" said Felicity.

"I love it" said Claire.

"Good" said Greg.

"It is" said Steven.

"We all change the future by making choices in the present" said Greg.

"We do" said Steven.

"I agree" said Amy.

"Me too" said Jessica.

"Same" said Robbie Jr.

"Same here" said Sean.

"I'm the same" said Felicity.

"Same here" said Claire.

"Okay" said Greg.

"It is" said Steven.

"Liverpool losing to Burnley was bad" said Greg.

"It was" said Steven.

"Yeah, I agree" said Jessica.

"Me as well does" said Amy.

"Me too" said Robbie Jr.

"Same for me" said Sean.

"Not a good result" said Felicity.

"I agree" said Claire.

"Okay" said Greg.

"It is" said Steven.

"Walk through the fire is a good song" said Greg.

"That it is" said Steven.

"I agree" said Amy.

"Me as well" said Jessica.

"Me too" said Robbie Jr.

"Not for me" said Sean.

"It's good" said Felicity.

"It is" said Claire.

"Okay" said Greg.

"It is" said Steven.

"Special fifty pence are good" said Amy.

"They are" said Steven.

"That they are" said Jessica.

"I feel that" said Robbie Jr.

"Me too" said Sean.

"They're good" said Felicity.

"They are" said Claire.

"Okay" said Amy.

"It is" said Greg.

"Paddington bear was on onc" said Amy.

"Good" said Greg.

"I like him" said Steven.

"Me too" said Jessica.

"Me as well" said Robbie Jr.

"He's good" said Sean.

"He's fun" said Felicity.

"He is that" said Claire.

"Okay" said Greg.

"It is" said Steven.

"Head warmth is good" said Amy.

"Yeah it is" said Greg.

"That it is" said Steven.

"It is" said Jessica.

"I agree" said Robbie Jr.

"Me too" said Sean.

"Me as well" said Felicity.

"Same" said Claire.

"Okay" said Amy.

"It is" said Greg.

"Rail journey holidays look good" said Steven.

"That they do" said Jessica.

"They do" said Robbie Jr.

"I agree" said Sean.

"Me as well" said Felicity.

"Me too" said Claire.

"Okay" said Greg.

"It is" said Steven.

"Molly's digestives were nice" said Greg.

"They are" said Steven.

"That they were" said Amy.

"I agree" said Jessica.

"I don't" said Robbie Jr.

"I do" said Sean.

"Same for me" said Felicity.

"Good" said Greg.

"It is" said Steven.

"I agree" said Amy.

"Euro shopper fruit and nut chocolate is nice" said Steven.

"I feel that" said Amy.

"Me as well" said Jessica.

"Me too" said Robbie Jr.

"I enjoy it" said Sean.

"Me too" said Felicity.

"I love it" said Claire.

"Good" said Greg.

"It is" said Steven.

"Wardrobes are good" said Greg.

"They are" said Steven.

"I think that" said Amy.

"Me too" said Jessica.

"I do" said Robbie Jr.

"I do as well" said Sean.

"I love them" said Felicity.

"Me too" said Claire.

"Good" said Greg.

"It is" said Steven.

"Blackpool looks nice" said Greg.

"It does" said Steven.

"I agree" said Amy.

"I do" said Jessica.

"Me too" said Robbie Jr.

"Not for me" said Sean.

"I like it" said Felicity.

"Me too" said Claire.

"Good" said Greg.

"It is" said Steven.

"Spa tortilla chips are nice" said Amy.

"They are" said Steven.

"I say they are" said Jessica.

"Me too" said Robbie Jr.

"Me as well" said Sean.

"Same as me" said Felicity.

"I feel that" said Claire.

"Good" said Greg.

"It is" said Steven.

"Display books are nice" said Greg.

"Yeah and useful" said Steven.

"Yeah they are" said Jessica.

"That they are" said Amy.

"I think that" said Robbie Jr.

"Me as well" said Sean.

"Me too" said Felicity.

"Me as well" said Claire.

"Good" said Greg.

"It is" said Steven.

"Brown is quite a nice colour" said Amy.

"It's interesting" said Greg.

"I like it" said Steven.

"I feel the same" said Jessica.

"Me too" said Robbie Jr.

"I as well say that" said Sean.

"Me too" said Felicity.

"Same here" said Claire.

"Good" said Greg.

"It is" said Steven.

"Dairy milk and dark milk salted caramel are nice" said Amy.

"It is" said Steven.

"Yeah it is" said Jessica.

"I feel that" said Robbie Jr.

"I feel it's nice" said Sean.

"Me too" said Felicity.

"Me as well" said Claire.

"Okay" said Greg.

"It's nice today" said Steven.

"Yeah it is" said Greg.

"It is that" said Amy.

"I feel that" said Jessica.

"Me too" said Robbie Jr.

"Me as well" said Sean.

"Me as well, I have to say" said Felicity.

"Me too" said Claire.

"Okay" said Greg.

"It is" said Steven.

"Aldi cheese topped buns sound nice" said Amy.

"Aldi cheesy buns, yeah!" said Steven.

"I agree" said Jessica.

"I do" said Robbie Jr.

"Me too" said Sean.

"Me as well" said Felicity.

"Same here" said Claire.

"Okay" said Greg.

"Norway pens are nice" said Amy.

"They are" said Greg.

"I agree" said Steven.

"Me as well" said Jessica.

"Me too" said Robbie Jr.

"Same here" said Sean.

"Same" said Felicity.

"Same goes for me" said Claire.

"I don't like surveys" said Greg.

"Me too" said Steven.

"Same" said Jessica.

"Me as well" said Robbie Jr.

"Same" said Amy.

"Me too" said Sean.

"Me as well" said Felicity.

"They're not nice" said Claire.

"Okay" said Greg.

"It is" said Steven.

"Andy Gray's 'premier league quiz' is good" said Greg.

"It's not my favourite" said Steven.

"I love it" said Amy.

"Me as well" said Jessica.

"Me too" said Robbie Jr.

"Same" said Sean.

"Same here" said Felicity.

"I enjoy it" said Claire.

"Okay" said Greg.

"It is" said Steven.

"Drugs is wrong as it wastes the mind and too much food is wrong as it wastes the heart" said Amy.

"True" said Greg.

"It is" said Steven.

"Yeah it is" said Jessica.

"I agree" said Robbie Jr.

"Same" said Sean.

"Same here" said Felicity.

"Me too" said Claire.

"Okay" said Greg.

"It is" said Steven.

"Free mobile phone games are good" said Amy.

"They are" said Greg.

"I think they are" said Steven.

"That they are" said Jessica.

"They're good" said Robbie Jr.

"They are" said Sean.

"I agree" said Felicity.

"Me too" said Claire.

"Okay" said Amy.

"It is" said Greg.

"I do" said Amy.

"I do too" said Robbie Jr.

"Me as well" said Sean.

"Same here" said Felicity.

"Same here as well" said Claire.

"Good" said Steven.

"It is" said Greg.

"Most people commit suicide because they kill themselves through the pain of hard work. Most people make breakfast in bed after sex so they're prostitutes" said Steven.

"Correct it is" said Greg.

"Correct" said Amy.

"It is" said Jessica.

"Yeah it is" said Robbie Jr.

"Same here" said Sean.

"Same" said Felicity.

"Same for me" said Claire.

"Okay" said Greg.

"It is" said Steven.

"I found all the humorous " said Greg.

"Me too" said Steven.

"Me as well" said Amy.

"Same here" said Jessica.

"Same" said Robbie Jr.

"Funny ha ha!" said Sean.

"Yeah it is" said Felicity.

"It is" said Claire.

"Okay" said Greg.

"It is" said Steven.

"Tony the Tigers Frosties is good" said Greg's partner Amy.

"They're great!" said Steven.

"They are and Tony's cute" said Jessica.

"True" said Robbie Jr.

"It is" said Sean.

"That it is" said Felicity.

"I agree" said Claire.

"Okay" said Greg.

"It is" said Steven.

"Spicy Pringles are nice" said Amy.

"Yes they are" said Steven.

"Okay" said Greg.

"I like them" said Jessica.

"I love them quite a bit" said Robbie Jr.

"Me as well" said Sean.

"Me too" said Felicity.

"Same" said Claire.

"Okay" said Greg.

"It is" said Amy.

"Debit cards are good" said Steven.

"They are" said Greg.

"I say the same" said Jessica.

"I agree" said Amy.

"Me as well" said Robbie Jr.

"Me too" said Sean.

"Good things" said Felicity.

"Good indeed" said Claire.

"Okay" said Greg.

Meanwhile the evil alien is flying a nuclear warhead shell filled with fire engine foam towards the heart of the sun.

Steven has a vision.

"Oh no! The evil alien is going to destroy the world" said Steven.

In moments later the sun is destroyed.

"Well Greg, it looks like you're not the only ghost" said Steven.

THE DESTROYER 3: THE END, NO SUN

"Ha!" Said Greg.

"It's going to be tougher now." Said Steven.

"It is." Said Greg.

"I agree with that." Said Sean.

"I agree." Said Amy.

"Me too." Said Jessica.

"Same here." Said Robbie Jr.

"Me as well." Said Felicity.

"Me too." Said Claire.

"Okay." Said Steven.

"It is." Said Greg.

Suddenly Adrian Domescu's spirit appears.

"Not you." Said Greg.

"Yeah, do you want to sport?" Said Adrian.

"Yeah, anything to beat you." Said Greg.

"Yeah!" Said the fellow superheroes of Greg.

"Good, so you're all in, I'll put a team together." Said Adrian.

"Okay." Said Greg.

"It is." Said Steven.

"Squad with me is one: Christopher, two: Satan, three: Stalin, four: Napoleon, five: Mussolini,

six: William Wallace, seven: The evil alien, eight: Herod, nine: Hitler and ten: Saddam Hussain.

"What sport." Said Greg.

"First, dodgeball." Said Adrian.

"Okay." Said Greg.

"It is." Said Steven.

"Our squad is: us and Manny, Sarah, and Father Robbie." Said Amy.

Manny, Sarah and Father Robbie appear.

"Hi!" Said the superheroes.

"Hi!" Said Manny, Sarah and Father Robbie.

"Oddball can be the ball." Said Robbie Jr.

"The referee will be the one from the match with the Nazis." Said Greg.

The referee mentioned appears.

Oddball turns into the ball.

> We took on the villains of life, to do what we needed to end
> that strife. It's a good way and we won, hey, hey.
>
> (Chorus: We won at dodgeball and we stood like a wall.
> We played well, so we've got a story to tell.)
>
> We won, we won, we had total fun. Victory at last, we played fast.
>
> (Chorus.)
>
> We threw the ball and hit you all. So that's it, we feel like a sit.
>
> (Chorus.)

"Why not speak in poetry?" Said Greg.

"Yeah!" Said the superheroes.

"We'll keep going, even when the wind is blowing.

Life is a garden, no weeds. Wimps are poo, they're going down the loo.

We'll be the best team, better than a dream.

We're great, better than hate.

We're the one and only, we're not lonely.

Great, we're not irate.

The best are honest, as well as modest.

We're tough stuff."

The superheroes play the game called hopping.

> *We lost at hopping and took a whopping. It*
> *didn't last long but we did no wrong.*

> *(Chorus: The hopping race was good like Elmer*
> *Fudd. We had fun like eating a bun.)*

> *What we did was lose, you had a cruise. We lost, we felt the cost.*

> *(Chorus.)*

> *What we do is chase you. When time was up, we were like a tired pup.*

> *(Chorus.)*

> *"No!" Said the superheroes.*

> *"We'll bounce back and attack.*
> *We've made great fate.*

> *We're the best, we're a strong test.*
> *Yeah, yeah.*

> *We're getting over adversity things; each one, everyone.*

Top gun fun.

*"We're all remembered differently, so evil is just technicality, so
everything's fun not very shitty. The Earth's spirit's our good bud.*

*It's normal that we're mad, it's not bad. We're
alive, we won't make this place a dive.*

We're great at a great rate.

We won't be forgotten, so we're better than cotton. Better than a tit bit.

*Life's about passing, passing work on and passing
away one day. We're the right bite.*

*We're better than Hitler's army, who were like
gristle from Peperami. Not nice spice.*

*We won at imaginary plane racing and you were left
chasing. It was good, the way it should.*

*(Chorus: imagination was part of the day and we did play.
Winning was a nice time, like hearing a chime.)*

*This could be Heaven and you took a sleavin'. We're
the best again and we let the dragon out the den.*

(chorus.)

*Our racing saw us come out on top and your hope
went pop. We won, we were top gun.*

(Chorus.)

We have hell but it's good that we're well. We've had the best test.

We've outrun the devil, in it we revel. We're alive like a beehive.

We're strong and our spirit is long. We'll continue to live well through hell.

Hitler was a bully, not like Holly Valance's Flick Scully. Bad not mad.

He was the worst, curry worste. He was all hate and ended people's fate.

We won't remember him fondly and we're lovely. Good mud.

We played ball and had a fall. Your result was best, you were a strong test.

(Chorus: You got the most points in the hoop, you made our energy droop. We fought back but you had the best attack.)

Your team was a dream, we don't feel like giving a smile that does beam. We lost and felt the cost.

(Chorus.)

You reached for the sky, that is no lie. Napoleon was too small to score a slam dunk, but you didn't do a bunk.

(Chorus.)

We play great and are masters of our fate. We're morally on top and have pop.

We kick back. We behave and stand like a cave.

We will never be completely beat and eat a treat. Yeah, Yeah.

We beat you at foot hockey, but didn't get cocky.
We played well and gave you hell.

(Chorus: We beat you, we beat you, that is what
we did do. We're the best, you're the rest.)

We gave our all and made you fall. One for all, we had a ball.

(Chorus.)

We had joy, like a child with a toy. You took a
beating, our hearts felt like heating.

(Chorus.)

We cut deep and don't wimpy weep. We are the best and like Friends fest.

We can fail but we'll be like a nail.

We hate dark fate. Do do.

We won at ten pin bowling, with the ball rolling.
It was good, we did what we could.

(Chorus: We struck you out, we put ourselves about.
We're the kings, we like our things.)

We played with passion is what we did, in our
tournament bid. We were as loose as a goose.

(Chorus.)

What we did was play on the everlasting day.
We've done well, our victory was swell.

(Chorus.)

We take action and are like a faction. Right on, life won't be gone.

We're fun, you run. Bye, bye.

We'll be up and you'll greatly mess up.

We played foot cricket, we avoided the wicket.
We played well and gave you hell.

(Chorus: We knocked it long and did no wrong.
We did it right and kept it tight.)

You bowled and fielded, our axe was wielded. We
played our best, we put you to the test.

(Chorus.)

We used our brain, we took the pain. Work is good, we did what we could.

(Chorus.)

We hurt and words you blurt. We have top pop.

We run free and we're like a bee. Ooh, we do.

We're crisp and some people have a lisp.

We showed our pace without a run and had loads of fun.
We scored goals and liked the way the ball rolls.

(Chorus: Walking football made us feel tall. We were honest, we
were the best. We were good, you were bad, we made you feel sad.)

We went mad, we were each like jack the lad.
Good, there was no dead wood.

(Chorus.)

We beat you and did it through and through. We
didn't get mentally tired, you were wired.

(Chorus.)

We run fast and will always last. We're a gun, shooting selfish fun.

We shoot from the hip and can spit a pip. We
act right and are up for a fight.

We are strong and are on song. We love life and go against strife.

We took the hits and lost the match but we'll be
back with our own vigilante batch.

(Chorus: Wheelchair rugby was rugged and tough, we did huff and puff.)

We played hard and moved our lard. There were tries
for both of us and each of us were not a wuss.

(Chorus.)

We did it our way, we just didn't win the day, part
of the day. We played on and we didn't con.

(Chorus.)

The superheroes get back at the villains by making fists.

"I like bullying and killing people." Said Hitler.
"You like bullying and killing people, do boxing!" Said Greg.

PAGE 1 OF CONTINUED BOOK:

"We're good humans and sometimes drink out of cans.
Yeah, we dare.

We're the best ones and don't like cons. We are free.

Earth is great, not yobbish hate. Yeah, yeah.

PAGE 2:

I'd never wear an earring, that's not my thing. No bling bling.

No tattoo, that's not something I'd do. I'm not a
trouncer bouncer.

We'll be ourselves now, like an honest horse or cow. True, true.

PAGE 3:

We're brains and hearts and there'll be not nice farts.
Yeah, we care.

We have feelings and dealings. We will thrill.

We see clearly, we love dearly. We're all for one like every swan.

PAGE 4:

We're a bowl of ice cream and we're a team. We love, like a dove.

We're different flavours, and different behaviours. Nice,
like rice.

We could be like rice pudding, better than gristly black pudding. We're great, not irate.

PAGE 5:

Life is like rugby passing, not yobbish harassing. You've got to be accurate and know where you're at.

It's tough and it's nice to be buff. Sometimes tough and rough.

It's hard and try not to get barred. Have real steel.

PAGE 6:

Life is like football passing, you'll be gassing. Nice times, good rhymes.

We stand together strong and we'll have lives that are long. Great, talk straight.

We are fabulous and don't like fuss. Yeah, let's care.

PAGE 7:

Cricket balls pass though the air and we overcome things that are not fair.

We can catch goals and gives bowls. We are wonderful and like being careful.

We can dance like we're human ants. Right on, we're as one.

PAGE 8:

We're happy and flush away the crappy. Happy chappies.

We're on top and try not to flop. We're Planetarians not violent fans.

We have hearts of confident cats and are not very sloppy like chip shop fat.

PAGE 9:

Life is like Christmas and is like war when people pass. Its crackers and extreme drug addicts are spackers.

There's nice food to put us in the mood. Farmers need a top crop. We're high and like pie. We like to touch much.

PAGE 10:

We are boredom haters and have fun like skaters. We are strong, though sometimes we're wrong.

We all have some love, that's consciousness from above. We are responsible and reliable.

Let the past be, let that be. Yeah, yeah.

PAGE 11:

Life can be cruel, like school. We know there's poop and don't want to droop.

We will carry on regardless and like to dress. We could dress looking like egg and cress.

Visions are better than dreams, we need to be in teams. Yeah, we like air.

PAGE 12:

Flowers smell better than paint and we are quaint. We do what we like and we have a spike.

We are hot, like hot pot. We are the great and the good, like clear mud.

We'll be free, yes, run free. We are like a chocolate topping and like shopping.

PAGE 13:

We are smooth we are, like a self-driving car. We're the strongest, like trees who have been here one of the longest.

We don't like lemmings and know their suicide is one of the worst things. True, true.

We will keep on at people now and forever as fight is forever and cowardness is meant to be never.

PAGE 14:

We will keep the Earth's spirit and not give in to bullshit. We love being free.

Life feels short and we need to make the most of it which will be hard fought.

Time after time life can be bitter and be like lime.

PAGE 15:

We need love and hate so use them at the right rate. Oh, don't get too low.

We fall, to fail is for all. We in spirit will be forever free.

We're nice, like doormice. Our chests are tittytastic, like some people think of Barbie dolls plastic.

PAGE 16:

We like what we like. This means we are freedom fighters and not little blighters.

We are nice like pies. Mince or apple ones, they taste great like cheese scones.

Time is great, so don't waste it by being late. We are very free.

PAGE 17:

Our time is precious forever and we will keep being clever. Life is a hotspot and can't be forgot.

Basketball is a great thing and we like to sing. Ring runs round people is what we do, in this zoo.

We get hurt, that's life's dirt. We are like a cup of tea.

PAGE 18:

Life is like boxing, it is, there's fizz. Ring, ring, ding, ding.

Right hook, left hook, whatever you are, you can go far. Fit, you're it.

You can hit hard anytime you like, it's better than the third Reich.

PAGE 19:

Running is like life, you can visit East Fife. There's hope so we can cope.

Running is fast, we will continue to last. Keep on, keep on.

We can show great speed and get over a bleed. Good blood.

PAGE 20:

Taekwondo is like life is what there is to say, we will keep evil at bay. It's good exercise, you can show enterprise.

A top sport, like a top resort. Keep being on song and limiting life that is wrong.

Sport is fun, like having a bun. It's great like a debate.

PAGE 21:

Kick boxing is furious, it's good like being curious. Yeah, like a bear.

It's hard stuff, better than fluff. We'll keep going, like a child growing.

We love living and giving. Yeah, like a care bear.

PAGE 22:

Baseball is where you play catch and you have to snatch. Great joy, like a child with a toy.

Could be funny, like a cat or bunny. Tough, like a top cop.

It's got fast running and needs good timing. Great, don't be late.

PAGE 23:

American football is offered to all. It's throwing and catching, and snatching. Marino and Brady are greats, like dates.

There's an oval ball and be like a wall. Nice, like using a vice.

You can kick and don't be too thick. You won't get sick, tackles will feel like a wall that is thick.

PAGE 24:

Ice hockey might be played by penguins or people on a rink, you'll be made to think. Positive game, avoid too much shame.

It's joyous and like going on a bus. It's superfast and will hopefully not put you in a cast.

There's punch ups which aren't for everyone, like a con. Toughness required and you'll get tired.

PAGE 25:

Sailing needs a mast and steering to make your journey last. It can bumpy, you might feel jumpy.

It's hard work, no room for a lazy burke. Fun it looks, like when food cooks.

The tide can be high and you may ask why? Have a will for a thrill.

PAGE 26:

Gaelic football is mad and a different football. There's several ways to score, like football and rugby, it's war.

People love it and it'll keep you fit. Sport eh, yay, yay.

It may be exciting, there's fighting. Yeah, don't expect it to be fair.

PAGE 27:

Aussie rules football was play in Neighbours, the soap, don't be too much of a dope. It seems to be like American football, probably same sort of ball.

There's love and shove. It could be like a fine wine.

It's hard, like lard. Greatness over lateness.

PAGE 28:

Wrestling is grappling. Like life, it cuts like a knife.

There's Olympic sort, humour that could make you snort. Fight back with an attack.

Be happy and snappy. Overcome being sad and mad.

PAGE 29:

Sumo wrestling is good, it does what it should. Carry on, be someone.

Japan looks amazing for creatures, woman and man. Nice times, like Big Ben chimes.

Don't have enough of being tough. Being happy is better than worry.

PAGE 30:

Javelin is like throwing a giant pin. You've got to be precise, better than head lice.

Be good at it, don't throw a hissy fit. Time for a throwing time, fun like a rhyme.

Have a great fate. Be kind and allow everyone to have dined.

PAGE 31:

Long jump is better than a pump. You need power hour.

You land on your bum, in sand, not bubble gum. Fun after a run.

You have to be like a grass hopper, confident, like a copper. Be right and fight.

PAGE 32:

Shot put requires muscle and mental hustle. Throw the furthest to win and avoid cheating sin.

Have great fun, get things done. Nice to grin and bear it keep mentally fit.

Sport is physical and methodical. Great to debate.

PAGE 33:

Archery keeps people happy. Keep on, fight on.

Life is a ball, make a good call. Think on, feel and go on.

Be feisty and tasty. Good taste is important, not a waste."

"We've had fun" Said Steven.